# THE HOLLY VILLAGE MURDERS

BENEDICT BROWN

Storm

ALSO BY BENEDICT BROWN

**The Marius Quin Mysteries**

*Murder at Everham Hall*

*The Hurtwood Village Murders*

*The Castleton Affair*

*A Body at the Grand Hotel*

*Arsenic and Old Lies*

**Lord Edgington Investigates…**

*Murder at the Spring Ball*

*A Body at a Boarding School*

*Death on a Summer's Day*

*The Mystery of Mistletoe Hall*

*The Tangled Treasure Trail*

*The Curious Case of the Templeton-Swifts*

*The Crimes of Clearwell Castle*

*The Snows of Weston Moor*

*What the Vicar Saw*

*Blood on the Banisters*

*A Killer in the Wings*

*The Christmas Bell Mystery*

*The Puzzle of Parham House*

*Death at Silent Pool*

*The Christmas Candle Murders*

*Murder in an Italian Castle*

**The Izzy Palmer Mysteries**

*A Corpse Called Bob*

*A Corpse in the Country*

*A Corpse on the Beach*

*A Corpse in London*

*A Corpse for Christmas*

*A Corpse in a Locked Room*

*A Corpse in a Quaint English Village*

*A Corpse at a Wedding*

*A Corpse at A School Reunion*

*A Corpse from the Past*

*To my wife Marion and our incredible children,*
*Amelie and Osian.*
*You make the hard work worthwhile.*

# READER'S NOTE

As with all my Christmas books, I've written this one to be spoiler-free so that new readers can discover and enjoy it. This does mean that I've had to pause a couple of plots that I will pick back up in the next entry in the series. To make up for this, I promise a big leap forward in the missing father, shadowy figures and murdered-suitor storylines the next time around.

As always, at the back of this book, you'll find information about my reasons for writing it, the incredible things I learnt while researching it, a character list and a glossary of the unusual vocabulary I used.

ONE

It had been a long time since I'd looked forward to Christmas with so much anticipation. Ever since the war, I'd convinced myself that such childish pastimes were no longer relevant to me. I might have been to festive parties in that time. I believe I even received the odd present or two but, like much in my life, my feelings had become numb to the very idea of it. I had replaced my sense of joy and wonder with a grim belief in the coldness and cruelty of life. I was, to all intents and purposes, a modern-day Ebenezer Scrooge.

It is difficult to say exactly why 1928 was so different. Over the last twelve months, I'd investigated conspiracies, thefts and more murders than I can recall. With my beloved friend Bella at my side, we'd encountered true evil, and lost friends and loved ones in the process. And yet, on hearing "I Saw Three Ships" played by a Salvation Army band in Trafalgar Square in early December, I found myself smiling from one ear to the other. I felt that special warmth filling up my insides and, rather than continuing with whatever inessential task I had set myself, I walked over to St Martin-in-the-Fields to enquire whether there would be a carol concert in the coming days.

The truth is that, as much as I was happy to have Bella back in my life after a decade apart, and relieved that sales of my mystery novels were keeping a roof over my head, the real change in me was something less easily defined. I think I'd finally come to accept that the war was over. I'd spent years living as though a grenade could go off at any second, and I'd have to jump on top of it to save the people I love, but that feeling had slowly faded. It was almost as if I were alive again. And life, it turned out, was rather good.

London looked beautiful in the cold light of December. The shops on Regent Street were decorated in greens and reds. Crowns, stars and mistletoe hung from the lamp posts and, once a day, just after dusk, a curate would light the candles on the tree in front of St Paul's Cathedral. Small families and groups of boys from the Hoxton Christian Mission stood in quiet awe of this stirring spectacle and, I must admit, I did the same.

I had other reasons to be cheerful, too. I'd finished my truly dreadful book after months of hard labour. *Murder at Pemblewick Manor* was a load of old twaddle, but I'd promised my editor that I would write it, and he was very happy with this early Christmas present.

Even better than that, on the Thursday night before the big day, I had rather a special appointment to keep.

"I feel like I'm doing something naughty," my uncle said as we awaited admission.

"Stop pulling on your tie, Stan," my auntie Elle complained.

"I'm not used to all this fanciness." Uncle Stan continued to pull on his tie. I'd rarely seen him wear one and, though it clearly chafed against the dear old fellow's sense of himself – not to mention his neck – he looked very smart in one of Father's old suits.

"There's no need to worry," my mother told them as we heard the sound of footsteps from inside the immense building. In truth, she sounded just as nervous as her brother- and sister-in-law, but she hated to see others ill at ease.

"There really isn't," I reassured them, tucking the present I had brought under my arm to put a hand on Stan's back. "Bella's family are terribly nice..." I thought about adding a small caveat but decided against it. "And it's only a party."

As I said this, the holly wreath on the huge wooden door went swinging away from us and there was Pullman, the Hurtwood Manor butler.

"Mr Quin and family," he sounded as though he were announcing our arrival to the other guests, but as far as I could see, there was no one else within earshot. "If you would like to follow me to the Great Hall."

Pullman ushered us inside, and Stan marvelled at our surroundings, as if we were in Buckingham Palace to see the King. Admittedly this is a lazy comparison, as we were in a famous manor house to see a duke.

"It's like..." Auntie Elle tried to describe the view before us, but she didn't have the words for it, and so I pushed her wheelchair after the butler.

Pullman silently crossed the flagstoned parlour towards the main gallery that cut across the building and led to various opulent staterooms. I was beginning to wonder whether it was such a good idea to bring my whole family. If they were that impressed by the gloomy entrance hall, I had to worry how they would react when we reached our destination.

My mother went with "My sainted aunt!" to express her amazement as we walked into the grand old space. Whereas my uncle opted for the slightly more archaic "Gadzookers!"

I'd always loved the Great Hall in Bella's house, not least because there was a secret passageway behind one of the intricate wooden panels where we used to hide when we were children. We never had so much fun as when jumping out on passing maids, unsuspecting footmen or – if we were unlucky and due for a telling-off – Bella's mother, the Duchess.

The floor was made of Italian marble, marked out with squares so that we were able to play life-size board games with some of the more co-operative servants. An impressively carved wooden minstrel gallery dominated one end of the room, and there were high, mullioned windows that started at head height and, during the day, allowed great shafts of light into the oblong space at regular intervals.

There must have been fifty people already there, not to mention the ten or so staff gliding around the gathering with trays full of drinks. There was no dancing to speak of just yet, but a string quartet played up on the minstrel gallery, and the guests lent a happy chatter to the room. I recognised half the people there from the local area but, judging by their clothes, there were more than a few well-connected friends of the Duke and Duchess mixed into the crowd.

"The Family Quin!" a full voice declared, and we were diverted towards the large, cheery character who was propped up in the corner of the room. Bella's father, the Duke of Hurtwood, had suffered a stroke some years earlier, and this was the first time I'd seen him on his feet since I'd left for war.

"It's so nice to be here again," Mother said, and I was happy that the once steely Duchess should hold out her free hand to greet her.

"It's lovely to meet you, Your Grace." Uncle Stan had been schooled by his wife on how to act, talk and stand in front of our hosts. He did a surprisingly good job of it.

"And you," Bella's mother replied, with her arm still under her husband's in case he should need her support. "Our daughter has told us all about you over the years."

"Marius doesn't tell us anything," my aunt teased me, but I must admit, I was only half listening to their conversation. I was still looking about the room, and my old friend the Duke must have noticed.

"Hello there, Marius." He wasn't mobile enough to poke me in the ribs but, as the Duchess was busy with my relatives, I'm sure he considered it. "Are you looking for someone in particular?"

His unexpected attention startled me a little. "Me? Looking for someone? What makes you say that?"

He had a bushy beard, a roguish grin, and he loved to keep me on my toes. "You seem a touch distracted."

"Christmas," I said, because I was sure it would be relevant to any discussion that night and gave me time to think of a better answer. "Which is to say I was looking at the decorations. They really are lovely." I pointed to the large Christmas tree in the middle of the room without turning round to it. "They're so... festive."

He beckoned me closer, and I could hardly refuse. Bella's mother evidently saw that I had taken over the guard duties, as she relinquished her husband and took the others across to see an old painting of some description.

"I'm glad you're here, Marius. You know, I don't think Bella would have organised the party if it hadn't been for you."

My heart raced at the idea that I was of such importance to the woman I'd loved since I was a child. "I'm sorry. How do you mean?"

His round cheeks pulled in a little as he sought the right words. "You took her mind off things. You know... You gave her something to live for after the loss she endured, and my wife and I are grateful for it."

I'm not one to blush, but I couldn't just accept this compliment. "I'm sure that whatever I did was entirely selfish. I don't know if you've realised this, but I rather enjoy your daughter's company."

"Oh, I've noticed, my boy." He elbowed me in the side. It hurt.

"What have you noticed, Father?"

This time I definitely jumped, not just in the air but out of my skin. "Bella!" I sounded like a startled woodcock.

"Good evening, Marius."

Dressed all in red, as she so often is, she was not just Christmassy but Christmas itself. She was the season personified; a being filled with promise and generosity. She had the power to make my jaw drop open, only for me to stand there dribbling like a foolish puppy. When her green eyes fixed upon me, I wished I would never have to look away again.

"We were just saying what a wonderful job you have done bringing all these people together," her father replied in his usual wise tone. "We used to have parties like this when you were children. You're a marvel to have brought the old place to life again."

She'd done the very same thing to me. Bella could infuse joy into any situation, which made the sorrow that had resided within her for the last few months all the harder to bear.

"I'm sorry, Daddy. But I must steal Marius from you. There are people I'd like him to meet." With an impish smile, she put her arm through mine to pull me away, and I had a sudden panic that the Duke's legs would buckle and he would fall to the floor. That was not what happened, as he was supporting himself with one elbow on the windowsill.

We walked through the crowd as she nattered, and I wondered whether she really was all right, or this was an act that rich young ladies put on to avoid unpleasant questions. "Daddy's exaggerating, of course. I didn't really do all this on my own. Having a staff of forty certainly makes throwing a shindig a lot easier. Now let me introduce you to my uncle Basil."

The evening passed in a whirlwind of new names and faces. I met each and every one of the Duke's powerful friends. The Foreign Secretary had made an appearance – though the Home Secretary was notably absent. There were also a few minor royals, the recently created Bishop of Guildford, and the West End actress Georgiana Cotton in attendance. It was a good thing no one tested me on their names, as I immediately forgot who was who. I did recognise our local postman and my teacher from my school days, but the place was so busy, and getting busier by the half hour, that it was all quite overpowering – in a good, chaotic way, at least.

"Marius, you dear, dear man!" my editor Bertie shouted across the room when he arrived. He was soon distracted by my elegant companion. "And my dear Lady Bella, has Marius told you what a genius he is?"

"Many times," she assured him, and I ignored them both.

"Hello, Margery," I said to the rambunctious fellow's wife, who I hoped would take my side in any discussion that was about to begin.

She kissed me on both cheeks but was evidently eager to hear of my brilliance. "Tell us all, Marius. We want none of your usual modesty."

Bella laughed at the idea that I would ever show such discretion, whereas I found it fascinating that two people could have such contrasting perceptions of me.

"I for one am eager to know what amazing new feat you've achieved." She put a hand to the bodice of her velvet dress.

I didn't have to say anything, as Bertie couldn't keep the answer to himself. "Your friend here has written the most engaging and brilliant mystery novel since... since..."

"*The Hound of the Baskervilles*, perhaps?" his wife suggested.

Bertie clapped his hands together. "That's it! *Murder at Pemblewick Manor* – title to be confirmed – is the best mystery novel written since Conan Doyle first picked up a pen. After some minor corrections, it is going to make Marius a household name if ever there was one."

Bella looked perplexed. "Didn't you say that the paper it's written on was barely fit to—"

I decided to interrupt her. "Didn't you say you wanted to dance?"

Margery winked at me as I hurried away from them, and Bertie looked disappointed that he wouldn't get to lavish me with any more praise. There was a whole room full of people with whom he would soon make friends, so I wasn't too worried about him.

"I didn't think to see you taking the floor this evening," Bella told me once we'd escaped, and we were waiting for the next piece of music to start.

"You're very persuasive."

I'd made her smile, but, when the music began, it was strangely slow for a celebration – especially after the joyous Yuletide melodies the quartet had previously been playing. We stood in a waltzing pose, but all we could do was sway ever so gently. I wanted to make her laugh. I wanted to tell her how much I was enjoying the continuing thaw of my heart thanks to her efforts organising the party, but instead we continued our spiritless shuffle.

I imagine we were both relieved when the piece reached its conclusion, and we could leave the floor.

"I should really make sure that Father is all right over there." Bella didn't need to tell me that the Duke had found greeting so many people quite exhausting.

"Offer him a chair with my compliments." I hadn't meant to say it quite like this, but she evidently thought I was trying to be witty and gave me a wry look as she hurried away. The train of her dress followed behind her like a puppy after its master.

Bizarrely, this made me miss my dog, but it didn't say anything on the invitation about bringing pets, and he'd only have upstaged me. I stood at the side of the hall, happy to be a wallflower as the musicians finished playing and, up on the gallery, a five-piece jazz band began to play. The change of style (and particularly the increase in tempo) sent a ripple through the room.

Young ladies dressed in shimmering outfits pulled on their partners' arms to get them to dance. The unsophisticated young gentlemen looked thoroughly frightened by this, but they largely obeyed and, a few moments later, the space reserved for revellers was filled. I was glad that I hadn't been sucked into the maelstrom, as I wouldn't have known what to do with music like that. I'm only twenty-nine, but seeing the youngsters from my childhood village down the hill let rip made me feel old before my time.

Bella's chauffeur, Caxton, had been roped into serving drinks, but he'd never liked me and went whistling past with his tray whenever I held up my hand to get his attention. A far friendlier footman soon brought me a John Collins as the band moved on to a speedy and stirring rendition of the 'Boar's Head Carol'. This had the dancers clapping with wild abandon. I had no idea young people were so fond of fifteenth-century songs featuring smatterings of Latin.

*"The boar's head, as I understand,*
*Is the rarest dish in all this land,*
*Which thus bedeck'd with a gay garland*
*Let us servire cantico,"* they sang along in time with the band leader.

I must admit, it was a catchy piece, and I found myself tapping my feet as I watched. Bella's three brothers had made an appearance, but they'd always been an odd bunch and kept to themselves. They were chattering away in a closed huddle until Uncle Stan found them and had other ideas. The old baker was a champion conversationalist, and he was yet to meet a person he couldn't pull from his shell.

Closer at hand, an old lady with perfectly white hair was standing beside the wall. Her hair was arranged in a neat plait, which ran halfway down her back, and she was dressed in an Asiatic style. The gown she wore was of black silk with a Mandarin collar and frogging down the front. She was a very well-turned-out woman, which made her sudden outpouring all the more startling.

"Who goes out walking so late at night in the snow? I don't know what she sees in that opportunistic good-for-nothing," she muttered to herself without paying me any attention. "He's surely after her money. That's the only thing that makes sense."

She kept shaking her head, then looking down at her hands and shaking it again. I could tell that she was quite disturbed by whatever dark thoughts were parading through her mind, and so I tried to talk to her.

"Is there anything I can do to help, madam?"

My interruption only served to unnerve her more, and she looked at me as though I were the one who had upset her. "I told the police today," she said in a nervous yet matter-of-fact voice. "I told them. I said, if anything happens to my friend, he'll be the one behind it."

My nerves began to tingle. My senses engaged, but I tried not to sound like a detective as I responded. "If you tell me what the matter is, perhaps we can find a solution."

She put her hand in mine and squeezed it, as if I were the one who needed comforting. "No, no, my dear. There's nothing anyone can do. I told them. I said, that man has the look of a killer if ever I've seen one."

TWO

I asked the lady to explain herself, of course, but she was suddenly quite shy.

"Oh, dear me," she said with her hand still in mine. "I'm sure I'm just being foolish. The police insisted there was no reason to worry. I don't know what's got into me this week."

She did look a little pale, and I made a quick decision. "Stay right where you are, and I'll fetch a glass of water." This was my first mistake, though there would doubtless be plenty more.

By the time I returned with refreshment, there was no sign of the panicked woman. There was a line of chairs against the wall, but she hadn't gone there to rest. A couple standing nearby told me that they hadn't noticed anyone, so I walked to the entrance to the hall. The footman on duty thought he'd seen a lady with long white hair pass through there, but he couldn't be sure. I followed her possible path, and the butler told me that the lady in question was well known to him and had left the party in her own car. Now I was the nervous one, and I needed someone to tell me not to worry.

"Bella, dear," I said when I found her surrounded by admirers. I didn't feel too jealous, as none of the crowd she had drawn was under sixty. "I'm sorry to steal her away from you, gentlemen, but I have something important to ask."

There were some groans of disappointment, but the whippersnappers soon found something else to amuse them.

"And how may I be of service, sir?" She had a light, frivolous tone that I'm fairly sure was due to the cocktail in her hand rather than her natural mood.

"I was talking to a lady—" I began, but she was really not herself and interrupted me with a giggle.

"Well, good for you, Marius. You can't spend your whole life a bachelor."

"Thank you, but I don't think that my prospects are too rosy in this case; she immediately ran away from me. She was wearing a Chinese dress in black silk, and her long hair was as white as the snow outside."

She clearly knew who I meant. "That's Auntie Addie." I must have looked blank as she added an explanation. "Don't you remember Adele Leach? She used to look after us when Nanny was on holiday."

A flicker of an image of a friendly, round-cheeked lady with curls came into my head. "That was twenty years ago," I reminded her. "She has changed somewhat. Is she really your aunt?"

Perhaps the conversation had sobered Bella as her blithe grin had disappeared and she pulled me over to the window where, now seated, the Duke was still entertaining his guests.

"No, no. She's just a friend of the family, but every such person becomes a dear relative when you're a child." She looked a little absent-minded herself then. Before I could ask another question, she answered it. "Adele was a friend of my grandmother's, so she was Daddy's auntie before she was mine. What's all this about, Marius?"

Instead of answering, I raised another doubt. "Is she..."

"What, Marius? Is she what?"

It sounded patronising, and I didn't like to say it, but I did have to know. "Is she all there? I only wonder because she said several alarming things and then disappeared when I went to get her a glass of water."

Understandably, Bella was insulted on her friend's behalf. "Adele is one of the most astute people I know. Now tell me what she said."

I paused to consider what I'd heard and, for a moment, I thought I was the one who was overreacting. "Perhaps it was nothing. She told me she'd been to the police because she believed that someone was in danger." I picked over Adele's words, which were already shifting in my brain. "She made it sound as though her friend's husband or boyfriend was after her money and would kill to get it."

"How astonishing." Bella's expression was more of concern than amazement. "And where is she now?"

"That's just it. She walked straight out of the party as soon as I'd turned my back. Pullman saw her driving off in her car before I went to look for her."

Bella's features seemed to move closer together in apprehension. I noticed a slight movement in her throat as she swallowed, and now I needed a drink.

"The poor woman, she must have been unimaginably upset to tell a stranger. Unless she recognised you, of course."

I considered the possibility. "I doubt it. In fact, I don't think she was telling me at all. She was merely thinking over the matter out loud. By the time she'd finished, she seemed resolved to the idea that it was all in her head."

This did little to reassure Bella. "Then why did she leave without saying goodbye?"

I could only shrug.

"I'll be sure to call her in a couple of hours when she's at home."

The same waiter as before was passing with drinks for the children, so I helped myself to two cordials that I felt would be more use to us than cocktails.

"Does she live far away?"

Bella didn't look at her glass before she tipped the contents down her neck. "In a curious little place near Highgate. She has a gorgeous cottage full of treasures, and I always loved visiting her when I was a child. I still meet her in London every month, but it's been years since I've been to Holly Village."

"Do you know anything about her life there now?" I asked, as I am a part-time detective after all. "Can you imagine to whom she was referring?"

She turned away to look through the dark windows above us. "Not really. Adele has always found the village to be a pleasant little community. And I know she has friends there, but I don't know many of their names."

It seemed that we'd exhausted the obvious possibilities for now, and I was uncertain what to do next. To save me from having to suggest another awkward dance, Bella had an idea of her own.

"I bought you a Christmas present." She was jolly and child-like once more and grabbed my wrist to pull me after her as she weaved in and out of the noisy congregation. We arrived at a table where people had left handbags and pocketbooks. She produced a wine-red box from underneath and held it flat on her open hands.

"Wait there for just one moment." I tried to remember where I'd left the one I'd brought for her. It was on a table near the door, and I hurried over to retrieve it. "I'm afraid it's just bath salts," I revealed, so as not to get her hopes up. "I wanted to get you something nice but made the mistake of asking an assistant in Gamages' Christmas Bazaar for help. She was presumably paid commission, as she insisted that I buy you a silver cigarette case. She was so unrelenting that I picked up the first thing I saw and said I was happy with it. I hope you like baths and the smell of dog roses, as I bought you enough of the stuff to last a decade."

I pulled the gift from her hands and put mine in its place.

It was heavy, and I can't say she was over the moon at my description. "It's just what I've always wanted."

I was about to open hers when she put her hand out to hold the lid down.

"What are you doing?"

"What do you think I'm doing?"

"It's the twentieth of December, Marius. Don't be so hasty." This prompted the question of why she had been so keen to give me a present that I wasn't allowed to open, but I didn't like to say anything, and her tone softened. "Open it on Christmas Day and remember me here and now."

"Of course," I said, trying not to look at her directly, just as most clever people avoid staring at the sun.

"Do you promise?" I couldn't imagine why she was so persistent and, before I could answer, my friends and family had barged in to involve us in whichever new jollity they were enjoying.

The evening passed like this. We bounced from one brief entertainment to the next. The band played. People drank and danced and nibbled on vol-au-vents and, at the end of the night, those who remained formed a circle around the hall, and we sang "Auld Lang Syne".

A good time was had by all, but when it was over, I didn't feel like staying in the countryside any longer. Mother and I picked up my basset hound from my old house. We said goodbye to Stan and Elle, and I drove us back to London, thankful that I'd only had one strong drink and that I'd put that down fairly swiftly after picking it up.

I'd never before understood why rich people have chauffeurs. The idea of paying someone to do something so pleasant on your behalf is incomprehensible to me. However, it presumably reduces the number of motoring accidents with drunken lords and ladies ploughing into things.

I thought about Adele Leach as I left the quiet countryside to enter the almost as quiet city. I couldn't forget the look of terror on her face as she rattled off her observations. I wondered whether that emotion really had passed, or she was unable to sleep in her house in Highgate, thinking about the danger to her friend.

I must confess that, when I woke up to my warm-bodied companion nudging my face the next morning, I quite forgot about the events of the night before and thought only of the fine Christmas ahead of us... until I realised that it was my wet-nosed hound who had disturbed my slumber and not the woman I love.

"Percy, you little cur. I suppose you're after some breakfast?" I looked at the clock and realised that I would not be spending much time editing my new book that day. In fact, I did very little aside from a spot of Christmas shopping and a visit to the Army and Navy Veterans' Society in Holborn.

I'd been trying to go there twice a week for the last two months as, though much of England had forgotten them, the limbs of the unlucky many who were wounded in the war hadn't grown back and psychological wounds were yet to heal. Giving up a few hours of my time talking over the past with my fellow Tommies was the least I could do.

I'd come to know the boys down there rather well, and they were just as excited about plum pudding, roast goose and stolen kisses under the mistletoe as I was – even if any such embrace would almost certainly be with Percy in my case. I went to bed quite merry that night and, when Saturday morning peeped its head above the horizon, I was ready to laugh at just how bad a writer I was and do what was needed to polish the unpolishable lump of coal of a novel I'd created.

I sat down in my writing room with a sigh as I remembered what had happened there two short months earlier. I pulled out the manuscript that Bertie had adorned with minor corrections and far too much praise. I had even picked up my fountain pen and dipped the nib when there was a knock on my door, and I not so regret-fully had to abandon my task.

"Marius," Bella uttered in a voice wracked with emotion.

"What's happened? What's the matter?"

"It's Auntie Addie." Her lip visibly quivered as she gathered the strength to answer. "She was found dead in her home yesterday morning."

# THREE

Percy thought this was the most wonderful development, not because he's a heartless monster, but for the simple reason that he adores Bella, and her arrival meant that we would have to go out in the car.

"I hope you don't mind driving," she told me, still drawing deep breaths between each sentence as she struggled to come to terms with the bad news. "I said that Caxton could have the morning off to visit his family in Streatham before Christmas."

I was a little surprised that her chauffeur had a family. I'd always assumed he'd been put together in a laboratory like Frankenstein's monster. If forced to guess, I would say that he was half bull, quarter pit-bull, and the rest of him was made up of left-over pieces of human that were found in the nearest operating theatre.

"That will be nice for him," I said, rather than appalling her with my true thoughts. "Now, tell me more about Adele. Did you manage to speak to her after the party?"

"I was really in no state to call, but I managed to get through to her just as she arrived home. She assured me there was no need to worry."

"Did you believe her?"

"Well, no, if the truth be told. She sounded dreadful." She watched the scenery flashing past the window of my bright red Invicta as we drove around Regent's Park. The bare horse chestnuts along the avenue had been dusted with snow overnight and there was just enough in the open meadow alongside us for a group of children to have a snowball fight.

"Then what did you say in reply?"

She looked straight at me. "What could I say? I'm sorry, beloved family friend who, without pay, did so much to look after my brothers and me when we were children, but I think you're fibbing?"

I had a sneaking suspicion that I would have said something very similar, but as you may have noticed, I've become rather good at keeping such thoughts to myself. I did it just then, and Bella continued.

"I tried to keep her on the telephone, in the hope she might finally confide in me, but she said she was tired and I let her go."

I stopped at a crossroads at the top of the park before driving on towards Camden Town. "How did you discover that she'd died?"

"The police called Father this morning. Adele didn't have any family of her own but he was listed as her next of kin when she bought her house."

"Do they have any idea what happened to her?"

"They weren't concerned that she'd been murdered, if that's what you're thinking. She was almost eighty, after all. A lonely old lady with a weak heart found dead in her home isn't going to arouse suspicions now, is she?"

I thought back through the cases we'd investigated since Bella had convinced me to set up shop as pretend detectives. Each of the killings we'd encountered had been clear-cut murders. It would take some skill to prove that a seemingly innocent death was really the work of a malicious hand.

"You must admit that it's something of a coincidence, though," I challenged her in the gentlest way I knew how. "Adele was so worried that she went to see the police. We have to at least consider the possibility that she was—"

"You're beginning to sound like me." She smiled for the first time then, but this brief sign of amusement was soon extinguished.

Once we passed Kentish Town, the space between houses began to grow and there were more greens, parks and fields about between the modern housing estates and the odd grand Victorian mansion. It was easy to see that Highgate had once been an entirely separate town from London. Located five miles from my house in the centre of the city, it had a different feel from the other neighbourhoods through which we'd passed. We'd jumped back in time an extra few decades for one thing, and much of the architecture was now notably Georgian.

We turned off the main thoroughfare towards the famous cemetery before coming to a broad junction on Swain's Lane. It was a good thing Bella knew her way around as I hadn't been to this part of London in years and would have got us quite lost – which is no way to start an investigation.

It struck me that I'd got the wrong end of the stick entirely and it wasn't my expertise as a detective that Bella needed, but my emotional support. To be on the safe side, I made every effort to be kind.

"Why are you acting so strangely?" was the first thing she said when I ran to the other side of the vehicle to open the door for her after she pointed to the exact spot where she wanted me to stop.

"This door sticks sometimes," I lied.

I held the door open, and she looked even more suspiciously at me as she swung her legs from the car and stepped out. Always well behaved around his favourites, Percy followed close behind her and stopped right where she stopped.

Bella didn't say anything for a minute. In fact, she stood in the middle of the road and her eyes became fixed on a strange building opposite us. If I described it as an Anglican church crossed with the gatehouse to a Transylvanian castle, I really wouldn't be doing it justice, as it was both more beautiful and far odder than that.

On one side of the iron-gated archway was a stone sculpture of a woman cradling a lamb, and on the other a woman with a dove. An author like me really should know what such figures are meant to represent, but I don't, so I'll imagine it was hope and charity and leave it at that. I couldn't help but notice the two large holly trees that bordered the wide building, nor the inscription on the Gothic arch which said HOLLY VILLAGE ERECTED 1865.

"Are you quite all right, Bella?" I asked, remembering my silent commitment.

"No, not really." She still hadn't taken another step. "I should have waited for my brothers to come with me, but I was so upset when Father explained what had happened that I found Caxton and we left immediately."

Even when she turned up at my house without warning, I hadn't realised just how moved she was by her friend's death, but then I'd never known before how close she was to a woman of whom I only had a vague memory.

"I used to spend a week here in the summer every year. Sometimes my brother Kenton would come, but more often than not, it would just be me. It was the most marvellous holiday with the most marvellous person, and I felt so lucky that Auntie Addie was my own special friend."

I didn't want to rush her, so I just waited for the story to continue.

"I wish you'd known her better. She was such an adventurous person and…"

I was very much looking forward to the story by this point, but Bella is never one to go along with other people's expectations, and it was at this moment that she marched towards the gatehouse and on through it. I watched her go for a few moments – her heavy woollen coat swinging around her ankles as she bustled away – before I snapped out of my trance and hurried after her.

The snow looked as though it had been painstakingly applied to the leaves of the holly trees by some patient hand. Red berries peeped out here and there, and the dark green undersides were suitably shadowy for their Gothic setting, so I could quite understand why someone would have named the area after the striking plants.

Passing through the arch, I felt as if I'd climbed into a children's picture book. The village within a town within a city that we had just entered was the very definition of picturesque. There were seven more buildings spread out around a large green with curling gravel paths cutting across it. Well, it was a white actually, but I had to assume there was green grass underneath the layer of snow.

The houses all matched the gatehouse in style, and yet they were quite different from one another. I thought perhaps someone had knocked down a large church and built a series of dwellings with the leftover masonry. Each had small, elaborate spires and pointed weathervanes, but whereas one resembled the tower of a medieval cathedral, others were more cottage-like, with pretty fluted gables and neat wooden porches.

"No wonder you enjoyed your holidays here," I said as I caught up with Bella, who was shooting along one of the paths faster than a Sopwith Dolphin. "I feel like I've travelled to another world where all the inhabitants are pixies."

She made no response but rummaged in the pockets of her oversized coat for the keys she apparently possessed. "Adele had no family left, so she always kept a spare set at Hurtwood in case something should happen."

With Percy padding along beside her, Bella approached the tallest of the eight buildings, its façade covered with leafless, flowerless vines that presumably belonged to a wisteria plant. She put the key in the lock, turned it, pushed open the door, took eight steps inside and then froze there for her tears to come.

"I'm sorry," she told me between jagged breaths. "It's just all too much. This on top of..."

There is something we no longer discuss. We did once, not so long ago, but we came to the unspoken decision that the only way for Bella to get over what happened was to pretend that it never had. At least a month had passed since we'd mentioned Gilbert – since we'd mentioned the man she loved and lost.

I went to stand next to her, but I said no more as I looked around the curious room that resembled an exhibition in the Horniman Museum. We'd passed through a tiny entrance hall with an equally miniature staircase in it to get to the stuffed drawing room. The walls were covered with shelves containing glass cases which held a curious assortment of treasures.

Perhaps I should have realised from the exotic outfit that Adele Leach wore to the party, but she was evidently well-travelled. In her collection, I could see artefacts from all over the world. You would need an expert to do the place justice, but I noticed a display of one hundred butterflies in fifty different colours – none of which you could find in Great Britain. There were tiny silver vessels which, judging from their etching, were from the Far East, and I thought they might have been used in a temple there. I saw pre-historic ammonites, the nacreous shell of a nautilus, a selection of exquisitely vibrant feathers and a line of small African figures with exaggerated proportions.

"I wish you had known her as an adult," Bella muttered, taking in the scene as Percy nosed at her affectionately. "She could tell you a story about every last object in here. Though I've barely set foot abroad, having spent so long talking to Auntie Addie, I feel I've travelled the world and flown twice round the galaxy, too. She was a true inspiration."

I didn't know whether it was best to let her enjoy those precious memories or ask more. She was clearly eager to talk, though, so I decided she wouldn't mind my asking a question.

"Who was she exactly? Or rather, how did she come to have such an adventurous life that enabled her to acquire these unique items?"

Bella didn't hesitate to reply and, as it was clear that we were distracted, Percy went to look for somewhere more comfortable to lie down.

"She and her husband were archaeologists. Well, officially he was the archaeologist, but she was there every step of the way with him. They spent much of their careers in Indochina before taking the longest route possible to come home. They thought they would get here and have children, but they were never so lucky. Her husband died relatively young, and she was already living here when I was born."

For a moment, I felt a little sad that an incredible woman's life could be reduced to just a few sentences, but then this was merely a summary; every object in that room provided an intriguing foot-note. Perhaps, in twenty years' time, Adele Leach would only be remembered by Bella and her brothers, but that didn't make her achievements any less significant, and I had no doubt that her name could be found in archaeological papers and history books that would be read for generations. I will be amazed if people are still reading my silly stories in a hundred years' time – dead but also amazed.

"She was evidently an exceptional woman."

Bella finally looked back at me. "Yes, she was one of my very favourite people. I feel just terrible for not spending more time with her on Thursday night. Sometimes you take people for granted, even when they are very special."

I said no more for the moment. I gave her the time she needed to come to terms with the hush we found there. Auntie Addie wasn't about to appear from the kitchen with a tea tray and a precious anecdote. Her spirit – in one sense or another – might have still been there, but Adele was no longer home, and she wasn't the only thing missing.

We wandered through a circuit of the downstairs rooms. Leaving the most interesting space behind, we passed through a small dining area and kitchen, the hallway once more and finally the sitting room. Each had its own exotic peculiarities and, had we visited in happier circumstances, I'm sure I would have had count-less questions to rattle off to our hostess. Instead, we were accom-panied by silence. Even Percy, stationed beside the front door, didn't make a sound.

I regarded Bella much as if I were watching a film in the cinema. She smiled at a series of large polychrome masks on the wall that evidently meant something to her. She frowned at times, though I can't say what sparked the reaction, and, more often than not, she looked as though she was trying her utmost best not to cry.

And then we made it to the largest room there, which was dominated by a three-piece suite arranged around an ox-blood-tile fireplace. Just as she had twice before, Bella came to a stop in the middle of the room and simply stood there without saying anything. I thought she was staring into space at first, then realised she was looking at a large, framed painting of a bucolic scene that was hanging on the chimney breast.

"That was never there before." She raised her hand to point at it. "There's a painting missing. It has been there ever since I was five."

# FOUR

"Was it valuable?" I had to ask, as that would surely put a different gloss on the situation.

"I should say so. I believe another of Manet's works recently sold for £40,000 in a London auction."

"It was a Manet?" I made no attempt to hide my surprise.

Bella walked closer to look at the replacement. "Yes. It was a small portrait of people enjoying themselves in front of a French café. If I'm remembering correctly, Adele once met the artist in Paris. She spoke several languages, and her French was first rate."

She was about to reach up to take the painting of sheep and hills and what have you off the wall when I stopped her. "Gloves, Bella. You must wear gloves. If the police are to find the thief's fingerprints, they won't want yours all over it."

She didn't take it as a reprimand, and I certainly hadn't meant it to be one, but she went to retrieve her soft woollen pair from the hall where she'd left them. For once, I hadn't brought any with me, so I left it to her.

"You see," she said once the landscape was removed, and a blank wall stared back at me.

"Do I?"

"Look at the way the paint is faded all around the small frame that was previously hanging there. It had been here for years."

I moved sideways to look at the wall in a different light and realised what she meant. It was only a subtle change in tone, but it was clear that a different painting had occupied that space for some time.

"Is it possible that she sold it?"

Bella once more paused before answering. "I don't see why she would have. Her husband came from money and left everything to her. She also lived quite modestly, and besides, she loved that painting. If she was planning to lay some valuable item up in lavender, her jewellery or silverware would have been the first things to go."

There was no doubt that she was already motivated to find out what really happened to her dear friend. I watched, both impressed and a touch hypnotised, as she plotted a course through the evidence to get to the truth.

She bit her lip as she drew her first conclusion. "In which case, I suppose we should check to see whether anything else is missing."

I held my hand out to show her that she should lead the way, but before she could, we heard the front door opening.

"Hello?" whoever it was called out, as she must have found a four-stone basset hound blocking her way. "Is anyone in here?"

The newcomer had a pleasant, working-class voice. When we reached the entrance hall, I saw that she was dressed in the clothes of a maid.

"Oh, Miss Bella," she said, curtseying. "You've come. I did wonder whether I should visit today, but I don't like to stray from my routine, even if it's about to be turned on its head."

"Maggie, it's so nice to see you." Bella hurried forward to join hands with her. The pair exchanged a meaningful glance before it all got too much, and she pulled her friend in for a supportive embrace.

"It's so sad, miss," Maggie declared, the tears already forming in her eyes. "I can't believe she's gone."

"I know. I know," Bella took a deep breath and looked for her words. "I can't tell you how much I will miss her."

"Should I put a kettle on for you, miss?" the maid enquired as they separated.

"I'll do that," I told her. "You should both sit down to talk."

I didn't give them the chance to object. I turned to the short passageway that led to the tea-making facilities (amongst other things). I must admit that I used the time the water took to boil to nose around in cupboards on the off-chance I'd find something important. I didn't.

By the time I'd brewed the tea leaves, the pair back in the sitting room were laughing.

"She was certainly no shrinking violet," Bella commented. "Adele could be fiery when it was required."

"That was one of the things I liked most about her." Maggie had dark hair, pale skin and a trustworthy smile. She puckered her lips and looked down at the dark Axminster rug. "She was full of character and treated me ever so well over the years."

I hadn't considered the woman's age until this moment but, while I would have assumed she was around thirty, the way in which she said this made me think that she was quite a few years older than me. The laughter lines around her eyes seemed to support this idea. Despite the sad topic they were discussing, I could see that her face was normally quite jolly.

"Thank you, Marius," Bella said when she noticed me in the doorway, and I wondered why I hadn't simply placed my tray down on the occasional table and taken a seat of my own. Maggie sat in the centre of the sofa, and Bella had an armchair, so I now occupied its twin on the other side of the hearth.

I poured the tea into three blue and white Wedgwood cups as I listened.

"I find it so hard to accept that she's really gone." Maggie shook her head and looked cut adrift. "I know she had her health problems; the doctors said for years that her heart weren't strong, but she was so young for her age – so active. I'd known her to walk home all the way from Kensington after a morning's shopping, just for the pleasure of the exercise."

I may have looked at Bella in a slightly too forceful manner, but she allowed the casual conversation to fade and posed her first serious question. "Do you mind if I ask who found Adele's body?"

Maggie looked a little worried for a moment, so I passed her a cup of tea as though this would solve the problem. "It were me, miss. I don't clean on a Friday, but I normally saw Adele shopping in Highgate. I like to think that she was more than just my employer. She was my friend, too."

Her voice suddenly went higher, and I was certain she was about to cry, but she did her best to control her emotions before continuing. "We would often have a cup of tea after we'd bought our bits and pieces, and I was worried she were at home in bed. I wandered down here and knocked on the door, but there was no answer. That wasn't like her, so I knew that something was wrong. She might have gone out somewhere special, I suppose, but she normally told me if she had plans."

"You'd heard where she went on Thursday evening, then?" I thought I should check.

"Oh, yes!" Maggie leaned closer to Bella to take her hand once more. "She was so excited about the party. Said you hadn't thrown one at Hurtwood in years."

Though I have known Bella for more than two decades and seen her in nearly every state of joy and distress, I can still never predict how she will react to a situation. She looked terribly morose at the mention of the party, and I felt I had to ask another question to get the rest of the story from the maid.

"I imagine you used your key when no one answered the door?"

"Well, the door was unlocked, as it happens. I came inside and listened. There was the stillness of an empty house, but her keys were hanging up where they always were. Her handbag was under the telephone table. I didn't know what to think, or what could have happened in the hall, so I came in here and—"

She held one hand to her mouth and Bella squeezed the other, before deciding that this was too impersonal and moving to sit next to her. "That must have been such a shock."

"It was, miss." It was finally too much for Maggie, and she let out a small cry. Most domestics are taught to show as little emotion as possible around their "betters". But Bella has never been so superior as to demand such a thing.

"I knew she were dead: her eyes were open, and I had a feeling she'd been lying there for some time. Maybe it were the colour of her skin or somet', but I knew there was no sense in trying to help her." The distressed, high-pitched squeak she'd previously produced sounded again. "I called the police as soon as I could move. There were a constable here ten minutes later and an inspector a while after that, but neither of 'em took it seriously. They called her a sorry old dear whose heart had finally given up on her. And for every point I raised, they had an explanation."

"But there was no sign of any wounds on her?" I asked, perhaps too directly. "The police didn't notice any bumps to the head, perhaps, or bruising of the wrists?"

"No, sir. Not that they mentioned to me."

Bella knew how to talk to the bereaved and asked the following questions in a perfectly measured tone. "Did the coroner come?"

"Only to remove her for burial, as far as I know. No one said nothing about suspicious circumstances or the like – even though a whole row of ornaments were dislodged up there." She pointed to a shelf that was above head height, so it was unlikely to have been disturbed in a physical altercation. "And the hall carpet were all dirty. I told 'em she was perfectly well last time I saw her, but they wouldn't listen."

"When *did* you last see her?"

Maggie took a moment to consider this. "It were Tuesday last. I normally come Thursdays too, but I had a day off to visit my mother in Potters Bar. I work in other houses on the days I'm not here."

I believe that it occurred to her that this was no longer true and her sorrow peaked. "I tidied up after the police had gone. They told me I could, and it were such a mess in here, I couldn't bear to leave it how it was."

This made me want to ask an obvious question, but Bella thought of a more important one. "What happened to the painting that was above the fire?"

Maggie's eyes narrowed, and she peered up at the chimney breast. I could see before she spoke that she hadn't noticed the difference. "Ah me!" She extended her hand to point at the rather ugly landscape. "I was so distracted the last time I were here that I didn't even notice. It's gone. Her favourite painting were right there on Tuesday. Who nabbed it?"

Bella glanced across at me. Her look spoke volumes, and I could see with every new question she asked just how convinced she was that we had stumbled across at least one crime, if not two.

"We were hoping you might know." She waited for a few seconds before moving on. "Can you tell us whether Adele had been in any kind of trouble recently?"

"Trouble? Adele wouldn't've known trouble if it jumped out of a bush and ran around her in circles. What kinda trouble did you have in mind?"

Bella sat back on the sofa and looked nonplussed, which suggested that she would be happy for me to take over.

"I spoke to her on Thursday night at the party, and she mentioned a man whom she didn't trust," I began. "Do you have any idea who that might be?"

Maggie released a puff of air and raised her eyebrows in puzzlement. "A man she didn't trust?" she repeated before attempting a real answer. "You know, her circle of acquaintances were a small one. Most of her friends lived here in Holly Village."

"She actually said that she feared for her friend's life and thought that this man might be taking advantage of her."

The maid leaned forward and picked up her teacup from where she'd left it on the table. "Adele said all of that?"

"She even went to the police with her suspicions," Bella

explained. "They apparently told her that she was worrying about nothing, but she was still distressed enough at the party to be thinking about whatever had happened."

"I don't understand it. I honestly don't."

There was a faint flash of something in her eyes as she said this, and I was glad that Bella noticed so that she could ask the necessary question.

"But there is someone who might meet that description? A couple from differing backgrounds or ages, perhaps?" It was a bit of a jump to assume this was the case, but I'd come to the same conclusion.

Maggie turned away to look at the painting again. I must say that it was ill-suited to the otherwise tastefully appointed house. It was so simple and unsophisticated that it might have stood out to me even if I hadn't known of the Manet that had previously hung there.

"I don't want to say anything which could get someone into hot water when, as far as I know, he's done nothing wrong."

If there had been any real question over the maid's involvement in the crime, I would have taken this moment to prod her a little more vociferously. I would most likely have launched a nice, testing, *Oh, really?* Or an *Is that right?* But I could see just how upset she still was at Adele's death and sought to reassure her instead.

"You needn't have any fear of that, Maggie," I said in a hushed tone that was almost as sympathetic as any that Bella had managed that day. "We aren't about to run around making accusations. We just wish to set our minds at ease that nothing untoward has occurred here."

Maggie held her response in for another five seconds before answering. "There is one person who immediately comes to mind. But like I said, I've no reason to think badly of him. He's just..." She searched for the right expression. "Well, it's just that the average age of the inhabitants of Holly village must be over seventy, and he's quite a bit younger."

"And his name is?" Bella was the one to push for the most important detail.

"His name is Presler." She puffed her cheeks out and I could tell how difficult it was for her to reveal this simple fact. "John Presler. And he lives at number three across the green."

FIVE

I must say that I had expected a more dramatic name for our villain than *John*.

Then again, I had also expected Bella to launch into a careful dissection of the facts as soon as Maggie left, but that's not what happened. I suppose that my friend was too occupied by her own thoughts to involve me in them. Normally we would have picked over a few key questions – the reliability of the witness and her various statements, what we thought of the theories that she had put forward, and whether she didst protest too much (or whatever the past tense of that phrase might be).

Instead, I took the teapot, tray and cups back to the kitchen, gave them a wash, and by the time I'd returned to the sitting room, Bella had gone upstairs. She was more distant than usual and reminded me of the generic replacement for the Manet that was now resting on the floor beside the fireplace.

I looked into a bathroom, a study and a small guest room before finding her in what was surely Adele's bedroom. Percy was with her, his head hidden beneath the valance, and his bottom sticking up in the air. Bella, meanwhile, though also under the bed, was in a slightly more natural pose.

"What have you found?" The excitement was plain in my

voice, but she didn't respond. All that came back was a lot of grunting, so I walked over to the dressing table and opened a few drawers. I'm no expert, but I was fairly certain that the diamonds, rubies and emeralds that I saw were real.

"I've already checked her jewellery. There doesn't seem to be anything missing," a muffled Bella revealed before rolling onto her back to slide something out from under the bed.

"Is that a ladder?" I asked somewhat foolishly, seeing as the long, wooden object on the floor was unmistakably a ladder.

"Do I know my grandmother?"

"Touché, Bella. From memory, both your lofty forebear and the piece of apparatus you've just extracted are quite unmistakable."

"Marius?" She put her hands on the bed's stone-hard mattress to pull herself up to standing. "Stop talking nonsense."

"What a good idea."

Rather than asking what she planned to do with the ladder, I seized it by one end to raise it to a hatch in the ceiling.

"Thank you, kind sir."

"You are very welcome, madam."

I debated for a moment whether it would be more gentlemanly to let her go up the ladder first while I averted my eyes, or remove her fear of any lascivious intentions on my part by going up ahead of her. I took so long that she decided for me, and I made sure to study the carpet at my feet. I couldn't imagine what we'd find in this hidden space, but she must have had a good reason to look for the ladder in the first place. Once she was clear of the hole in the ceiling, I followed her. Puzzled and a little amused by the presence of a hidden space in the house, I poked my head into a fully furnished room with the same thick, fitted carpet as in the one below. There was also a desk, an easy chair and, less predictably, a telescope.

"What function did this room have?" I was coming to wonder whether Adele Leach had a secret identity.

"It was my aunt's retreat from the world." Bella was already standing in front of the window, looking down at the frozen court-yard and the various houses around it.

We were in the tower that I'd noticed when we arrived. There were narrow, arched windows on all four walls, and I saw the same grey-blue pointing on the windowsills as there was downstairs. It was the perfect place from which to spy on one's neighbours.

Bella spotted the right house before I could. "That's number three." I assume it was the presence of a comparatively young man on the doorstep rather than any prior knowledge that helped her to this understanding.

Before it was too late, I grabbed the barrel of the bronze library telescope and spun it around to look at the fellow. The instrument had evidently been set for short distances, as I could make him out without having to adjust the focus wheel. He conveyed a certain smugness as he stood looking around the tiny garden village. I couldn't say what was going through his head, but I was happy to guess. If this was our thief – and (why not?) Adele's killer – he might well have been wondering which of the houses he would target next.

"Have a look," I told Bella, and she skipped back to peer into the eyepiece. "Do you think this is the Presler chap that Maggie mentioned?"

Bella was in no mood for conjecture – whereas I had already constructed an elaborate tale around the man. She closed her free eye, and I went to the window where she had previously stood. The door opened behind him and a lady who looked twice his age appeared. He didn't turn around as she put her arms around him and kissed his ear. I thought perhaps she was whispering some-thing, but I couldn't say for certain.

"Had you heard of him before?" I asked when my first question went unanswered.

"No, but then I've hardly been here over the last decade." She pulled back from the telescope but stayed where she was. "People have come and gone since I was a regular visitor. There's possibly one couple I know who still live here, but I've tended to meet

Adele in the city recently or she's been to see my family in Surrey, so I didn't have any reason to come here."

There was that same flatness to her voice that had been noticeable for much of the day. I wanted to put my hand in hers, just as Maggie had, but it wasn't my place. The best thing I could do to comfort her was to find out what really happened to her adopted aunt.

"But, yes, I think that must be him," she finally told me. "This house is number eight, so counting around the other buildings, it stands to reason that their house would be number three."

She walked a few steps forward and looked through the double of the window at which I was stationed. The man to whom we would henceforth refer as John Presler – unless we found out we were mistaken – had his eyes closed as his significantly older paramour squeezed him tightly, then sent him on his way. I tried to form an impression of him as he wandered along the path, turning back three times to wave goodbye.

I couldn't say that he was a particularly remarkable man from so far away. His ears were large to match his nose, and he had greased black hair in a sharp parting that seemed to cut diagonally across his head. But it was his walk to which I instantly felt something approaching revulsion. He had the confident swagger of an itinerant salesman, going door-to-door with a wink and a smile to sell something that no one needed. In his checked yellow jacket and pleated blue trousers, he had the look of a two-penny conman.

I glanced back at his lover, who looked impossibly pleased with her lot. I knew then that he was either very good at what he did, or as innocent as my dog downstairs – who was moaning because we had most unreasonably deserted him. Percy would have followed us up there, but climbing ladders (or large steps, for that matter) has never been his forte.

Bella had finished her brief bout of surveillance and walked over to the desk to look at a pile of papers.

"Anything interesting?" I asked once Presler had disappeared through the gatehouse. A royal-blue Morgan Runabout three-wheeler rolled off along the street a minute later, so I could only assume he'd driven away.

"I think she really was spying on her neighbours." She frowned as she read from the topmost piece of paper. "There are notes here on the comings and goings on the estate."

"Are there any names?" I asked as I stepped away from the window.

She took a few moments to consume the page of hastily scribbled notes. "No. She uses pronouns – he and she for the most part. And some of the comments are in shorthand."

I moved around the desk to read the first line.

*Tuesday 11 p.m. He's out in drk. Dd of nt. Y?*

That was easy enough to understand, as was:

*She nos nthng.*

"Something must have happened since Maggie last came to clean on Tuesday. Adele would have shared her suspicions otherwise."

"It looks that way," Bella replied, sounding a little distracted. "But nothing here proves that a crime was committed."

"She must have seen something significant to have been in the state she was at the party on Thursday."

"What about this?" Bella paused as she reread one of the notes in her head before saying it out loud. "'He leaves early aft lst nt'. So, that's *after last night*, presumably, which would mean this was written on Wednesday morning. Perhaps whatever led to her murder happened on Tuesday."

"Or she saw something when she came back from the party right before she was killed. If only she'd written everything out in full."

I looked over the pages of tiny, scribbled handwriting. The times were laid out very clearly, but some of the comments were impossible to understand.

*Wednesday 7.15 p.m. He's weaselling off in darkness while She's out till late.*

"She wasn't writing this down as evidence of a crime," I decided. "These were notes to aid her own memory. She already knew about whatever dramatic event had precipitated all this. If she believed that Presler was capable of murder, then she was watching him to see what would happen next. This may be the key to unlocking the whole case."

When Bella's response came it was cautious and controlled. "So you really think Adele was killed?"

I took my time to be sure of my answer. "Yes, I believe she was. We need to watch the Preslers for a while before approaching them. But first we must speak to the local police and find out what she told them."

I could only think that she was about to agree with me when there was a knock on the front door and we both froze.

"I can't help feeling as if we're the ones breaking the law," Bella muttered as the sound became a little more insistent.

"We're coming!" I shouted down, before admitting to my friend, "It's funny you should say that, as it would never have entered my mind. After pretending to be a detective for the last year, and occasionally doing a good job of it, I feel that the term *out of bounds* no longer applies to us."

This time, there was no question of who should go down the ladder first. With Percy holding the bottom rung, Bella safely descended to Adele's bedroom, and I slid down after her.

"We're almost there," Bella called as she launched herself from the bottom of the staircase and Percy deftly – for my lolloping pup at least – copied her. "Sorry we took so long," she was saying as she pulled the door open to reveal a woman with henna-red hair springing out in ringlets all over, "we were up in the tower and—"

"I know you were. I saw you up there!" the visitor interrupted in a judgemental tone. "Now I'd like to know what you think you're doing in my dear friend's house."

SIX

We stood in the doorway staring out at the woman who had mistaken us for the intruders that Bella imagined us to be. Percy pretended to be a guard dog and poked his head between us to growl, but this was the only response she would receive for a moment or two.

I looked at Bella, she looked back at me and, while I would have been more than willing to answer, she took that responsibility upon herself.

"It's not what you must be thinking," she finally began. "We haven't taken advantage of the death of a kindly old lady to break into her house." This really wasn't the best way to allay anyone's fears. "I'm Adele's niece, Isabella Montague."

The woman was not convinced. "She never mentioned a niece to me."

Perhaps spurred on by this challenge, my normally confident friend found the guts and gusto to stick to her claim. "Nor did she mention *you* to me. Who are you?" She looked down at the interloper with all the imperious composure that comes with being the daughter of a duke.

"My name is Ivy Frazel." Never had a name better suited a person. Ivy looked particularly frazzled. Her eyes had a wild quality, and she made me think of one of those small mammals who are far stronger than they have any right to be. She was a mongoose, weasel and honey badger rolled into one. "I live at number one on the green."

"Well, Mrs Frazel, how can I help you?" Bella had already turned the tables, which proves, if it needed proving, just how powerful a self-assured approach can be.

"It's *Miss* Frazel actually," the neighbour replied, attempting to regain some of the authority she'd previously possessed. "And if you really are Adele's niece, tell me what her husband's name—"

Bella answered before the question was complete. "It was Mortimer Leach, and he was a pioneering archaeologist."

Frazzled Frazel crossed her arms high over her chest so that her hands hid away in her armpits. She wore a blue blazer, with a posy of silk flowers pinned to the lapel, and a long blue skirt. She reminded me of my grumpy schoolteacher – but then that is a common occurrence, and I've come to realise that Mrs Abbot still holds an outsized influence over me even now.

"Now, Miss Frazel, if you've no other accusations to make, we would like to be alone at this difficult time." To make her point, she put her arm through mine and pulled me closer.

Sensing the chance to get in her good books, Percy barked in a tone very similar to his beloved Bella's.

"Wait!" Miss Frazel shouted as we moved to close the door, and I realised I hadn't said a word. "I'm sorry, Isabella."

"It's Lady Isabella, actually." She sent Frazel's previous comment back to her in an even snootier tone. Though we were no closer to solving the mystery that had brought us there – or understanding the events of Adele Leach's final days on earth – Bella held herself at this moment as if she had accomplished a great deal. I, meanwhile, like the obliging assistant that I wasn't, still hadn't made a peep.

"My apologies, Lady Isabella." Frazel became a fraction more deferential and looked up at the new mistress of the tiny house. "I really only wished to welcome you to the village. It's neighbourly to welcome newcomers, wouldn't you say? When the Preslers arrived... Well, I admit that I thought it funny at first that there was such a..." She leaned closer to whisper her first nugget of gossip. "You know... such a large age difference between them. But when they arrived, five years ago now, I made sure to welcome them with wine and bread and the like. Of course, since then, we've had several other new neighbours."

Bella could see what a potential goldmine our visitor was, and her face brightened. "Perhaps you should come in for a cup of tea. You're clearly the person to know if we wish to ingratiate ourselves in the neighbourhood." I believe she chose the word *ingratiate* to tell me exactly what she thought of Ivy Frazel, but the lady in question just smiled and mounted the first step.

"How terribly neighbourly of you, Lady Isabella." She nodded first to my friend and then to me. "And you, Lord Montague."

I gritted my teeth and returned the nod as I stepped back into the house. "I suppose I should be the one to make the tea, then."

Bella ushered our no longer uninvited guest into the house, and I happily retreated to the kitchen. I could already tell what sort of case this would be.

When I'd completed the most important task of any detective, Bella was sitting opposite Miss Frazel with her hands in her lap, as though she was gripped by whatever she'd just heard.

"Are you saying that the Baroness released the parakeets to fly free over London, and they haven't been seen since?"

Frazel nodded excitedly. "That's right! She said she couldn't stand the noise every morning and had to do something about it. It certainly ruffled some feathers. You know I'm not one to gossip, but I'm sure she won't mind my telling you." She paused to reflect on this as I handed her a steaming cup. "The Baroness and her lovely husband are ever so generous with their time. They are the very best of people, and I don't know how this village would function without them. Of course, not everyone around here is the same."

"Are you referring to the Preslers?" Bella was quick to ask.

Ivy Frazel peeped out of the window in case anyone was listening. "I wouldn't use any such criticism myself. After all, they've never done me any harm, but there is a certain..." I believe that she searched for a word that wouldn't make her sound like a snob. "... roughness to their personalities that makes them stand out here."

"Do you have any idea what John Presler does for a living?" The overly eager detective did nothing to hide her suspicious nature.

Like so many people (and canines) before her, Ivy had fallen head over heels with Bella, and I could tell it would be easy to find out what we needed to know from her. In fact, it was too easy, so I interrupted to make it a little less obvious.

"What about you, Miss Frazel? Have you lived here long?"

"Me? Long?" She puffed out her lips and shook her head as if my question had tickled her. "It will be six years this coming January."

"Where did you live before that?"

"I was over in Godstone in Surrey. Do you know Godstone, Lord Montague? It's a lovely little place with some of the worst people you could ever find on this sceptred isle." She shook her head again; she was a woman who had experienced all kinds of wonders in life and was surprised by every last one. "It is a particularly poorly named village, as every last person who lives there is quite *God*-less. The stories I could tell you about my former neighbours!"

A little voice in my head said, *Please don't!* But I'm a polite man really and returned to my regular occupation of pouring the tea for Bella.

"So what brought you to Holly Village?" my friend asked, having realised the wisdom of not immediately asking our witness whether there were any killers on the estate.

"Me? Here?" Frazel pointed at herself but did not require confirmation. "As it happens, I inherited the house from my grandparents. That's how I know everyone so well. I'd been coming for years before I moved. Lovely little spot, isn't it? The people here are... Well, the people are really quite nice, actually. Not that the folk from Godstone would admit such a thing. You know, there was one woman back there who—"

"Do you work, Miss Frazel?" Bella had got in on the interrupting act. It seemed necessary if we wished to hear more about Holly Village and less about a rural community some twenty-five miles south.

"Work? Me?" It's hard to describe the shock in her voice whenever she questioned our questions. "Yes, I do actually. Not so much for a living, as I inherited rather well – Grandfather was a major in the army, don't you know. He made a killing from some clever speculation over in India when he retired. My parents died young, and I was the only grandchild, so I got the lot. As a hobby, however, I make silk floral arrangements for funerals and the like."

She pointed to her buttonhole and awaited the obligatory praise.

"Oh, how lovely," Bella and I said as one.

I was trying to imagine how old Miss Frazel was. She had a rather youthful face, but the manner and attire of an elderly woman. I wondered for a moment whether it wasn't just her grandmother's house she'd inherited, but her personality and role in the community. I decided that she was perhaps seventy, but I couldn't be certain.

"I've come to like them more than the real thing. Real flowers die."

I don't think either of us were ready for the gloomy way in which she pronounced this last sentence. She had abandoned her light, frivolous tone to reflect on the impermanent nature of plants.

"I've always thought it a strange idea that we put flowers on graves." I had hoped that this observation might lighten the mood, but halfway through, I could already see my mistake. "It's almost as if we wish to draw attention to the momentariness of human existence. We'll all end up like dry, shrivelled roses before long."

"How very morbid, Marius." Bella tutted and did a much better job than I had at keeping the conversation flowing. "When the time comes, I will place flowers on my aunt's grave. They will be bright and beautiful and, even when they wither, their initial vivacity will live on in my mind, just as Adele's will."

This boosted my spirits, but Miss Frazel's glum countenance was unchanged.

"It is terrible the number of people I've known who have died. My parents and grandparents of course, and even after I arrived here, there was old Mrs Anderson in number seven. She expired just two years after I moved to the village. That was around Christmas time, and now every time I see the first snowfall of winter, I remember how fleeting life is. So many die in this long, dark season, it's as if the snow itself is a harbinger of death and destruction."

Percy went to comfort the poor, morose woman who stared into her cooling beverage. I cast a look in Bella's direction with my neck muscles tight and my mouth stretched wide, as if to say, *Well, what are we supposed to do now?*

I did not imagine that she would echo Miss Frazel's blue-devilage. "Yes, our time on this earth is short, which is why I was so keen to pay my respects to—"

"I don't mind admitting that I was expecting a bleak and lonely Christmas this year." The old lady rose without spilling a drop of her drink, her sorrow now even more pronounced. "And now I can share it with you."

"Yes..." Bella was rarely fazed by the eccentrics whose paths we crossed on our cases, but Miss Frazel was in a class of her own. "Obviously we're very excited to spend Christmas here at Holly Village, despite all that has happened."

"I must be going." Ivy stared out of the window as she poured the whole cup of tea down her throat. "I won't keep you any longer, but if you have any questions, you know where to find me." Moping from the room with all the enthusiasm of the last mourner in a funeral parade, she left the house and disappeared out into the cold.

# SEVEN

"At least she's friendly." Bella stayed right where she was, staring after the woman who had worked her way through at least four distinct moods in the space of ten minutes.

I was beginning to feel that we were trapped in a play with only enough money for one set, so I put my hands on her shoulders and pushed her towards the front door. "Put your coat on. We're going to see the police."

She did as commanded, still recovering from the impact of Miss Frazel's visit.

"I don't understand it," she muttered as we stepped back outside, and Percy trotted along proudly ahead of us like a postilion leading the royal landau. "I was sure she would be a font of information and tell us all we needed to know. Why did she end up so miserable? And how did she make us agree to spend Christmas here?"

"Never mind that," I said as I saw Mrs Presler waving at us from her house across the green. "More importantly, why is it that, wherever we go, we end up having to act as if we're engaged, married or in love?" I can't imagine why I objected to this. Perhaps the gentleman didst protest too much.

Bella was not impressed. "Is that your biggest problem?"

"No!" I was quick to respond. "My biggest problem is that now I have to carry on as if I'm a toff."

"You can hardly blame me for that. It was natural for Miss Frazel to assume that the husband of a lady would be a lord."

"But I'm not your—"

"Bella?" someone called from the house closest to the path. "Bella, is that you?"

"Oh, Mr Wandle! It's so nice to see you."

A nattily dressed, red-cheeked man sporting a simply superb moustache with twizzled ends was leaning against the front door of the biggest building there. He had a plummy voice, but a warm manner, and he was clearly very fond of Bella.

"Merry Christmas, dear child."

"Merry Christmas, Mr Wandle," I put in when Bella just smiled at the jolly old fellow. "My name is Marius—"

"I'm so sorry." Bella finally remembered I was there. "Marius and I have been friends for so long that I sometimes forget that he doesn't know everyone that I do. Marius, this is Herbert Wandle, a dear friend of Auntie Addie and a confidante of mine whenever I spent my holidays here."

"It's an honour to meet you, young man." He extended his hand in my direction. "But I'll have none of this standing on ceremony. Bella called me Herbie when she was a child, and I would expect no different today."

"Herbie it is, then," I was happy to reply, and I thought, *What a lovely man. He's bound to be a killer.* Try writing murder mystery novels and not having such terrible thoughts! Go on. I bet you can't!

"I was so sorry to learn of your aunt's passing." His good cheer instantly vanished but, unlike Miss Frazel's strange performance, it was proportionate to the change in the conversation. "We both were."

In my mind just then, I put a small tick mark in the column which said, *Wife whom he's almost certainly swindling?*

Bella took his hand and squeezed it tightly. "How is the Baroness?"

He looked over his shoulder into the house. "She is very well. Thank you for asking." His smile was so wide that I could only conclude it was put on to hide his evil nature. "Now, tell me. Are you staying here long? Will we have the pleasure of your company?"

"Actually, yes." She put her hand on my arm and looked adoringly at me. I had hoped we might be spared this act with her friends, but no. I tried to forget how tetchy I had become and enjoy the chance to stare back just as lovingly. "My new husband and I have decided to spend Christmas here."

"Bella, my darling!" He came down from the front step to kiss her on both cheeks and I noticed that he walked with something of a limp. "That is the most magical news I could wish to hear. Congratulations to you both."

"It all feels so recent," I said to tease the woman I loved, whom I couldn't admit to loving, whom I was currently pretending to love. "We're practically still on our honeymoon."

He shuffled his shoulders and clutched his hand to his breast. "I very much remember how that feels. My beloved wife and I have been married for forty years, but I will never forget the first blooms of our romance."

Bella smiled, then frowned. It was a common occurrence that day. "I'm sorry, Herbie, but we must be pressing on."

"Don't worry, my child. I quite understand." He bowed to us one after the other with a sense of theatricality. "You must come in for tea very soon."

"We will. I promise." She looked down the path along which we'd just walked in case there was anyone near to hear her. "And I might need to consult your expert brain before long."

"I am always at your disposal."

We both said goodbye, he waved us off, and we continued towards the gatehouse.

"He seems very nice indeed," I commented in an apparently sarcastic tone, and Bella hit me around the back of the head.

"He is!"

There was clearly no sense in hiding my baseless theory. "You don't think he was trying a little too hard to convince us of his sterling character?"

She took a step away from me. "He has no need to do any such thing; I already know him well enough. This is a man who volunteers at the local church and gives up his time to help his neighbours whenever they need it. He was one of Adele's very best friends. He even designed the bookshelves that adorn her cottage."

"So he's a carpenter?"

"Among other things."

"Very well, I take it all back." My tone was too jovial for this to be true.

She gave me another clap around the back of the head and grinned at me. This was much better than the heartbroken expression she'd worn for much of that day, and I felt I had achieved my objective.

Mrs Presler – the wife of the suspect that Adele's maid had put forward – was trimming a hedge in her front garden. This struck me as strange behaviour when said hedge was covered in snow. I could only think it was an excuse to look at us more closely.

Further along the path, there was a woman with thick glasses and a small stepladder tying green bows on the ornate iron lamp posts. She was readying the place for Christmas, and I wondered what other festivities were planned for the week.

"Should we drive or walk?" I asked Bella when we got to the street, but Percy didn't look as though he were in the mood for motoring and walked off along the road. He did not know that part of London and was going in the wrong direction, so I ran after him and turned him the right way.

With this task complete, I noticed that Bella hadn't answered me. She was in one of her distracted phases again. It wasn't just since we'd had the bad news about her honorary aunt. Her dips in mood had been happening off and on for the last two months. So far, our cases had helped to take her mind off her worries, but investigating the death of someone close to her was apparently too much for my normally irrepressible friend.

I wanted to offer my arm and walk together through the normally leafy streets of suburban London, but that was not on the cards this Christmas, if you'll excuse the pun. We travelled in silence all the way to Archway Road. I'd like to say that I was picking over the sparse facts of the case with my detective's brain, but I'm afraid I was mainly enjoying the scenery, wondering what it would take to have the confidence of a basset hound and peering into Highgate Cemetery as we skirted the boundary, in case I could spot any of the famous graves there.

When the station came into view – with its bands of red brick and Portland stone like a miniature version of Scotland Yard – and I saw the blue lampshade of the police light, it filled me with a sense of security that I rarely feel. Our world isn't perfect, but if there's one thing on which you can rely, it's the humble British bobby.

Two minutes later, I came to question this belief.

"She was a batty old lady. What did you want us to say?"

I was struggling to understand the attitude of the spotty young constable on the desk. "Are you saying you ignored the fears of a member of your community for the simple reason that she was a woman in her eighties?"

The sergeant appeared from the back room to intervene. "Easy there, fella. I will not allow anyone to speak to my officer in that hostile tone." I had rather hoped he would be on our side, but he was spoiling for a fight from the outset. "It seems to me that you've come in here with a chip on your shoulder. If you're not careful, I'll toss you out like a bag of rubbish."

Before I could lose my temper or yell in frustration, Bella pushed me away from the polished wooden counter. "I'm sorry for my friend, Sergeant, but you must admit how curious it is that a woman came to share her suspicions of a potential crime and, the very next day, she was found dead."

The hulking, rubber-faced superior was already a head taller than her, but he puffed himself up before replying. "You know what's curious, miss? There's a fellow what lives in Kentish Town who's been arrested seven times in five different towns, and he still thinks he can get away with pinching bicycles. That's what I call curious."

I didn't quite grasp his point, but Bella at least pretended to understand. "Yes, but my aunt is dead, and we're asking for your help."

"Now, now, miss. I does not like what you are insinuating." He tipped his head back to glare all the more angrily. He seemed to hate the part of his job in which he had to have contact with the public. "Tell me, did officers attend the scene of her death?"

"They did."

"And was there a detective despatched to investigate the possibility of foul play?"

"There was."

His voice suddenly rose. "Then what are you bleedin' complainin' about?"

It was Bella's turn to show her temper. "I can't believe your attitude. I have come here in good faith to—"

And it was my turn to pretend that I was the reasonable one. This was only slightly undermined by my earlier comments. "Let's start again, shall we? Adele Leach came here just last week and spoke to one of you."

The sergeant looked at his underling, who was willing to accept this much at least. "Tha's right. It were me." He couldn't have been more than twenty-one and projected a strange mixture of shyness and slyness.

"Very good. And she told you that she suspected one of her neighbours of a crime?"

"Correct again," the constable said. "And we had a good laugh about it. Di'n't we, Sergeant Bulmer?"

His superior elbowed the boy to make him stop talking. "We listened carefully to the information she wished to share and formed a reasonable conclusion that the case was not worthy of our time."

"Tha's right!" The constable was even more cocksure now, though the older man obviously wanted him to keep his mouth shut. "You said she were off 'er rocker, di'n't you, Sarge?"

"Pike!" the sergeant snapped. "Why don't you see to the important work you do in the room beside my office?"

"Eh?"

"Tea, boy! Make me a cup of tea!"

The constable wandered off muttering to himself, and his superior spread his hands on the counter and leaned over it menacingly. "Do you need anything else? Or will that be all?"

"You haven't told us anything," I marvelled. "Could you at least let us know what Mrs Leach said?"

He breathed out through his nose so that his nostrils expanded. "Well, let me think... What did the confused pussycat – the like of which we get ten of a day coming in here to make unhinged accusations – actually say?" He tapped his fingers on the smooth surface. "I remember. She was babbling on about the winter coming and some fella who couldn't be trusted. I believe it was at that point that we stopped paying too much attention."

"So you didn't find out who the man was?"

"No... I... didn't."

"Does the name John Presler mean anything to you?"

"Does the name John Presler mean anything to me?" He looked up at the ceiling to consider this. "D'you know what? I think that was the name she mentioned."

Bella had been speechless for some time but found the strength to fire another question at the man. "And you didn't think to ask why he would want to kill anyone?"

"Like I said, I did not find the information that the old biddy— my apologies. I did not consider the information that the highly strung coot presented to be credible." I won't deny that I contemplated jumping over the counter to drive home my argument, but I managed to resist.

Bella dropped her voice and seethed in the despicable fellow's direction. "You're a disgrace to your profession, Bulmer. Do you know that?"

The sergeant was so happy to be the focus of our ire that he showed his teeth as the skin across his face stretched tighter. I could tell that he was the sort who lived for such attention, and there was no sense in continuing down the same path.

"Thank you so much for your time," I said with just a dollop of menace. I pulled Bella away from the desk before she could get us both arrested. "You have been so kind."

# EIGHT

As much as I like to complain about my dog's peculiarities, I must say that (thanks to my uncle) he is a very well-trained creature and always waits patiently outside shops. He was overjoyed to see Bella after our frustrating foray into the police station, and his tail flicked back and forth as he walked around us.

My friend, on the other hand, was in a less buoyant mood. "Marius, why did you give up like that?"

"I didn't give up, Bella," I insisted. "I realised what kind of person the sergeant was and beat a tactical retreat."

She gritted her teeth for a few seconds before redirecting her anger where it deserved to go. "The very gall of the man. I can't quite believe that he could be so incompetent, not to mention bigoted."

"I wish I could be the voice of experience and say that I've come across such people before, but the officers we've met have always been..." It was at this moment I remembered a less than brilliant detective down in Hampshire and searched for the right expression. "They've always been dedicated to their jobs."

"Then what should we do now?"

I looked down at Percy as he chased his tail, presumably to

keep warm more than anything. "If I can find a coin for the tele-phone, then I have an idea."

We went to the red telephone box on the opposite side of the road to place a call to police headquarters at Scotland Yard. With this done, I knew exactly what our next task should be.

"We have some time to kill. Would you care to join me for lunch?"

"I suppose it's better than standing here feeling angry with the world."

"Wonderful. You can take out your rage on some scones."

She smiled for the first time since we'd left Holly Village, and we walked along the high street until we found a tea room. I saw another dog sitting by its owner's table, so I knew we'd have no trouble bringing in our four-legged companion. In fact, everyone turned to admire the proud pup as he strode past.

"I must confess that I have a passion for such places," I told Bella once we'd been shown to a table by a middle-aged woman with a squint, a black and white uniform and a paper doily bonnet on her head. "It's not just the usually excellent sandwiches and cakes that I love. Something about tea rooms makes me feel at home."

"It must be the attention of the women who spend their days here." She looked around at the smiley clientele, a few of whom could have been born before the Crimean War. "It's the perfect place for an eligible bachelor like you to find a wife."

"Perhaps it is." I stretched my legs under the table and leaned back in my chair. "And perhaps you should put less stock in people's age than the officers in Highgate police station do."

She pulled away, clearly feeling guilty. "Please don't. I'm still furious at them. I really hoped they would point us in the right direction or at least listen to what we've learnt so far."

"Yes, but what have we learnt so far?"

Before she could answer this, the waitress returned to show us the menu, and we ordered forthwith. I couldn't remember the last time I'd eaten a mince pie (though it was presumably twelve months ago) let alone three, plus a helping of ham and mustard sandwiches and a slice of Christmas cake. Bella looked disapproving, much as she did every time I ordered the appropriate amount of food for my level of hunger.

"We know that something wasn't right at Holly Village," she answered my question some time after I'd forgotten what it was. "No matter what the police might think, I have no reason to question Adele's sanity or mental fortitude. She sat in her tower and observed her neighbour doing something that he shouldn't have – that much is clear. Furthermore, she told you that a man she knew was taking advantage of one of her friends."

"I believe the expression she used was 'he's surely after her money'."

"Which more or less fits with the limited information that the police confirmed for us. At the very least, we've been able to confirm Maggie's suspicions that John Presler is the one Adele suspected."

"Yes, but what's to say that she was actually murdered? A doctor or coroner must have inspected the body. Even if a full post-mortem examination wasn't conducted, he still determined that she'd had some kind of heart attack. It couldn't be poison because that would have been noticed, and it couldn't be strangulation either. Even suffocation, despite what crime novels and poorly made films would have us believe, leaves its mark."

"That's not what I'm suggesting." Bella picked up a teaspoon and ran her fingers along the stem. "Although I believe there are poisons which leave little trace. I had something else in mind."

"Oh, yes?"

She was deadly serious as she laid out her idea. "Perhaps you'll think I'm silly, but I wondered whether she could have been scared to death."

"You mean that someone dressed up as a ghost and jumped out at her?" I immediately regretted sounding so flippant.

"No, Marius. It's Christmas, not Hallowe'en. Unless the killer was a devotee of M.R. James or Sheridan Le Fanu, I doubt that would have been the chosen method to despatch Addie."

"Then what did you have in mind?"

"Well..." I could see how nervous it made her even to express the idea. "I know it might sound ridiculous, but do remember that Maggie described the scene as being chaotic when she found the body. She said that there were ornaments knocked over on the shelves. So what if the killer made a loud noise to wake Adele after she returned from the party and, when she came downstairs, he pushed her over, and the sudden scare it gave her led to the heart attack? I'm not denying that she had problems with her health. I just think that it's too much of a coincidence that she would happen upon a conspiracy in the village, then die that very same week."

"And I have no wish to disagree."

"Really, Marius. I stand by—" She had been preparing for an argument and had to stop herself. "Oh, I'm sorry. We normally take differing viewpoints before coming to accept the other person's. I see you've skipped over that stage."

I took a moment to make sure of my own thinking. "We can't say for certain that she was murdered, but I know for a fact that people can die from heightened stress brought on by fear. I heard of it happening to soldiers during the war. Perhaps it was just hearsay, but I was told a third-hand tale about a lieutenant who died without a scratch on him. A bomb exploded a few feet away, his captain was cut in half, and he simply expired where he stood."

The waitress returned with a well-laden tray which she soon unloaded onto the round, white-tableclothed table.

"Now, you two, have a lov-er-lee meal!" she sang to us, then disappeared back to the kitchen.

Bella looked perplexed by our discussion and, for some unfathomable reason, tried to dissuade me of the value of her own theory. "Of course, we can't say that anyone set foot in the house. It's still possible that Adele herself dislodged the items from the shelf. She was almost eighty and—"

"Stop," I told her, a touch too firmly. "You're forgetting the missing painting. Manet, wasn't it?"

She didn't reply. She looked perturbed by the whole matter and nibbled on a sandwich in the birdlike manner that the upper classes find more polite than eating like ordinary humans.

"There are fifteen things we could be discussing at this moment that would be more useful than questioning whether there is any crime to investigate in the first place." I passed a piece of ham down to Percy and realised that I would need to get him some proper food before long. This was not one of the pressing topics I needed to address. "With each of the three suspects we've spoken to this morning, a question arose which I didn't have time to ask you."

"Three? I'll accept that Ivy Frazel is an odd bird, but Maggie and Mr Wandle can hardly be considered obvious suspects."

She had almost answered one of my questions without knowing it. "Really? Why not?"

"Because..." She shifted her weight from one side to the other. "Because... Oh, bother you, Marius Quin! If I say I trust them implicitly, you'll tell me I'm a soft-headed innocent. If I say they wouldn't have gained anything from killing Adele, you'll bring up that blasted painting again. And if I tell you I've known them most of my life, you'll claim that I've been taken in all that time."

I couldn't resist a brief flash of a smile. "You're doing all the work for me today. I barely need to be here. But let's start with Maggie, shall we?"

"I'd rather hoped that John Presler's prominence would make him the only suspect." She looked askance and handed Percy some more meat. "But if you insist..."

"Aside from your general impression of her as a decent sort – which I promise I'm not dismissing out of hand – is there any concrete reason we shouldn't regard Maggie as the potential killer, or perhaps an accomplice? She had the opportunity: her own key to the house, no less. And while she can say the front door was unlocked, we only have her word for it. Furthermore, she knew the victim personally and, had she stolen the Manet and replaced it with the tasteless composition that now hangs there, she could have made a real packet for herself."

Bella remained reluctant to consider her friend a suspect. "Yes, but if she had stolen the painting, she would simply have told us that Adele had got rid of it herself. She could have made up a perfectly believable story for why her employer had tired of looking at the same picture for so long. Instead, she described how the Manet was in its place the last time she cleaned the house. I say, therefore, that Maggie is innocent."

She brought her fist down ever so softly on the table to make her point – it was not the kind of establishment that approved of unnecessary brouhaha and several heads turned.

I bit the inside of my cheek as I looked for any holes in her logic, then admitted defeat. "Very well, what about Herbert Wandle?"

"The same basic arguments go for him, too. He and his wife the Baroness were Auntie Addie's treasured friends. The three of them played bridge twice a week with another lady from the estate. Would she really have spoken of him in the manner she did at the party?"

"Proximity makes the heart grow murderous," I dared mutter, and she gave me a gentle kick under the table to keep me in line. I suppose it might have been Percy, but I'm quite familiar with the feel of her pointed leather toes on my shin.

"Don't be wilful, Marius. It suits you far too well."

I took this to mean that she couldn't entirely rule out her friend's involvement in the death. I decided not to vex her anymore and asked a practical question. "You said that we might need to consult Wandle on a matter that fell within his expertise. What would that be?"

"As well as designing furniture, he also sells antiques. In fact, he has a shop just across the road from here."

"Oh, then there's clearly no way he could have murdered

someone in order to steal a valuable painting and sell it to one of his shady contacts."

"What did I say about being wilful?" She could be quite steely when the feeling took her. I admit that I found it both unnerving and a tiny bit exciting.

"Let's move on, shall we? Is his wife really a baroness?"

She looked at me as though I'd just asked whether the petits fours she was eating were made of Bakelite. "Of course she is, Marius. That's why everyone calls her the Baroness."

"No one calls you the..." I began before realising that, as the only time we were ever introduced was when we were both five years old and our parents thought it might be nice for us to play together, I hadn't a clue what category of aristocrat she actually was.

"That's because I don't have a title of my own, Marius. As the daughter of a duke, I have the honorary—"

"Actually, I'm not very interested." I winked to show her I was at least partially teasing.

The fact was that I missed this kind of conversation. We'd fought and bickered and teased one another from that very first day playing in her house. It was probably selfish of me to want my old friend back. The past year had pulled us in a thousand different directions, but I simply loved passing a few carefree minutes with her, and if there were refreshments on offer, all the better.

"Now that I think of it, most baronesses are merely referred to as ladies, so it is a little—"

"Will this have a bearing on the case?"

"It's hugely unlikely."

"Will there be a test for me at the end of the day?"

"Definitely not."

"Then perhaps we should move on to the next point."

She stirred her tea. "Fine. As far as I know, she had no brothers and must have inherited the title from her father by writ. Or perhaps she was married before she met Herbert. I really can't remember. I do know that her parents were from Scotland and they do things differently up there."

As fascinated as I wasn't by the inheritance of English peerages and titles, I was even less enthralled by those of our northern neighbour, but at least I had time to try a mince pie whilst she talked. It was delicious. The fruit was rich and piquant. The pastry was just the right side of buttery to crumble in my mouth. It made me wonder why we don't eat them all year.

"How riveting." I tried to sound earnest. I thought we might get to the point more quickly that way. "So, your aunt was good friends with them, and you don't think they can be involved. Let's just say they are possible candidates for the moment. What about Ivy Frazel? Had you heard of her before this morning?"

She pouted, and the subtle red of her lipstick became more noticeable. "No, but neither had she heard of me, which I thought odd."

"Yes, that was curious, especially as she claimed to be a good friend of Adele's and knocked on the door as though she owned the whole village. First, she wished to accuse us of trespassing, then she became incredibly deferential to you, and finally she grew morose and hurried from the house. I've probably met more peculiar human beings in my life, but no one comes to mind."

We both fell silent then. It was a strange way to start a murder investigation, let alone the Christmas season.

After a sip of her Darjeeling, Bella looked across the table and announced, "There's nothing out of the ordinary about our suspects being an eccentric bunch. But what about the mystery man of Holly Village? We should be talking about John Presler."

"I've only just got here, and you've already found a mystery man," a newcomer interrupted, and I was pleased to see that reinforcements had arrived.

# NINE

"Detective Inspector Lovebrook!" Bella was evidently pleased to see him. "I'm so pleased to see you." See?

"And you, dear Lady Bella. Now, tell me what I've missed." Our good friend from the Metropolitan Police took a chair from the neighbouring table and sat down so that Percy could sit on his feet. "I came as soon as I could."

"How did you know we were in here?" Bella was surprised to see him, though she'd heard my phone call outside.

"I know Marius's feelings on tea rooms. I saw this place and immediately knew where you'd be waiting. Perhaps I'll order some refreshments of my own before we go any further."

He did just that, and we discussed the few suspects that we'd already considered before finally getting to John Presler.

"Presler," he murmured. "Obviously you can't read too much into a name, but there's something rather unsavoury about it."

"That may be," I replied, "but all we know about him at the moment is that he is much younger than his wife. He lives in a house opposite our victim, and she was making notes on his comings and goings in the days before she died."

"Well, I've heard enough. With a name like Presler and an older wife, he's clearly the killer. If you give me his address, he'll be before a judge by the end of the day. This may be the easiest case we'll ever investigate."

Lovebrook is terribly well spoken for a police officer, and has a friendly air about him, which makes everything we do seem simple. It also makes it hard to know whether he's being serious. Bella sent an apprehensive glance across to me, and our friend set our minds at ease.

"I'm only joking. We can't really arrest the man without evidence. Do you happen to have any?"

She looked no less nervous now. "I'm afraid not. There was nothing in Auntie Addie's notes to suggest what she suspected her neighbour of doing."

The inspector turned to me. "But she said she thought he was a killer?"

"Not quite," I told him. "She said he had it in him to kill, and she thought he was taking advantage of her friend."

He thought for a moment and then asked Bella another question. "And so Mrs Presler was your aunt's friend?"

All Bella's drive from a few minutes earlier had dissipated. "I'm afraid I don't know very much about Adele's life in Holly Village. I did once, but it has been a long time since I visited her there. However, her maid came twice a week. Maggie was the one who told us that John Presler was the likely suspect, and the local bobbies confirmed she mentioned his name."

"Perhaps you should tell me everything I need to know from the beginning," Lovebrook suggested, and we did just that.

"The reason we really need your help," I said, having laid out the details of the case as his tea was served, "is because the police here have been so unhelpful, not only to us, but Adele Leach too when she took her suspicions to them."

"That's not a problem." He poured himself a cup without waiting for it to brew. I suppose that, in the life of a professional detective (as opposed to a hobbyist imitator) there is little time for such luxuries. "I will simply fire the men responsible and see what they think of Mrs Leach's suspicions when they're on the bread line."

Bella was horrified once more. "No, that isn't what—"

"I really am sorry," he interrupted. "I was trying to lighten the mood during what is clearly a difficult time for you. I've never been much of a comic and will now retire altogether."

I actually thought of him as quite a droll fellow, but he was probably right about not making jokes at such a sensitive moment. Perhaps he assumed that our regular habit of finding dead bodies had desensitised us, but Bella needed a gentler touch this time.

"Would you like me to talk to them? Is that what you're suggesting?" He had an ever so endearing expression and, like everyone else that day, reached across to take Bella's hand in his.

I could see the good it did her. She nodded, and it was apparent just what a weight had been taken off her shoulders. The poor soul had been through so much, and she needed more than a couple of jokers to help her through the experience.

"Most concerningly of all, they didn't even investigate John Presler after my aunt presented her fears to them. I would greatly appreciate it if you could speak to them yourself."

Lovebrook needed to hear no more. He tipped the scorching tea down his throat without a wince, wrapped a triangular egg and cress sandwich in a paper serviette and stood up from the table.

Percy had been soundly asleep – I could tell from the snoring – and he looked most put out to have been roused. I, meanwhile, had finished my food and was happy to make a move. It was Christmas, and I didn't want to spend the holiday looking for a murderer.

Bella was just as animated by Lovebrook's verve as I was. We paraded from the tea room like Winnie the Pooh and his friends going for a walk. We continued along the pavement, waited for the tram to rumble past on its way up the hill, and then crossed the road towards the pleasingly designed police station, with its rounded entrance and temple-like porch.

"If you wait here," Lovebrook told us as we came to a stop outside, "I'll do what I can."

"Excellent." I tried to be optimistic for Bella's sake, and the inspector brushed off his hands and walked through the open door to the station.

Bella, Percy and I stood in a line facing the traffic. I now knew how my dog felt to be left on the pavement so often.

The shopping street was busy, even with the snow turning to slush. A cooper's wagon crept up the hill, forcing the car behind to toot angrily as another tram passed in the opposite direction. On the pavement, various hawkers displayed their goods to passing shoppers. An onion man from Brittany had a stick over his shoulders with strings of his produce hanging from it. Further along the pavement, a small crowd of children had gathered around a stall selling fumsups and mechanical chimney sweeps who would poke their brush up and down if you wound them with a key.

The flat-capped salesman sang to get the attention of the wide-eyed infants and their harried parents.

*"Good wares do I bring*
*To you and your kin.*
*Great toys for this Christmas*
*And they won't cost you dear."*

It wasn't the most festive reinterpretation of "We Wish you a Merry Christmas", but it raised a smile from more than a few reluctant purchasers. From their reactions, it was clear who would give in to their children's demands and who would resist. The singing merchant was doing a roaring trade, even though there was a toyshop selling a larger, more reliable selection just a few doors away. The fact he was charging half the price surely didn't hurt.

"I think I saw a dog food man with a cart just past the bank," I told Bella when we'd been waiting there for a few minutes without any word from Lovebrook. "I should get something for Percy while I have the chance."

This obviously made my dog happy, but Bella was barely aware that I'd spoken. I left her with her thoughts (and Percy).

There were no decorations adorning the lamp posts in this part of the city, but the feel of Christmas hung in the air. The bustle and busyness of the place made me think of my own trips to the city with my parents when I was a child. One Saturday each year, in the middle of December, they would take me to Hamleys on Regent Street, and I was allowed to choose one toy for myself (within reason). I can still remember the excitement of entering the busy toyshop filled with children just like me, our hearts overflowing with anticipation.

A less joyful image greeted me on Archway Road that lunchtime. A man of perhaps fifty was playing records on a gramophone which he pushed around on an old perambulator. He would let one carol play, then change the disc and wind the contraption once more. It made a jolly, raucous noise as "Ding Dong! Merrily on High" blasted across the scene, but I mainly noticed the man who was reliant on strangers' generosity for his living. I had no doubt that he'd been in the war like me. He wound the gramophone with his left arm, but his other sleeve was empty. I gave him a pound note, and he looked at me like I was playing a trick on him, presumably because people had done that very thing before.

"A Merry Christmas to you," I told him, and he made the effort to extend his good arm to me and looked me in the eye as he returned the greeting.

The cart selling meat for pets was stationed in front of a quiet shop. The name on the sign was "H. Wandle & Company Antiques" and the window display was made up of imported French furniture, porcelain figures and silver watches. When I'd heard that Adele's friend Herbert was an antiquarian, I'd imagined him selling priceless treasures and fine art. The reality wasn't nearly so glamorous, and it was hard to imagine a Manet going on sale there.

I paid for the package of meat that the boy had wrapped in wax paper and returned to the station. Bella was far more alert than when I'd left. She was listening in at the doorway with an impressed mien.

"What's—"

"Shhh!" She put a finger to her lips, as though the shushing wasn't clear enough.

"Well, that isn't good enough," Lovebrook's raised voice carried out to us. "Your job is to serve the public, and yet you let down a vulnerable old lady, neglected your duties and compromised the investigation of a potential murder."

"Really, sir—" Sergeant Bulmer began, but the inspector wouldn't let him speak.

"Thank you, but you've said enough." I'd never heard him so incensed. It wasn't just a hiding he was giving them; this was a full tanning. "I expect you to look into this man John Presler, as you should have done from the beginning. And let me leave you with this final thought: if I were your direct superior, you'd be lucky to keep your jobs."

Bella and I hurried back to the spot where Percy was keeping his patch of ground warm. Why we should have felt the need to pretend we weren't listening, I cannot tell you, but our parents' insistence that we weren't to eavesdrop, and our youthful habit of doing so whenever we got the chance, meant that such guilt had stayed with us.

To my surprise, Lovebrook emerged with a radiant smile. "By Jove, that was fun."

"What did they tell you?" I had to ask him.

"They communicated quite clearly what incompetent officers they are. There's no place in the force for men who put their own selfish needs before the welfare of the community."

"We were thinking more of Adele's visit here in the week," Bella pointed out.

"Ah, that." His enthusiasm faded as he thought back over his encounter with the arrogant pair. "I don't think they were keeping much from you. The only thing they recalled when I turned the screw was that they asked your friend for evidence of her claims. All she could say was that she'd seen the suspect out of the house at all hours and he had an untrustworthy look about him."

# TEN

Lovebrook returned to Scotland Yard to speak to the detective who had been called to Holly Village after Adele was found dead. He also promised to look into John Presler, but I couldn't help feeling a touch deflated by our exploratory trip to the nearest high street.

At first, I'd wanted to believe that the police would tell us something significant that Adele's notes had failed to capture. Then I'd hoped that our inspector friend could get the truth out of them. But the only really positive thing I'd gained from the excursion was that I was no longer quite so hungry as I had been. Of course, such satisfaction is, by its nature, fleeting.

"What's next?" I asked my partner in detection.

"It feels like you keep asking that question."

"That's because I keep asking it."

We'd turned off the high street to navigate the quiet roads back to Holly Village. A man was shovelling the snow off the pavement in front of his house, and the scrape of metal on tarmacadam caused the filling in my tooth to tingle unpleasantly.

"First things first," I said decisively, "when we get back to the village, we'll interview every last person we can find."

"Yes." She nodded and chose a similarly optimistic tone. "Then we'll look around Adele's house for any other clues."

"Perfect. And after that, it will be time for tea, and we can visit your friend the Baroness."

She frowned again. "Is the source of your next round of sandwiches always the most important thing to you, Marius?"

"Not always. For one thing, I spend most of my time coming up with new ways to kill my characters that will confound and amaze my readers. And for another, I also enjoy pastries, flans, salads... The list goes on!"

She turned her head at an angle to appreciate the incredible human being at her side. "You really are quite witty sometimes."

"You didn't laugh."

"You're not *that* witty."

She may not have shown her amusement, but I did.

By the time we reached Holly Village, I was feeling a good bit brighter. The sky was a shade further from gunmetal grey than it had been when we left. The decorations were now in place on the elegant old lamp posts and, as soon as we walked under the archway in the gatehouse, the bespectacled woman we'd seen up the stepladder came hurrying towards us.

"Lord and Lady Montague!" She was most excited and gave a full curtsey with her nose pointed to the ground. "My name is Ruth Haskell, and it is an honour to have you as our new neighbours."

She was an excitable, jerky sort of person of around seventy-five. She wore plus fours, high leather boots and a waist-length coat with a velvet collar. She looked as though she'd been in three minds whether to play golf, head to the country or pop to the theatre.

She returned to her full height but continued to speak in the same fawning tone. "May I be so bold as to enquire whether you plan to attend our little gathering this afternoon?"

"You may," Bella responded most regally. In the time I've known her, I've come to realise that the Duke of Hurtwood's daughter has little regard for rank, but that doesn't mean she can't play along with others who do. She can be a real Marie Antoinette if that is what people expect from her.

"Thank you, Lady Montague." Ruth Haskell cleared her throat before her big moment. She was even plummier than the Duke himself. "Would you possibly consider honouring us with your presence at the gatehouse, where we will be assembling for some light Christmas refreshments and a carol or two?"

This decision was Lady Bella's to make, so I stood and waited as the question travelled around her brain.

"We would like that very much," she declared, still playing the part of the arrogant aristocrat.

Ruth Haskell furiously wrote our names down on a list that was pinned to a wooden board, and this gave me an idea.

"In fact, we can do better than that." Once she'd finished writing, I took the board from her. "Why don't we go around the village asking everyone to come at..." I looked at the piece of paper. "Six o'clock, is that right?"

"Oh, Lord Montague. You really are too kind. I have my work cut out for me here. I am what you might describe as the social secretary of Holly Village. I try to keep people busy and offer regular entertainment, especially for the older, single ladies we have here. The Baroness is a great help, of course—"

Pushing her thick glasses up her nose, she broke off what she was saying to ask a question that she wouldn't give us time to answer. "Have you met the Baroness? She is a wonderful woman, and so generous. She is forever lending me her husband when my work gets too much for me. Together, the three of us have decided upon our programme of Christmas activities. They are just the sort of people we like to have around here."

As she said this, she glanced at the house to our left, and I believe I understood her meaning.

"Yes, I'm very fortunate to have known Herbert and the Baroness since I was a child," Bella replied just as formally as before. "Whereas I don't believe you and I have ever met before, Mrs Haskell."

"Actually, it's Miss." She spoke these words with a certain pride, as if to say, *I am an independent woman. I need no man to help me organise a Christmas gathering (unless the Baroness can lend me her husband).* "I've been living here for seven years now. I'm at number six, where Mr Hardwick lived before he died. Did you know him?"

"His name definitely rings a bell."

Miss Haskell adopted a wistful expression and turned her eyes to the sky. "That's the only sad thing about living here. Holly Village has traditionally housed older residents. I'm sure you see the attraction, but it does mean that we tend to have people coming and going rather regularly."

"I can imagine," I said almost instinctively. She was the kind of person who gave you answers to repeat rather than questions to answer.

"Of course, now that you're here, things may be changing!" She was most taken with the idea that we would outlive her.

"Wonderful," Bella said in that ever so smooth tone. "We must be getting on if we wish to call on everyone before six o'clock. It was a real pleasure to make your acquaintance, Miss Haskell."

Just as with Ivy Frazel that morning, who happened to be sitting on a bench over on the far side of the square, Bella had charmed our new acquaintance. The sound of her name falling from the smart young lady's lips provided a great thrill.

"Thank you so much for your immense generosity!"

I was frankly amazed that she didn't curtsey again or perhaps pledge allegiance to Bella like a knight of old. Instead, she walked to a door in the back of the gatehouse, where I saw a grubby man in overalls with long leather gloves on his hands that made him look like a falconer.

Apart from Miss Frazel on the bench near her house, the village was dead, and the snow had started to fall with some intensity for the first time that day. Something about the way the flakes followed a winding trajectory to the ground, like feathers from a burst pillow, made it seem even quieter. The only sound was our feet on the path as we walked towards the first house, intent on carrying out the task that offered the perfect excuse to get to know our suspects a little better.

Sadly, there was no response at number three, and that was the address we most wanted to visit. At number four lived a very nice old lady called Betty, who showed us her less nice collection of porcelain pigs. She also owned what looked very much like a Ming vase, but it was mainly the pigs that she wished to discuss. She was only too happy to be reminded of the Christmas party, especially as she was just getting over a long and persistent bout of the megrims.

The next house along looked as though no one lived there. Then came number six, which belonged to Ruth Haskell, though it turned out the building was split in two, and 6b was occupied by a dear old fellow who was the soul of hospitality.

Clive Whitworth didn't have to tell me that he was the son of a marquess. I could tell from the way he held himself – not to mention the standard of furnishings in his well-kept cottage. He was a veteran of the first Boer War and had some colourful opinions on the men who'd led him into battle. I doubt such language had been used in Bella's presence before, but she didn't seem to mind. He had a truly beautiful library, full of exquisite first editions and ancient manuscripts, which I could have killed an hour or ten reading. Sadly, the time to leave soon arrived, but Clive did promise to come at six o'clock with everyone else.

House number seven was also divided in half, and we met another very civil woman named Carrie, who collected Fabergé eggs. Christmas party: yes. Useful information about Adele: no.

Our last call of any note was on a rather blunt gentleman who didn't like people knocking at his door.

"What is the meaning of this?" he shouted, waving his cane at us as though he thought it was a machine gun. "I didn't pay to live in a sheltered, secluded, fenced-in village just for every Tommy Talks-too-much and Mary Mouths-a-lot to come intruding on my privacy!"

I don't mind telling you that I found him something of an oaf. "We're sorry to bother you, but we've—"

"What are you doing here? Begging for the poor? Drumming up names for a petition to knight the local butcher? Or are you some sort of religious loon and I'll have to go back inside to get my bayonet?"

"We're none of those things." I spoke more forcefully now. "We are your neighbours as of—"

"I know every last person here, young man." He stepped clear of his doorway in order to poke me in the chest. "You won't pull the wool over these eyes."

There's a reason I don't investigate crimes on my own. Bella has always been better at talking to people, and she walked closer to do what I couldn't. "As it happens, Mr..."

"The name's Freddy Ponting, if you must know."

"Well, Freddy, as it happens, I am Adele Leach's heir, and we are staying in her cottage."

He studied her face for a moment, then looked back at me. "So you're not Shakers, Quakers, Keswickians or Radical Pietists?"

"I doubt that our religious denomination is relevant at this juncture. All we wish to know is whether you'll be coming to the Christmas party this evening?"

He screwed his face up as though he found this even more appalling. "Are you saying that Ruth Haskell sent you?"

Bella looked oddly anxious for a moment. "That's right."

"Then why didn't you say!" He was suddenly full of bonhomie. "Ruth and I are firm friends. I like her much better than most of the yahoos and busybodies who live around here." He closed his eyes to reel off his opinion of his neighbours. "Herbert Wandle is a horrific windbag. The Baroness expects us to fall in line and treat her like a queen. Talking to Ivy Frazel is as intellectually stimulating as dashing your brains out with a mallet. Clive is conceited, Carrie's a nincompoop, and taking tea with Betty is as much fun as a dose of scarlet fever."

"Well, now we know where we stand at least," I replied in as dry a tone as I could produce.

"Talking of tea. Would you like a cup?" Freddy smiled for the first time and looked at us expectantly.

"That would be lovely," Bella replied, and, to my surprise, the belligerent villager led us into his cottage.

Much like the others we'd seen, it was stuffed full of valuables. Unlike the other houses we'd entered, I left with no desire ever to visit again. Freddy Ponting had few good words to say about anyone in Britain. He clearly loathed poor Adele and, while he gave nothing away about her death, I had no doubt that the two of them had butted heads in the past. It was amazing he liked anyone, and I had to question why he made an exception for Ruth Haskell.

If that weren't bad enough, he used only the cheapest tea leaves and I'm fairly sure the milk had turned. He agreed to come to the party, though I already wished we could retract the invitation.

"There we go," I said, feeling both satisfied with our work and vexed to have had to put up with Freddy's misanthropy. "We've been around all the houses and achieved what we set out to do."

Bella clearly agreed with me, and even Percy let out a contented yip.

"Yes, it feels quite rewarding to complete our task," she said with a serious expression. "Now let's get back to the case."

# ELEVEN

We'd tried our hardest to find out what we could about the goings-on in Holly Village. Bella had been particularly good at working Adele's death into the conversation, but the dear folk who'd so kindly admitted us to their houses just shook their heads and said, "Terrible business."

Even mentioning our suspect, John Presler, did nothing to set tongues wagging. The locals apparently regarded him as an uncouth, though benign, presence in the village, and it was hard to get anything more out of them. I was tempted to wait outside his house for my chance to interrogate the man, but I felt that our case was built on such shaky foundations that I wouldn't know where to begin.

I employed my every ounce of cunning to get the truth from his neighbours, but it was no use. Freddy Ponting was the only person who let slip any sign of animosity towards Adele. It was possible that one of the friendlier residents would turn out to be a criminal genius who, in the guise of a quiet, law-abiding pensioner, had conspired to murder and rob, but it was difficult to imagine. With the obvious exception of the owner of 7b – who saw the worst in everything and everyone – the people we visited seemed quite oblivious to any danger.

Carrie in 7a, for example, had mainly tried to get us to eat her Christmas pudding, and shown little interest in Adele, of whom she talked fondly but could tell us little. And I realised after we left Freddy's house that he'd only let us in because he wanted me to help him tune his radio set. He paid us very little attention once he could listen to the results of the previous night's greyhound race in Glasgow. I suggested that, if he put a sausage on a stick and threaded it through Percy's collar, my dog might run a few laps of the green, but neither Percy nor Freddy seemed interested.

We arrived back at Adele's house feeling dispirited once more.

"It's hard work getting nowhere," Bella said as she sat down at the bottom of the staircase to untie the laces of her high, black boots. She paused the task to stare out of the cloverleaf window in the front door. "What if we're wrong and the only thing we're chasing is our tails? What if Adele really was bored with the painting and sold it before she died? What if—"

"We're not wrong," I said without hesitation. "And I feel certain there is something here that can prove it."

I didn't take my shoes off – bad form, I know. I simply walked into the sitting room to look up at the high shelf which Maggie had told us had been disturbed when Adele died. A small figure there appeared to be chipped, but everything else had been put back in place, so I searched on around the room for some new clue. In time, I returned to Bella, who was still looking glum.

"It's no good," she told me, and I raised one hand so that she would keep her negativity to herself until I'd had the chance to fail further. I can only think that Freddy's grumbling pessimism had rubbed off on her.

I had a look at the hall and something that Adele's maid had told us came back to me. With a spring in my step, I ran to the end of the room and pulled up the runner in order to examine the plain cream carpet underneath.

"What are you doing?" Bella hadn't expected me to do something useful just then.

"When we spoke to Maggie, she talked about the state of the

hall when she first came to check on Adele. I knew that there had been some kind of disturbance which the police chose to ignore. Well, this is the proof we need."

Bella instantly got to her bootless feet to examine the black streak which ran the length of the room. It was clear that Maggie had done her best to scrub it clean, but it was more than just a stain. The carpet had been scorched.

Bella knelt to touch the mark, and Percy gave it a good sniff. I think he probably knew what had happened, but it was Bella who spoke the words, "It looks like a burn."

I looked across the hall to the sitting room where the body was found. The entrance was in line with the high shelf where the objects had been dislodged.

"The killer really did want to terrify her," I concluded. "Perhaps there was a confrontation when she came home from the party. She said in her notes that the killer was always out late. He knew that Adele was suspicious, so he slipped something through the letter box or a crack in the door."

"But there was no guarantee it would kill her."

"Yes, but he could have waited at the door to do it if she came out. This was the cleanest option, but he had brute force or perhaps a weapon in reserve."

Bella walked to the other side of the room to look along the line of the damage just as I had. "What could have done it?"

"I've been thinking about that. It's definitely some kind of explosive. When I was in France during the war, I knew men who made grenades with gun cotton. They experimented to find out just how much of the chemicals to use to make the biggest explosion. A simple fuse could be added to delay it. We called them jam-tin grenades, because my friends made them using the left-over tins from our rations."

"Are you saying we're looking for an ex-soldier?"

"It's a possibility, but gun cotton only came to mind because, at first, I couldn't think how else someone would obtain an explosive device."

"Fireworks," she said, because she just loves ruining the end of my fascinating observations.

"That's right." I may have sounded a touch put-out. "Fireworks."

She explained her reasoning. "They're very easy to get at this time of year, and no one would think too much about one going off in the days before Christmas. Children are forever playing with them."

"It's still a risky method. This house is quite far from the others, but a loud noise in the middle of the night is still a loud noise. It doesn't make any sense to select a mode of killing that could be mistaken for natural causes, whilst simultaneously making such a racket that it could wake up everyone nearby."

"It's arrogance." Bella had to purse her lips then. I believe the emotion of what we were discussing had come back to her. "The monster who did this wanted to feel he could get away with the crime against the odds."

This matched a thought I'd had when we were going around the houses refusing tea and cake. In each of the murders we'd investigated, there was a certain overconfidence on display. In war, you kill because there is no other choice; in the wealthy suburb of Highgate, I doubt it is ever the necessary option. It takes a special kind of madness to go down that path.

"The assailant must have lit the rocket then thrown it straight into the house." I took this opportunity to follow the presumed firework's path. "It started on the floor, burning the carpet as it went, then flew up towards the shelf."

Bella looked down at the spot where the maid's eyes had told us she'd found the body. "Adele spent the last seconds of her life in terror. She would have already been scared after she crossed paths with the murderer outside. When a firework exploded in her home, it was too much for her. She suffered from angina and arrhythmia, though I believe her condition was so complicated that no one quite knew what was wrong with her. The doctors had been telling her to take things more slowly for years."

"This is a tight-knit community, and gossip travels quickly," I replied, taking time to consider the ramifications of what she'd revealed. "We must assume the killer knew that. He knew a real scare could finish Adele off, and the cold weather would only help."

Through the sitting room window, I noticed the resourceful Ruth Haskell, hurrying along a path between two of the houses with a large box in her arms. Freddy Ponting watched her from the other side of the square but turned away when Herbert came out of his house to help.

And that was when I caught my first glimpse of the Baroness. In a long grey dress with a full, bustling skirt, she looked like a cross between Queen Victoria and a blushing bride. Her hair was arranged in a complicated structure on top of her head, and she was carrying a tiny Yorkshire Terrier who licked her face as she walked up to her husband. In short, she was the very image of the person I'd imagined when I first heard that she liked to be referred to as "the Baroness".

Almost everyone we'd met had mentioned the domineering figure, and I was very much looking forward to hearing what she had to say for herself.

# TWELVE

"Are you certain that it's a convenient time?" Bella asked after we'd invited ourselves into their house.

"Of course it is. You're practically family." Mr Wandle was full of warm words, but I still felt out of place. He kept peering up the staircase as though afraid of his wife finding us there. "Please, children. Come through to the sitting room." He paused at the newel post to call up to his better half. "My angel? Sheena darling? We have visitors."

We didn't wait for our hostess but continued through a doorway set into a wood-panelled wall. Percy had decided he'd had enough of the cold and stayed behind for a nap in Adele's drawing room. This was probably a good thing, as the Baroness's Yorkie was positively furious at our intrusion and would surely have terrorised my poor pup. To reduce the noise, Herbie put him safely away next door.

"It's nice to be back after so long," Bella said as she placed the painting from Adele's lounge on the round table in the middle of the tastefully decorated space.

It bore some similarities to the same room in Adele's house, in that both were packed full of objects, ornaments and artefacts, but I felt that the display we now examined held far more valuable pieces than the dead woman's eclectic collection. I noticed several metal figures which resembled the work of famous sculptors I'd seen when I was living in France. There were paintings, too, and though I am no expert on art, I was certain that one of them was a Gainsborough and another a Turner.

Twice the size of Adele's main room, it was still like a shrunken-down museum, and it struck me again that people on the estate possessed all the trappings of luxury in some of the smallest houses I'd ever visited. I suppose that, like the Baroness, they had come from wealthy families who had lost their fortunes and were left with little but fine furniture and *objets d'art* with which to pack off the younger heirs.

Another important distinction between this house and Adele's was that there was a large fir tree standing in the corner of the room. It was decorated with shiny baubles and trinkets. On the floor around it were a number of prettily wrapped presents ready for Christmas Day.

"Oh, you've noticed my little gallery, have you?" a full, slightly masculine voice boomed from the doorway, as we looked at the artefacts on the shelves. Our hostess had arrived. "Whenever we travel to Paris or Lyon for Herbert's work, I train my eye to look for bargains. My father was something of a collector, and we have added a few select pieces over the years."

For a moment, I asked myself whether they'd recently acquired a Manet. No matter what I'd told Bella, I wasn't going to dismiss these two perfectly suspicious characters on the basis of old family ties.

"Whereas the painting you've brought with you is no great work of art," Mr Wandle told us as he removed a pair of glasses from the breast pocket of his richly embroidered jacket. "I don't wish this to sound offensive if you are very attached to it, but was it painted by a child?"

Bella allowed herself a brief smile. "It might well have been for all we know. It was hanging in Adele's house. Her maid can't understand how it got there."

I had expected her friend to say more, but it seemed that, when his wife was present, she was the one who did the talking.

"How peculiar." Her voice was still just as loud as when she arrived, even as she huddled with us to look at the officially terrible painting. "Do you mean to say that it just appeared there, and no one knows why?"

"That's exactly it," I replied, perhaps showing a little too much suspicion that she had worked this out so readily.

She stared down at the amateurish artwork, looking just as puzzled as her husband. "It looks like the kind of artless piece you might buy in the Caledonian Market. I was down there just the other day myself."

She certainly showed no guilt. Though in her quick, attentive gaze, I noticed a certain reticence that was hard to read.

"The longer you look at it, the uglier it becomes," Bella said as she examined the simple fluffy clouds that closely resembled the sheep in the field below.

"Where did you find it?" Herbert asked as though we'd brought a dead rat into his house and laid it on the table.

"It was there when Auntie Addie died, but I'd never seen it before."

"Where are my manners?" the Baroness eventually asked once we'd stood there for some time looking at a painting that had no intention of giving up its secrets. "I haven't formally introduced myself."

She held out her hand for me to kiss, and I could see that she took her role as the aristocrat of Holly Village to heart.

In the end, she wasn't the one to do the introductions. That fell to Bella. "Baroness, this is my husband Marius Quin."

I kept a yelp of surprise to myself. The truth was, I'd quite forgotten we were married.

The old lady's round cheeks puffed up in excitement. "Marius Quin, the mystery novelist?"

"The very same." Bella looked unusually proud of me. My

fame had apparently grown recently as people had begun to recognise my name – if not my face.

"What an honour it is to have you here." Though she was not very tall herself, the Baroness's architecturally constructed hair brought her up to my height. She put a hand to her chest and looked suitably impressed. "I'm just sorry that you're here under such sad circumstances."

She pointed us to the nearby sofa, and Bella and I sat down as she crossed the room. Her elaborate lace dress, with its many skirts, swept the carpet behind her on the short voyage to a Chesterfield armchair in dark brown leather.

"I'm afraid that's the real reason we've come here." Bella's brow was crumpled and her usually bright eyes were full of sorrow. "I was wondering whether you could tell me in what frame of mind Adele was during the last weeks of her life."

The Baroness's expression mirrored Bella's. "I wish I could shed some light on the matter, but she had been quite her usual self. Wouldn't you agree, Herbie?"

Her broad, rather grandfatherly husband stood at the arm of her chair. He hesitated for a moment, and I decided that the Baroness was painting a rather too simple picture. "I would indeed, my darling."

"We lived our lives just as before, and dear Adele was very much part of our daily routine."

"She was the picture of health and never missed a game of cards," Herbert added before receiving a look of disapproval from his wife.

"That's right. We pursued our usual habits. She would come here for afternoon tea on a Monday, and we played cards most mornings in the gatehouse. Two weeks ago, we even went Christmas shopping together. We passed a lovely few hours in Piccadilly, enjoyed elevenses in Fortnum and Mason's, then took the number sixty-nine electric tramway back home with all of our purchases."

There's something uniquely British about people like the Baroness, and I was aware just how much I missed such eccentricity when I lived abroad. Just as an example, I hadn't heard anyone describe the local transportation system as the "electric tramway" since my grandmother had died. But it was her tone and bearing that I found most curious. I felt as if I'd travelled a hundred years into the past.

Bella released a brief gasp as her sorrow now mixed with shock. "Her present!" She put her hand out towards me but immediately retracted it. "She left me a box when she came to the party, but I put it to one side and totally forgot about it."

"Don't take that upon yourself," I insisted. "She wouldn't have wanted you to open it until Christmas anyway."

"It's true, Bella," Herbert agreed. "Adele loved you like a daughter. She wouldn't be upset because you came here to see her old house rather than tearing open her gift."

The Baroness didn't appear to have heard much of this, and when she spoke again, her voice was weaker. "It's hard to believe she's really gone. Just a few days ago, she was full of life and passion. She was so looking forward to your party."

"What happened is a tragedy, but you mustn't blame yourself." Herbert wouldn't give up on making Bella feel better. "Some things are unavoidable."

"I'm afraid we can't be so sure." Bella didn't look at them as she uttered her response. "We have found evidence to suggest my aunt's death was no accident."

Adele's friends wore similarly stunned expressions, and Herbert put his hand on his wife's arm to prepare her for what was to come.

I hadn't expected to be the one to say it, but Bella couldn't shoulder that burden alone. "We think she was murdered."

Herbie's lips parted slightly, whereas the Baroness showed no emotion whatsoever. She gripped the arm of the chair, but her expression didn't change even as she replied.

"Murdered? You can't possibly mean that—"

"Murdered means murdered," I told her firmly.

"We heard it was her heart..." Not for the first time, I could tell that she wanted to say more but stopped herself.

"We're not denying the facts," Bella took over. "But we think that someone set out to scare her to death."

"Come, come." The Baroness shook her head as though our ideas were too silly to bear contemplating. "That's the sort of thing that happens in ridiculous serials in the newspaper, not real life."

"Someone threw a firework into her house." I could have minced my words, but I decided against it. "That would have made even the fittest fellow's heart race. As she had existing problems with her health, it's really no wonder it killed her."

Herbert looked troubled. "A firework?" He kept peering into his wife's face for reassurance that was not to be found. "And she died on Thursday night?"

I nodded, unsure what he might have extracted from any of this.

He raised one trembling hand to point at me. "I heard it. I heard an explosion."

"Was that the night of the opera?" she asked, sounding less sure of herself. "No, the opera is usually on Wednesdays. You're right. That was Thursday." Her face seemed to turn a little paler in the shifting light. "You woke me up when you jumped out of bed. That was the night she died."

I could see that the scene was playing out in Herbert's memory. "I found it so alarming that I ran to the window to see what was happening."

"What time was that?" I asked, to get the facts straight, and he looked across at the Baroness for confirmation.

"It was around midnight."

The pieces were starting to fall into place, and I gripped the back of the sofa as I answered. "That would have been an hour or so after she arrived here."

"Did you notice anyone in the village?" A new sense of urgency had entered Bella's voice, but Herbie shook his head.

"I'm afraid not. A bright light flashed across the snow, but by the time I'd found my glasses, there was nothing for me to see."

The Baroness turned her head to one side as her husband tried to remember the hazy details of what had occurred.

"I'm afraid I went back to bed and forgot all about it. I really should have made the connection the next day when we found out that Adele had died. I was so flustered by the news that the disturbance quite escaped me."

Their roles had switched, and it was Bella's turn to reassure him. "That's hardly your fault. You had no reason to think she was murdered when the police were unwilling to consider the possibility."

"Did they at least ask you about the explosion?" I pondered, remembering the angry halfwits we'd met at the station.

"The police?" The Baroness shifted in her seat. "They were useless. They took no interest whatsoever in who our friend was or how she'd died. They asked us nothing."

"But a firework? What kind of fool would draw attention to himself like that?" Herbie asked in amazement. "What kind of monster would hurt a good, sweet person like Adele?"

"Very well, my love, that's enough," the Baroness suddenly snapped. I couldn't understand why she would have reacted in such a way, as I wholeheartedly agreed with her husband's sentiment.

I decided to act as though she hadn't said anything. It was either that or sit there in painful silence. "For the moment, we don't know who could be behind her death, but our friend from the Metropolitan Police is looking into the matter."

"Oh, yes?" The Baroness retained the stern tone she'd used to address her husband.

"For one thing, he's going to see what he can discover about the other residents of Holly Village."

Before I could move on to the next obvious point, Bella raised it for me. "Is there anyone here who stands out as different?"

Far from putting our hostess more on edge, this question served to relax her a little.

The husband and wife looked at one another, and it was no surprise that she would be the one to answer. "I suppose you're referring to the Preslers? They're the ones who tend to cause trouble around here."

"We really don't know a great deal about your neighbours." Bella needed to find out the truth rather than the widely distributed version of it. "What can you tell us about them?"

The Baroness looked away, and so Herbie answered for the two of them. "It's not strictly what they do that offends, but the way they interact with everyone else here."

"They're not our kind of people!" the Baroness barked, and the flesh around her neck gathered together in folds.

Herbie was more diplomatic. "What my dear wife is trying to say is that John and Silva Presler could be classified as vulgar sorts."

"If he's not cursing, she's blinding!"

Herbie winced a little but continued his explanation in a measured voice. "Adele, Sheena and I tried our very best to befriend the Preslers when they first came here five years ago. They seemed like, if not nice, then at least friendly folk, but it went horribly wrong."

Before I could ask yet another obvious question, the Baroness provided the answer. "They accused me of being disparaging!" She looked at Bella and me as if to say, *How could anyone think such a thing?* "I went out of my way to be kind to them, and that bustling polecat of a woman told me that I was only being nice to show them up."

*Were you?* I thought but didn't say, and Herbert soon provided a little more context.

"You see, we invited the Preslers here to dinner a week after they arrived. It seemed the neighbourly thing to do, and we like to make the effort with newcomers even if they aren't—"

"They're not our kind of people in the slightest!" the Baroness reminded us.

"I suppose they must have found the occasion overwhelming." Herbert had a thoughtful look on his face, and I had to wonder whether, had he not been married to such a high-handed woman, he would have taken against the Preslers quite so strongly. "Whatever the reason, they were less than appreciative of our hospitality."

"Herbie is being polite." The Baroness finally fixed her grey eyes upon us again. "They came here, ate our food, drank our wine – wine that my husband slaves away in his shop to afford – and then they insulted us."

I could see the trepidation – and perhaps just a hint of amusement – on Bella's face as she considered how to ask what had happened. "Would you mind telling us what they said?"

The Baroness raised her chin and looked up at the ceiling to show that uttering any such explanation was beneath her.

"Well..." Herbie glanced at his wife for a moment, perhaps checking that he would not be shouted at for answering our question. "They found it most amusing that we had laid the table so formally and paid our maid to stay late that night to serve us. They said they weren't the kinds to have people wait upon them and then—" The words died in his throat, but he gave it one more go before his wife interrupted. "And then—"

"And then they walked into *our kitchen* and washed the dishes themselves!"

This was hardly the revelation I'd been hoping to hear. Bella normally kept her feelings hidden during interviews, but even she couldn't resist a glance across at me which said, *I doubt the police will accept that as evidence of a murderous nature.*

Herbie must have understood something of our reaction, as he added, "I believe you had to be there to understand why we found this so offensive. I can promise that they were most disrespectful."

"Yes, but—" I tried to interrupt, but we were in the Baroness's house, and she was holding court.

"That was just the beginning." She had large, owlish eyes that only grew when she was incensed. "Silva Presler said some terrible things about me. Her sorry excuse for a husband is a troublemaker, and the pair of them together have made this a far less pleasant place to live." She crossed her hands in her lap and would say nothing more, which made me wonder why they had fallen out in the first place.

We hadn't had our tea yet, and it was at this moment that an elderly woman came into the room pushing a laden trolley. She was dressed in an outfit which was not so very different from the girl who had served us that afternoon on the high street, but when she saw the expression on her mistress's face, she turned straight back round again and disappeared from the room, leaving the trolley to roll closer to us.

"So you can tell us nothing more definitive than that?" Bella sounded unimpressed by their answers.

"It's hard to say exactly what we find so suspicious about them." Herbert had a good brain in his head and, as he regarded a weathered marble bust on the shelf, he gave us a more nuanced impression of his scandalous neighbours. "I'm sure you'll see it if you have the misfortune of speaking to them – or stepping inside their garishly decorated abode. If you get to know them in any way, you'll soon see what I mean. It feels as if they are always plotting something, always trying to get one over on their fellow men. He in particular is an undeniable schemer. I've noticed him skulking about the village at all hours. He comes back here in the middle of the night sometimes. You wait and see."

"So your opinion of them has nothing to do with the fact that Mr Presler is a good bit younger than his wife?" Perhaps this was a provocative question, but I felt it bore asking.

The Baroness scoffed, but did not deign to answer.

"I would hope you can see that we are not that sort of people, Bella." That's right. I had posed the question, but he addressed his response to my companion. "We have friends of all stripes, and we are not the kind to judge other people unfairly."

"Yes, of course, Herbie," she replied, regaining something of her usual charm. "We're merely interested in what happened to Adele."

He left his wife's side for the first time to walk around the back of the sofa. I felt that he was considering the situation before delivering his verdict. "I would like to tell you something more substantial, but I cannot. If she really was murdered, I am not the man to tell you who is responsible."

"Herbert!" the Baroness finally muttered, but her husband would not be silenced.

"No, my dear, this is something I must say." He paused again to consider his piece. "I have no way of proving that one of the Preslers is a killer. All I can tell you is that, as soon as you revealed that our poor Adele had been murdered, it was not simply that my mind went to our unwelcome neighbours; I was frankly unsurprised that someone here had been killed."

# THIRTEEN

This discussion cast a pall over our time in the lavishly decorated home. There really is no coming back from the revelation that a close acquaintance has been callously slain. Admittedly, Herbie did his very best to lighten the mood by reminding Bella of her trips there when she was a child.

I can't say that I was so fond of his wife. She was proud and prickly and, despite their claims to the contrary, the Baroness seemed like just the kind of person to look down on those around her. Her practically regal affectations made me wonder what sort of person she was underneath.

It was hard to say whether Bella felt the same as I did. Once we'd had our tea and said farewell to our hosts, she fell oddly quiet. I popped the unlovable painting back in the house and checked that Percy still didn't want to come with us. When I returned, Bella was still standing in front of the grandest of the eight houses, looking around the village.

"I always thought this place was so innocent. I imagined it as a toytown – a mystic place I could only visit once a year when the magic portal opened to me. But now I wonder whether there's something rotten here – something hiding behind the climbing ivy and well-trimmed, snow-covered hedges."

"It's not your fault, Bella." I don't know why I told her this. It sounded quite incongruous in response to her observation, and yet it was the right thing to say. My friend had clearly taken the responsibility for the old lady's death upon herself. "Whatever was happening here went unseen until Adele stumbled across it. You haven't visited in years and—"

"That's just it. I hadn't taken the time to come here. We used to meet each month for tea in Harrods or a walk in Regent's Park, but I didn't think about checking on the world in which she lived. I assumed that it would never change – that it would remain, in perpetuity, quaint and sweet and..."

Her words tailed off, and I imagined them being caught by the wind to go flying over the rooftops and chimney pots of the snowbound city.

"It probably sounds fantastical," Bella continued once she'd gathered her thoughts, "but I can feel that something is wrong here, and I think it might be down to us to discover what it is."

She ground to a halt once more, but in the middle of all this, a thought had come to me. "What we need is a break from the madness."

"The carols and what have you start at six o'clock."

"Don't worry," I told her, already steering her towards the arch to leave the village. "We'll be back in plenty of time."

We reached the car, and I got my prize possession started. Even on that cold day, the Invicta purred. I'd never known another car like it, and when it started so reliably, I couldn't help but remember the reluctant trucks and even the Lanchester armoured monstrosity I travelled in during the war. Back then, if a vehicle didn't start first time, especially in those frozen winter months, it could mean the difference between life and death. I'm happy to say I no longer face such challenges, but I still find the instant growl and hum of the engine as I turn the ignition to be terribly reassuring.

"Where are we going, Marius?" Bella asked from the passenger seat after we'd been driving for some minutes.

"Don't worry about that for the moment." I thought she would object to my dismissive reply, but she barely noticed. "What did you make of Herbert and the Baroness? Would you say they were acting differently from how you remember?"

"Yes, I suppose they were," she replied most temptingly before dashing my hopes that I'd missed some vital clue. "Herbie in particular seems unsettled by Adele's death. He's not the type to make a scene, especially when his wife is present, but I remember him being such a jolly figure."

I didn't know how to phrase my next question without upsetting her, but I did my best. "I was curious about the change I noted in him when his wife came downstairs."

She looked troubled for a moment, then her features evened out a little. "That's certainly nothing new. I always thought it sweet that he was so deferential to her. I suppose there is some inequality in their marriage."

Her words pricked me, as she and I were almost as different as it came. "You mean in terms of class and breeding?"

A half smile appeared on her lips then vanished just as quickly. "Well, yes, but also financially. Of course, I can't say whether the Baroness retains any of her family's wealth."

I had pondered this question myself. "Holly Village is a strange place. You evidently need a substantial amount of money to buy a house there in the first place. And yet the buildings are so small that they only suit people in reduced circumstances – metaphorically and then literally."

"It's more about the atmosphere, surely. I can only think that people move there because they want to feel safe in a big, dangerous city. Perhaps the sacrifice of space is worth it. I can imagine that's why Adele went to live there after her husband died."

We had reached the busy junction at Tufnell Park, where the almost absurdly ornate Boston Hotel advertised its "foreign wines", as if there are really any other kind worth drinking. We waited for a rag and bone man to cross ever so slowly and then continued south towards the city.

"Perhaps that's the case, but I doubt that someone like the Baroness would make such a compromise."

She smiled again. It was almost as if the sadness inside her had melted like the snow on the pavements. "She is a real character. I've met less majestic marchionesses."

"I'm sure there are less majestic kings and queens than Baroness Wandle." I didn't actually know that this was her surname, but I needed some way of differentiating her from any other baroness who happened to be nearby.

"Now, are you going to tell me where we are going?"

I considered it for a moment, then shrugged. "We're almost there."

We caught sight of the enormous clock tower first. It was standing over the Caledonian Market like a cyclops on sentry duty. I found the sight of it rather reassuring. I suppose it was the idea that, when planning London's largest cattle market, some bright spark had decided that it should look grand and beautiful. Instead of simply knocking up a quick corrugated-iron shed, a whole complex of buildings was designed, with the central market resembling a cross between a Roman temple and the Crystal Palace.

We were not in the area to buy beef for Christmas dinner. With the winds of commerce having blown in a different direction for the last thirty years, much of the space there had been taken over by a pedlars' market selling just about everything you might – or might not – wish to buy.

"The Baroness mentioned she'd been down here recently," Bella said. "Is that why we've come?"

"I can't deny she gave me the idea." I climbed out of the car and walked around it to let her out. "The door sticks sometimes," I lied like last time, and she once again looked at me as though I were planning to rob her.

We left the car in front of the Bull public house and headed towards the open space which would once have been covered in livestock pens. There were still animals sold in the market, and the smell of cattle was unmistakable in the air, but half of the immense area was now set aside for the daily rag-fair. Second-hand wares of every kind were displayed in long lines. Piles of once-loved books marked our entrance to the market before sellers hawking suitcases, car parts, carriage wheels, gramophone records and every imaginable piece of bric-a-brac from ships' anchors to train pistons called to the passing foot traffic.

One might have expected the clientele of such a place to be from the lower end of the economic spectrum, looking for bargains to stretch their limited income as far as it would go, but the people there were just as varied as the wares on sale. I'd spotted two Rolls-Royces and a rather elegant Humber tourer out in the road, and each had its own chauffeur waiting for his employer to return.

As we walked up and down the aisles of goods, I noticed a few men I took to be antiquarians, along with several well-dressed denizens of London, searching out treasures like explorers in some distant land. A woman with a gigantic ostrich feather in her hat was whispering to a man with a gimlet eye as they loitered in front of a stall which sold sculptures. They were quite conspiratorial, so they must have believed they'd discovered something worth keeping to themselves.

Coming in the opposite direction just then was a man with a monocle and a fur-collared coat fit for a tsar. He was declaring to a man who looked very much like a valet that the market was a secret that only he had discovered, despite the presence of hundreds of other people all around him.

"Are we here for last-minute Christmas shopping?" Bella eventually hazarded.

"Not exactly."

"You really don't need to buy me another present. You got me those lovely bath salts, which will surely last me a lifetime."

She was distracted by the stalls and, despite what she'd just said, her eyes alighted on a shell cameo of a woman with long hair in a complicated plait that hung over her shoulder. It was rather sad to think that, perhaps fifty or a hundred years earlier, someone had loved the woman on the locket so much as to have the piece commissioned. I had to wonder what route it had taken to end up tangled up with thirty other chains and necklaces in a pile on a trader's table in Islington.

I didn't think about it for long, however. At the next stall, a woman was selling large, ugly paintings. Bright, bold and simple, they were housed within cheap wooden frames that looked as though a child had been paid thruppence a day to daub them with a gilt substitute. This work was still superior to the paintings themselves.

"Good afternoon, miss," I said, raising my cap. "I believe that we came across one of your artworks in a friend's house."

The seller wore a black padded jacket and matching pleated skirt. She had the look of a bohemian and the overenthusiastic manner to go with it. "Then your friend clearly has good taste, sir. I painted every one of these m'self."

She was young, and I took her to be an opportunist rather than a serious artist.

"I don't suppose you could tell us when you sold a painting of a hillside scene with sheep and clouds." Looking around the stall, I realised that my description fitted many of the pieces there.

The painter smiled. "Hmmm... let me think." She put one finger to her chin to illustrate this action. "I can't say that rings a bell." She let out a laugh and shook her head as though she couldn't believe how funny she was. "I'm sorry. I'm sorry. I'm just pullin' yer leg, mate. You'd 'ave to narrow it down a bit. I'm fortunate enough to 'ave made a good few sales over this most magical season. It was just yesterday that the Countess of Stockport snapped up three of m' works. She's quite taken with m' oeuvre."

I had never heard of a Countess of Stockport, and had she existed, I doubted that she was in the market for such sloppily painted landscapes.

I remained polite, nonetheless. "This was quite a large painting, easily as big as any you have here."

She leaned back on her stool and eyed up Bella, who did not seem to have noticed that I was interviewing a potentially crucial witness but was still looking at the neighbouring stall.

"That's the thing with me, y' see." The artist raised her hand to the sky with the air of one who is contemplating the wonders of nature. "I am a capable craftsman, no matter the size of the canvas. It's what appeals to many of m' patrons. M' hand is just as deft at miniatures as it is at…" She looked for the right term. "… them big ones!"

Bella must have been listening, at least subconsciously, as she turned to look at the *artiste* in our midst, then asked a more direct question. "We were wondering whether a short man with black pomade in his hair and a very straight parting had bought anything from you recently."

The young woman must have been born around the same time as Bella, but I could only imagine how different their lives had been. She had a knowing look on her face as she said five words I could have predicted very easily. "What's in it for me?"

"I beg your pardon?" It was quite possible that no one had ever said such a thing to Bella before. The world of the upper classes is built upon the idea that everyone underneath will stoop and bow to their every need and sensitivity.

"I'm asking why I should tell ya who bought m' goods. The fact is that I 'ave the confiden'shoeality of m' customers to consider. If it was your friend what bought the painting, why do you need me to tell you who bought the painting?"

I answered before the emotion behind Bella's alarmed expression could be converted into words. "What do you want?"

The woman rubbed her hands together. "Ooh, now. Let me think what would be fair recompense for such private and sensitive information." She came to a sudden stop and smiled. "I got it. I got it. Ya can buy one of m' paintings at full price."

"No," I was quick to reply.

She grimaced. "Why not?"

"I think you know why not. I have no wish to offend you when

I say that there are cow pats in the cattle market that would look better on my wall than most of your work. If I bought one, I'd then have to decide which of my enemies most deserved to receive it for Christmas, and I'm just not sure I'm cruel enough for that." Admittedly, one potential recipient did come to mind.

She held her hand up to her chest. "Ooh, that stung did that. Your words are barbed, young gentleman, but I appreciate your honesty. I'll accept a shilling for the identity of the man you need."

"So you do know him?" Bella eagerly retorted.

The painter held out her hand and raised her eyebrows. Bella was still distracted, so I went looking in my coat pocket and fished out a two-bob bit. "I'll need change."

The savvy negotiator laughed through her nose as she searched her table for the necessary coins. She brought them together with the ends of her fingers that peeked out through her well-worn gloves before handing over the handful of pennies.

"Pleasure, sir, madam. Now, if you're describing the person I think you are, I can't tell you 'is name. But my boy always delivers this fella's purchases to a cottage up near Highgate."

"In Holly Village?" Bella jumped in before she could say it.

"So that's your friend, is it? The ratty little bloke with a wife who 'as a very large..." She didn't say the word but pointed to her chest, and I couldn't decide if it would be polite for me to acknowledge this.

"That's him," I said when Bella looked away. "But wait. You said he always buys from you. Has he made a lot of purchases?"

"Oh, 'e loves what I'm selling." She leaned forward once more. "To be quite honest, 'e's got terrible taste. Just imagine buying more than one of these! Clearly 'as more money than sense. It takes me about five minutes to knock these out and, when I can't be bothered to paint the back'rounds I just stick a brush in m' dog's mouth and get 'im to do what 'e can."

Her great laugh sounded once more, and I have to admit that she'd made me smile. She pointed under the table, and I noticed a gigantic, slobbering head sticking out from beneath the black cloth.

The Alsatian looked up at me without moving, and I was glad I hadn't said anything worse about his handiwork.

"Who knows," I told his mistress, "perhaps one day people will pay large sums for such innovatively composed works."

"That's right, matey!" She rocked in her seat with amusement. "Bonzo'll be the first canine maestro. The toffs'll pay millions."

She was still laughing as she waved us away from her stall.

"What she lacks in talent," Bella declared sotto voce, "she makes up for in cynicism."

"To be quite honest, if people are willing to buy from her, then I don't blame her one bit for making the most of her abilities."

In front of us, the same mix of scrap, junk, knick-knacks and crafts stretched out some fifty yards, and Bella had seen enough. "Is that why we came here? To find out whether John Presler bought the painting in Adele's sitting room?"

"That was one of the reasons," I replied, cutting between the laid-out blankets of a man selling crockery that had been reclaimed from a closed-down hotel and another flogging third-hand suits. "The other is just over there."

# FOURTEEN

The seething mass of humanity had surely reached its peak for the day. It was a struggle to push through it to the part of the market we needed. In the far corner, there were stalls selling food and refreshments on one axis and plants and gardening tools on the other.

"Are you telling me that you've brought me here for a plate of eels?" Bella was becoming impatient.

To be fair to her, there was a particularly long queue of hungry customers at the eel stand. My father had once talked of Londoners' adoration of that slippery anguilliform as being akin to a cult. Much like him, I had never understood the attraction of a cold, jellied fish, and this supposed treat was not what I had in mind that afternoon.

"We're not here to eat," I reassured her, though, to my surprise, she gazed at the eelman, doling out his delicacy, with a certain curiosity. "We've come to buy one of those."

I waved my hand a little more insistently towards the part of the market where plants were sold.

"Oh, Marius. You are sweet." She gripped my arm, and I knew that our quest would be worthwhile.

The call of the holly and mistletoe sellers filled the air like birdsong at dawn.

"Not too late for love this Christmas," one fellow hollered, as he winked across at us, but that wasn't why I'd been scheming.

I walked up to the first Christmas tree in the two long rows of them and pulled it up to standing. "This one will do," I told Bella as I admired its conical shape and deep greenery. "I thought that, if we must spend the next few days in Adele's house, we could at least make it festive."

"And I admire the sentiment. However..."

I waited to discover what the problem was as she looked the specimen up and down.

"We can't take the tree that, in your words, 'will do'. We must find the very best one available."

I could already see that I'd underestimated our task and just how seriously my friend would take it. "It's a tree, Bella. They're all the—"

"If you say the word *same*, I will take the car and leave you here." She was presumably only half serious, but I didn't dare take the risk. "We're inviting a living being to spend Christmas with us."

I really hadn't expected her to be so sentimental towards what, by most people's standards, was a bush that had been watching its figure.

"It's not a living being, Bella. It's a dying being. Someone chopped its feet off so that we could cover it with shiny things and make it stand in the corner of the sitting room as it dries from the outside in before we finally dump it in the street."

She turned a look of thunder upon me. "I take it back. You're not so sweet after all."

I stood holding the tree I'd so carefully selected as she wandered along the row, pausing in front of each to inspect its worth.

"The least we can do is give this ancient custom its due attention."

I considered reminding her that this ancient tradition had come to Great Britain less than a hundred years earlier, but I could see that my concept of decorating for Christmas and hers were quite distinct.

She made it all the way to the end of the stall before turning back and examining the selection just as thoroughly on the way back. I waited quietly for her to return and showed not a hint of amusement when she seized the first tree and said, "It looks like this is the best one after all."

I let her choose the holly wreath.

As we were leaving, we found an enterprising fifteen-year-old who had set up a pitch selling tinsel, bows, stars and silver bells all in a row. I could tell that, had I not been there, Bella would have given in to her childlike impulses and bought the lot. She watched me through the corner of her eye to check whether I was judging her as she picked up garland after garland. I had to wonder whether she'd forgotten which house we would be decorating – or that we had a murder to solve.

When I got back to the car, I put my hand in my pocket and pulled out the coins I found there. "I'm sorry, Bella," I told her, having already secured the tree in the Invicta's luggage compartment with a length of twine. "It turns out that the woman who sold us the piece of information we'd already inferred has chiselled me. I'll have to have a word with her. I won't be a minute."

She barely noticed that I'd gone as she was busy trying and failing to squeeze the large crate of purchases between the two seats. I ran back to where we'd had the conversation with the unartistic artist and my task was soon complete, which meant we were free to whistle back across the city to our new temporary home.

People were buzzing around the gatehouse as we passed through with the Christmas tree. A few of the residents we'd visited cheered and clapped as though we had brought it there for their pleasure. Freddy Ponting, meanwhile, just scowled as if he disapproved of such things.

Ruth Haskell had a new list in her hand and was giving instructions to the same workman I'd previously glimpsed there. In front of their cottage, I could see that the much-discussed Preslers had returned from whatever nefarious task they'd been doing. John Presler seemed quite happy perched on a low wall, watching the comings and goings of his neighbours with a glass of what looked like London porter in his hand. I could well imagine that such behaviour would not endear him to the other inhabitants of Holly Village. How I wished to put our every question to him, but that was no simple task with Bella continually poking me with the end of a Christmas tree.

When we returned to Adele's cottage, Percy viewed the verdant newcomer with no small amount of suspicion. Considering the number of trees against which he'd relieved himself over the years, you would think that he would regard them as allies, but nay. Perhaps his long-understood dominion over them had been brought into question when he saw one walking into the house. The fact that I placed it in a metal cauldron in the very spot where he had previously been sitting probably didn't help matters, and he conveyed his feelings through a series of growls, moans and howls.

"Maybe he thinks we should have taken longer to choose the right tree," Bella said to exact some modicum of revenge on me.

"Or perhaps dogs practise an entirely different religion which does not observe Christmas at all. I've rarely seen one in church."

She poked me in the ribs, presumably to avoid having to admit that I was funny. We returned to the car for the last of our purchases – and thankfully no new ugly paintings – and got to work with either our least or most important task of the day.

If the truth be told, the tree was too nice for that poky sitting room. It looked even bushier in the cottage than it had in the market and only just failed to touch the ceiling.

Bella's hands went diving into the tea crate to extract first the long chains of beads, then the tinsel and then the bells. The tree already looked quite busy when I returned from appeasing Percy with a plate of beef shin.

"Come along, slowcoach," Bella badgered me. "I'll have finished before you pick up your first bauble."

I said nothing but accepted the challenge. I threaded each of my fingers through the silken loops attached to the various ornaments and, in this ever so efficient manner, was able to make a good start on the process.

The only problem arose when the tree began to tilt.

"I told you we were buying too many decorations," I muttered.

"No, you didn't," she replied quite honestly.

"Fine, but I thought it." I looked up at her as she stood on a chair to reach the higher branches. I must say, I immediately forgot about the tipping tree and how much we'd spent on decorations. I was captivated by the look of concentration on her face and almost jealous of the tree for the attention she lavished upon it.

She achieved her aim – placing a small golden camel near the very top of the tree – and glanced down at me with a contented look. I was certain that she had forgotten her troubles for a moment or two. Whenever this had happened over the last few months, a rush of guilt had overwhelmed her, but this time she continued smiling.

"What are you looking at?" A sense of achievement radiated from her. Even on the day she'd learnt of her adopted aunt's death, this brief break had done her good.

"The tree," I lied. "I'll have to get some stones from the garden to prop it up better."

I looked away from her at last, but Percy had finished his food and unashamedly stared at the woman he longed to have as his mistress. So now I was jealous of him, too.

I went to the front garden and took a deep breath. The air was crisp as it entered my lungs, and I noticed more flakes of snow falling. On the far side of the green, John Presler and his wife were what can only be described as canoodling in their front garden. He kept kissing her on the cheek then pinching her somewhere I shouldn't mention. Silva slapped his hand, then giggled as she waited for him to do it again. The Baroness was not far away and evidently noticed what I had, as she was pointing in their direction and complaining to Ruth Haskell.

Grumpy Freddy was moaning about something, and the lady with the list looked quite unsure how to react to her testy neighbours. I had to wonder how much the Preslers' performance was designed to stir up just such trouble. It was a far from harmonious environment, and so I picked up a few large stones from a snow-piled rockery by the front door and returned to help Bella.

# FIFTEEN

Caxton, my friend's oafish chauffeur, arrived with the requested provisions just in time for us to get changed before the Christmas party. He glowered at me whenever Bella wasn't looking but was all charm the rest of the time.

"It's really no trouble, Miss Bella. I had a very nice morning with my family, and I had to collect your case from your brother's flat anyway. It's just a shame that Mr Quin's home was in the other direction entirely."

Glower, glower, glower as Bella put the case out of the way.

"You did find it without too much difficulty, though?" she concluded, and Caxton bowed his head obligingly.

"Oh, yes, miss. Your directions were first-rate, and Mr Quin's mother was most accommodating." Glower, glower, glower, as if to say, *Unlike you, Quin!* "She had everything ready for me when she arrived and even offered me a cup of tea."

"I can't thank you enough, Caxton." Bella has never been able to see what a thug her driver is. She is one of the finest judges of character I know, but even she has a blind spot. "I hope you have a truly wonderful Christmas."

He pulled his neck in like an overgrown turtle and looked quite shocked. "I'm sorry, miss. Are you saying that you won't be coming home to Hurtwood Manor, even on Christmas Day?"

His mistress gave a shy smile, and I could see how hard it was for the man not to reach out one of his brawny mitts and grab me about the throat.

"I hope to return swiftly, Caxton. Of course I do. But our priority must be to find out what happened to Auntie Addie."

"The police..." the big man desperately mumbled.

"We've already recruited Detective Inspector Lovebrook to our cause," I told him most reassuringly, but he still seemed unhappy with my response.

"But, miss!" He glanced back and forth between us. "What will people say? An unmarried lady of high standing spending the night in the same tiny hovel as this..." He didn't finish his sentence. His eyes did the talking, and they spoke in disgusted tones.

For her part, Bella had to suppress a laugh. "Oh, don't be ridiculous. For one thing, everyone here thinks that we're married, and for another, Marius and I slept in far smaller 'hovels' a hundred times when we were children. For a few years of our adolescence, there was barely a summer night that went by when we didn't fall asleep in the treehouse together."

Caxton swallowed down whatever furious reply he had formulated.

"I really am grateful for your concern, Malcolm." As is often the way with servants – with the exception of footmen for some inexplicable reason – it is rare to hear their first names, and I'd genuinely forgotten that Bella's chauffeur was called Malcolm Caxton. It was a truly unfortunate name for a truly unpleasant man. "But Marius will be here to make sure nothing goes awry."

I was frankly amazed that Caxton's massive head didn't explode, especially when I reiterated Bella's point. "That's right, Malcolm. I'll be here twenty-four hours a day to make sure no one lays a finger on our beloved Bella."

She did her best to comfort him with a smile. How she failed to see the steam piping from his ears and fogging up the windows was a true wonder to me.

"Very good, Miss Bella." He bowed with a little more inclination this time and stayed down there so long that I thought he'd got stuck. "I wish you a very Merry Christmas."

"And a Happy New Year!" I put in to remind him that there was no limit to the time Bella and I might have to spend under that roof together. "I hope you have a jolly fine one."

He was obliged to bow to me too. Bella would have seen how rude he really was otherwise, and he was nothing if not careful. "Feel free to call if you require anything at all, Miss Bella. Anything!"

We were too busy to extend the conversation further, and so she gave a thankful nod and waited for him to leave.

"There's just time to dress before our suspects kindly congregate for us to watch their every action," Bella told me as she hauled her suitcase up the stairs.

She was evidently happy to be hurrying on to the next stage of the investigation, but I had started to worry about what my mother had packed for me without clear instructions. I opened my expanding Revelation suitcase and was relieved to find plain white shirts, and two perfectly sensible suits in different shades of brown. I lifted them up to discover a less welcome sight. It was truly the ugliest item in my possession, but it was so cold outside, I had no other option but to wear it beneath my coat.

"I'm almost ready," Bella called down to me a few minutes later. This wasn't quite true. She was entirely ready and descended the narrow, curving staircase much as if she were making an appearance in the glittering Opera Garnier in Paris.

"Are you really going to wear your tatty old officer's coat?" She looked down at the svelte gown she was wearing, and I must say that I felt she was the one who had failed to dress for the occasion. Some carols and a few mince pies hardly called for haute couture.

"Yes, I definitely am. It's freezing out there, and I've been cold all day without a jumper."

"And your mother didn't send one with Caxton?"

I really didn't know how to answer that, so I said, "Percy? Are you coming with us? There are often sausage rolls at this sort of do."

Although he'd been keeping an eye on the Christmas tree since it had arrived, he was up on his feet before I'd finished my sentence. If he'd had a hat and scarf, he would have already donned them.

Bella swished over to him, the skirt of her ivy green dress just a few inches above the floor. I don't know whether she'd read my mind or was simply trying to make the most of the glut of decorations that we'd bought, but she reached down to attach a bow to his collar.

"There you are, my dear creature. You look wonderful."

I was doomed to spend my life upstaged by my own dog.

"Come along, Marius," she called back to me when I didn't move. "We're waiting!"

We headed out into the cold once more, with the sun having set, and the lamps now lit. They cast a comforting glow across the snowbound square and turned the falling flakes a golden orange hue.

There were even more of the locals gathered around the gatehouse now. The man in overalls was dealing with something on the green. If I'd been cold all day without several thick layers, I could only imagine how he was suffering with his shirtsleeves rolled back and his muscly forearms bulging against the cold. He appeared to be arranging empty wine bottles at regular distances in the deepening snow.

"Lord and Lady Montague!" Ruth Haskell, the oddly attired social secretary of Holly Village, was happy to see us once more. "We couldn't commence without you, but we do have a busy programme of events planned."

"We were supposed to start five minutes ago," the man I took to be a caretaker called over his shoulder in a deep Scottish accent as he continued his task. "If w' say we're starting at six o'clock, I'd like tae start at six o'clock."

"Yes, yes, Mr Dumfries. We're almost all here. If Ivy doesn't come in the next ten minutes, we'll have to begin." She turned to the group and asked, "Has anyone seen her? I did remind her this morning of the plan."

"I have nothing to do with that obnoxious woman," Freddy reminded us with a scowl.

"I'll look in her house, shall I?" Clive Whitworth, the cheerful old soldier whose cottage we had visited that afternoon, slowly shuffled along the path in the direction of Ivy Frazel's abode on the other side of the village.

I took this opportunity to approach John Presler and his wife. We'd put off interviewing them for too long, but I felt I had a firmer grasp of the case now. I was just wondering how I might initiate conversation when he did so for me.

"Hullo there, fella. It's about time we introduced ourselves. The name's Presler. I'm John, and this is my Silva." He pulled his wife closer. She looked quite shy compared to the previous times we'd spotted her. "Don't worry about my missus," he continued with a wink. "She's not used to being around the upper crust. Not like me, at least. I've got friends from all walks of life."

Silva Presler curtseyed to us and, for some reason, I found myself waving to her like a benevolent monarch who preferred to stay some distance from the plebians.

"Pleasure to meet you, m'lordship, m'lady." Silva Presler had a real cockney accent – as if she were born not just within earshot of Bow Bells, but right next door. She did not immediately fit my image of the rich victim of her husband's schemes, which was largely based on what Adele had told me at the Christmas party.

"There's no need for such formality." Bella stepped forward to offer her hand. "It's lovely to meet you."

"Don't get me wrong." The funny little man touched the short hair at the side of his head as he spoke. "It's not that she don't come from money. Silva's dad were the Eel King of the Isle of Dogs. He's got a whole fleet o' ships and employs a hundred men. She grew up in an absolute palace, but your sort don't always take to us self-made types. Am I right?"

"Indubitably so," I replied, already wishing that I didn't have to pretend to be upper class around these seemingly ordinary people.

"And what about you, Mr Presler?" Bella was better at maintaining any pretence than me. She made it sound as if she were only mildly interested. In truth, we were both dying to know all about our preferred suspect. "Did you make your money from seafood?"

"No, no. Can't stand the stuff. I'm more of a corned beef man, me." He had apparently forgotten the earlier question, as his wife had to nudge him and he spluttered into life once more. "I'm what you might call an entrepreneur."

We gazed back blankly, which he evidently took to suggest that we had never heard the word before. "That means that I have very specific skills," he incorrectly explained. "If a person needs a special kind of service, I'm the man for the task."

"So you're an odd-job man?" I injected a little bafflement into this question, as I hoped to discover more.

"Nah, nah. I'll leave that to old Dumfries over there. I'm someone that..." He struggled to find his words and, for a moment, I wondered whether even he knew what he did. "... that a person may call upon when she – or he, in principle – needs something seen to that no one else can... see to."

"Yes, like an odd-job man," I continued. Putting on a posh accent lent itself to a more eccentric character, and I found that I was becoming quite insistent.

"Nah, nah. You're not listenin'. I do things that aren't strictly—"

"John, my love," his wife interrupted with that same coquettish giggle I'd previously heard. "They don't want to know about all that. It's Christmastime. There's no need to discuss work."

She wore a luxurious mink stole atop a long cashmere coat, and yet she'd still found a way to display a good portion of her extensive décolletage. I believe that she wiggled her chest a little at this moment to get her husband's attention.

"I suppose you're right, doll," he reluctantly conceded. "There's a time for business and a time for pleasure." He tapped his nose with one finger and gave another wink. "You know what I'm talking about, don'tcha, Lord Montague?"

"And to that end, you must come to our house for a drink." Silva Presler had lost a little of her apprehension, or perhaps she just wished for her husband to shut his mouth. "We would be only too 'appy to welcome a nice couple like you to the neighbourhood."

"To be quite honest, you're helping to bring the average age down." He leaned in closer and put one hand on my shoulder. I realised at this point that he was yet to address a comment to Bella. "It's hard work being the youngest amongst a bunch of grumblers and tiresome bores."

The suddenness of this comment, not to mention the bitter tone with which it was delivered, set Bella on edge, whereas I hid any feelings I might have had on the matter.

Silva tried her best to act as though there was nothing strange in what her husband had said. "Say you'll come for a little glass of swizzle? You choose when." She stepped closer to convince us, and I saw just how thickly the foundation on her cheeks was layered.

It was hard to know whether it was her husband's unappealing personality, their three-decade age difference or something we were yet to discover that had turned their neighbours against them.

"I'm no' waiting any longer." The Scottish caretaker had finished his task and went looking for the organiser once more as the other villagers chatted in a huddle. Several of them beat their arms to fight against the cold, and I had to hope we wouldn't be out there for too long.

"We'd love to see your house," Bella told Mrs Presler once that disturbance had subsided. She must have felt that this gave away too much of her thinking as she amended the statement. "By which I mean to say... it would be lovely to share a drink with you over Christmas."

"The day itself is almost here." John put a hand to his forehead in disbelief. "Where has December gone? It feels like only yesterday children were running about the streets calling 'Penny for a guy'. It feels like last week that the summer sun were shining down on us."

Even as he reminisced nostalgically over the recent past, there was a certain intensity to John Presler that I believe Herbert Wandle had been trying to describe to us. He had black, beady eyes that were set deep in their sockets. His brow was the prominent kind from which a man like Sherlock Holmes could have inferred any degree of criminality, and his thinning hair was so slick with pomade that children could have gone skating on top of it.

He gave my shoulder a painful squeeze. "I look forward to having you to myself, Lord Montague. I think that you and I could get on rather well."

He was oddly menacing for such a diminutive figure. I looked at his hand and noticed that there were cuts and scratches all over his knuckles, as if he'd recently punched a wall. His squeeze was more like a pinch, and he gave it one last go before releasing me.

"Very well, everyone," Ruth Haskell emerged to tell us. "If you'd like to file inside, I think everything is ready."

There was a pleasant murmur of excitement and, for a moment or two, I forgot about our murder investigation. A feeling of child-like wonder came over me, and I thought only of the promise that the candlelit gatehouse offered. Until we stepped inside, there could be anything there to find. A whole stack of presents might be waiting for us – no doubt containing every expensive train set and wind-up car I had so craved as a boy but gone without.

John Presler hurried off ahead of us, as though he wanted to have the pick of the imaginary presents, whereas his wife lingered behind with an apologetic look on her face. My juvenile fantasy was already forgotten, and I found myself wondering whether Silva Presler was the reason we'd come to Holly Village. If her husband had been taking advantage of her in some way – or was even planning to murder her – and Adele Leach had discovered his plan, that would surely explain her death.

"Merry Christmas, everyone," Miss Haskell said in an authoritative voice. If someone had bet me ten bob that she was a retired schoolteacher, I would have turned it down, as it was a bet I could only have lost. "Welcome, all."

The room wasn't exactly as I'd pictured it, but it wasn't far off. A tree standing in the corner must have just been lit by the caretaker, as there were twenty small red candles burning upon it. The swaying flames reflected off a series of silver glass baubles, which made the small hall all the cosier. I could only assume it had been built as a communal space for the village to enjoy, and I wondered whether it was normally used for the card games that various residents had mentioned.

The Baroness had taken a throne on the far side of the room. As ever, her husband was at her side, and he smiled at his neighbours one by one as they entered. In return, however, John Presler sneered at Herbie, and it was clear that the animosity between the two couples went both ways.

"Ladies and gentlemen..." Miss Haskell had moved to stand on an upturned crate in the middle of the room and, with first one hand and then the other, she coerced us into a grouping that was more to her liking. What had been a snaking line was soon transformed into a loose huddle. "That's better. Thank you all for coming. Before we start the carols and enjoy some refreshments—"

"Dinna forget the surprise," the caretaker interrupted, much to Miss Haskell's annoyance. "We mustn't forget the surprise."

She actually snapped at him this time. "It won't be a surprise if you keep talking about it, Hamish!"

Dumfries did not seem worried that she would object to his comment and began to whistle "The Coventry Carol".

"It's so nice to have you all here," Miss Haskell tried once more. "Especially you, Betty. I know you've been ill recently, and it's wonderful to see you back on your feet in time for Christmas." A yard or two away from us, the nice lady we'd visited at number four couldn't help blushing. "Before we begin, I feel we should mention the person who could not be here tonight."

"Ivy?" a voice in the crowd suggested.

"No, Carrie. Not Ivy!" Our leader was becoming quite frustrated. "I'm sure she'll be along in a minute. I'm talking about Adele." She tutted and released a long, steady breath before finding the energy to start again for the third or fourth time. "I feel we should spare a thought for our dear departed friend."

"She was too good for this world!" Silva Presler declared with a tear in her voice, and this at least answered the question of whether the two of them had been friends.

It did nothing to calm down the much-interrupted speaker. "Thank you, Mrs Presler. As I was saying, we have lost a lot of cherished friends over the years. There was Agatha at number four, dear Mr Parsons at 6b, and how can we forget Mrs Anderson? All of them were taken from us too soon, but we could never have imagined that spritely and youthful Adele Leach would be the next to go. I really can't remember anyone else with such vivacity and spirit living in the village."

"Hear, hear!" John Presler chanted, which drew an angry look from the Baroness, who gripped the arm of her chair a little tighter.

Her anger was mirrored on the face of the woman who was leading the event. Ruth Haskell would allow no more interruptions and swept her piercing gaze across the crowd before speaking again. I must say that, as her eyes drilled into me, there was a touch of fury in her. I wondered to what ends such a single-minded woman would go to achieve her goals.

"If someone would do the honours, I think we should start this..." She stopped herself then, as the candles on the tree were beginning to die out, and she presumably realised that this was no longer accurate. "I think we should baptise this evening by raising a toast to Mrs Adele Leach, who was so important to all of us."

Grumpy Freddy sniffed at this comment but went to open a bottle of wine. Cheery Betty from number four picked up a tray of precariously perched wineglasses. They clinked and shuddered as she transported them from one table at the side of the room to another in the centre. Ten or so servings were poured, and we were soon ready for the toast.

"To Adele," Bella spoke before Miss Haskell could. "My treasured aunt and friend of the family. To a truly good person who died too soon."

It took me a moment to realise why she had jumped in like this. I generally think it best practice to hide our intentions as much as possible, and we certainly hadn't made it known that we were looking into Adele's death nor that she had been murdered. Bella must have been tired of this pretence, however. The undertone to her words was clear, and a few of our new neighbours shivered as her eyes landed upon them.

"To Adele." Miss Haskell's voice rose over the subsequent chatter. "Now, let us sing 'Deck the Halls' and then we'll treat ourselves to a mince pie."

At the mention of mince pies, Percy, who had been hiding under a table until now waiting for the food I'd promised him, poked his nose out, had a sniff, and returned to the shadows.

Miss Haskell raised her hand. The singers looked at one another to check on their timing and then we joined together as one.

*"Deck the hall with boughs of holly,*
*Fa, la, la, la, la, la, la, la, la!*
*'Tis the season to be jolly:*
*Fa, la, la, la, la, la, la, la, la!*
*Fill the mead cup, drain the barrel,*
*Fa, la, la, la, la, la, la, la, la!*
*Troul the ancient Christmas carol.*
*Fa, la, la, la, la, la, la, la, la!"*

Most people sang very sweetly, and I was suddenly aware of my own less than dulcet tones standing out from the others.

Despite this, our conductor now looked pleased with us and, before long, I drifted away on the heartening melody.

I've always found it entertaining that so many Christmas songs feature that pleasantly universal custom of filling a bowl, cup, glass or barrel with alcohol and slurping it down. I'm sure there are as many carols that mention jolly drunkenness as there are that describe choirs of angels or the friendly beasts. It lends another meaning to the expression *Merry* Christmas.

To confirm this theme, when we reached the end of the song, I raised my glass and several others copied me. Bella wasn't one of them. She was still observing the revellers and there was no joy or festivity left in her. It occurred to me that she had not sung a single note of the song. Her thoughts were ticking over. Her head was full of the crime we had gone there to investigate, and I felt certain that she was considering the most important question of all: which of these respectable characters was responsible for her aunt's death?

"Clive never came back," Freddy muttered rather cheerfully when an awkward hush had settled.

We looked up at Miss Haskell on her box, and though she raised one hand as if to say something important, she turned to look outside. "It has been a rather long time. Are we certain that he hasn't come and gone again?"

In response, a negative mumble travelled across the room. The tension increased, and I doubt I was the only one to jump a little as a great explosion sounded outside.

"Not now, Hamish!" Miss Haskell jumped down from her podium and marched across the room as great flashes of light bounced off the snow and into the hall where we stood. Forgetting all about Clive, our party rushed to the windows as rocket after rocket took to the air.

There were oohs and aahs, as was to be expected, and I now understood why the caretaker had been planting bottles across the green. He was out there as we watched the display, moving from one spot to the next with a length of smouldering rope to light each fuse.

Bella was holding on to me, and I wished to ask what new idea she had formed, but as the fireworks coloured the low clouds red and green and yellow, and the snow fell, my eyes were drawn to something else. On the far right of the scene, in the light of a Catherine wheel that had been pinned to the trunk of the largest holly tree there, I made out a figure stumbling along the path.

I didn't wait; I ran out of the gatehouse and, forgetting the very real risk that one of the bottles could fall over and I'd end up with a rocket pointed at my head, I shot along the path around the village. The whistles and explosions were deafening, but I ignored them to get to the cheery old soldier who had welcomed us into his home a few hours earlier.

"Clive," I called out to him when I was just yards away. "Clive, what's the matter?"

It's hard to say how I could tell he was in distress. His uneven walk maybe? The way his shoulders were hunched and his head dipped? All I know is that I'd moved like smoke as Dumfries's display set the sky alight.

"It's Miss Frazel." Clive Whitworth was out of breath. "It's Ivy." He sucked great mouthfuls of air into his lungs between each sentence. "She's dead."

# SIXTEEN

For a moment, I was back in France – back at the battle of Amiens. The bangs I heard weren't fireworks, but bombs raining down on me. The yellow starburst of the rockets transformed in my mind into the fog of mustard gas, and I was constantly waiting for the grenade that would blow me off my feet.

When that really happened to me in 1918, I woke up a few hours later on a stretcher in a tent. The nurses couldn't see any major damage, and so they didn't send me off to a hospital away from the front line. They hoped that I would wake up unscathed, and, physically at least, that's how it went. They said I'd merely banged my head when the force of the explosion knocked me backwards. My friend Jimmy wasn't so lucky. He was there in the medical tent, too. Only he was under a sheet, waiting for a makeshift hearse to take him to the nearest Allied cemetery.

Perhaps this explains why I was frozen as I looked into Clive Whitworth's eyes. I was gripped by the fear that I saw there. Being around death – as I had been for much of the last year – I had lived through several similar moments before. Yet none had been so visceral. I don't know whether it was the smell of gunpowder in my nostrils or those flashing lights prompting the experience, but I felt quite removed from the here and now.

"Where is she?" I eventually managed to ask.

I could see that Clive was just as lost as I was. He was too old to have served in the Great War. He'd talked to us of his time as a soldier during the Victorian era, when Britain was still turning the map of the world pink. And yet, I was certain that he had a collection of memories like mine, and that each of them was bursting into his head in time with the bang- bang-bang of the fireworks.

"I looked in her house first." It had taken him so much energy and concentration to utter this that I doubted he'd be able to say anything more. "There was no sign of her, but that's when I remembered where I'd seen her earlier."

My departure from the gatehouse had been noticed, and Herbert was the first to reach us. "What is it, Clive? What's the matter?" He put one arm around his friend to support him.

John Presler was next and, though he gave just as good a performance as Herbert, I could tell he didn't have the same empathy. "Is it Ivy? Has something happened?"

I didn't need to listen anymore. I knew where the unusual old lady who had banged on Adele's door that afternoon would be. As Clive caught his breath and Bella arrived, I continued along the path past the Wandles' tiny mansion. Ivy's house was in the corner beyond it, but I kept going to the bench where I had last seen her. There were no lamp posts nearby, but the occasional illumination showed that she was no longer sitting there, and I could make out Clive's footprints in the snow. They kept going a little way, and there on the ground, just past where I'd last seen her, was Ivy's body.

"Is it her?" Bella called from behind me.

I turned to nod as she arrived. I didn't know whether to approach the dead woman or wait until the police came. The only footprints I could see stopped some distance from her.

"They must belong to Clive. The killer would have had to get a lot closer," I said to finish my thought aloud.

"So you think she was murdered?" Bella moved around me to look at Ivy in the faint light from the nearest cottage.

"I saw her sitting here in the snow this afternoon and was too busy thinking of the woman who had already died to question whether anyone else was at risk."

"You weren't to know, Marius," she insisted, but I wasn't convinced.

"There's no doubt we would have had a better chance of catching the devil responsible if we'd come straight here. Whatever evidence there might have been has been covered over by this evening's snow."

She could see it would do no good to comfort me further, especially as that should have been my role in the first place. I'd seen just how upset she was, but I was the one showing my frustration.

Still on the path, a yard away from the body, I knelt down to take a closer look. Ivy Frazel was lying on her side, having presumably slumped off the bench after some time there. Why hadn't I just gone to check on her? Why had I been so fixated on whatever task we were busily doing? Of course, the real question should be, why had I gone off to buy a Christmas tree when there was a killer to catch?

"Can you see how she was killed?" Bella asked, as a blast of slowly falling light exploded overhead.

"She was garrotted, I think. There's a wide band of red on her throat. Probably caused by fabric rather than a piece of wire."

"She couldn't have been throttled?"

I turned my head but kept looking at Ivy. "I don't think so. The mark is too consistent all the way around her neck."

Bella looked off towards Ivy's cottage. "I wonder if she was actually killed here."

"Why would you doubt it?"

She turned around entirely to examine the crowd that had spilt out of the gatehouse. Half of the residents had surrounded Clive, and the rest were hanging back near the entrance as though afraid of what he'd found. Dumfries appeared to have concluded his display as he was no longer darting around the green to light the rockets. Even the Catherine wheel had slowed its spin and would soon fizzle out altogether.

"Why don't you think she died here?" I repeated in case she hadn't heard.

"It's too public. If she'd cried out, anyone could have seen from the windows of the various houses." I followed her gaze with my own as it traced a path around the dead woman's property. "Why would the killer have taken that risk?"

I couldn't answer her question, so I asked one of my own. "Do you remember exactly when it was that we first saw her sitting here?"

"It was..." She had to think before answering. "It was after we returned from the high street. We were speaking to Miss Haskell near the gatehouse when I noticed Ivy over here."

"We'll have to ask everyone else, but if she died shortly before we came back, that would make it around two o'clock. I remember noticing the clock as we left the police station for the second time."

"There we go then." Bella was trying to sound bright and positive for both our sakes, but I hadn't forgotten the distraught look that she'd worn as we sang the first and, as it turned out, only Christmas carol. "It shouldn't be difficult to confirm our theory."

I hated to leave a dead body. Especially one in such a sad state. With her curly hair poking out in all directions and her glasses still perched on her nose, Ivy looked as though she had been entirely forgotten. And so, before I rose from my crouched position, I whispered a small promise.

I hadn't known her well. I'd learnt little of her background or what she had achieved in her life, but I still felt responsible for her, so I said, "I'll try my very hardest for you, Ivy. That is the most and the least I can do."

Bella and I walked along the path in silence as the two groups melded into one before us.

"We should get Clive inside," Ruth Haskell instructed. She was a good instructor – quite the boss of the village, in fact. I remembered the flash of anger she'd shown in the gatehouse, and I wondered how she reacted when people went against her will. "He's had a real shock, and he'll be better off in the warmth."

No one disagreed with this, so she jerked her head at the normally uncooperative Freddy Ponting. To my surprise, he didn't object but hobbled forward to help his neighbour to the nearest building, where he could enjoy a nice mince pie – assuming that Percy hadn't found and eaten them all.

Despite Miss Haskell issuing the orders, I realised that most people were watching us. Eventually, John Presler stepped forward, still with a note of concern in his voice as he asked, "Is it true? Is Ivy dead?"

It seemed impossible that he wouldn't know this yet, as I'd already seen him talking to Clive, but I said nothing, and Bella nodded.

She started explaining what we'd seen when Miss Haskell stamped her authority on events once more. "Now, now. There's no need to discuss the details until the police get here. This is obviously a very sad state of affairs, but—"

"Tell us what happened," Presler demanded. "Tell us what you found."

"How did she die?" Sweet little Betty copied his demanding tone.

I looked at Bella to see whether she wanted to answer, then replied in her stead. "It seems she was murdered." The recipients of this news were quiet and, in some cases, frail folk in their seventies and eighties, but they produced quite the din in response. I decided to make the most of the moment. "And what's more, I don't believe that Adele's death was natural, either."

Now the noise really shot to the heavens like Dumfries's fireworks.

As the discussion became indecipherable, the Baroness, who had said nothing until now, managed to raise her voice over the tumult. "It was you, wasn't it, Presler? I've always known you were a savage."

"How can you say such a thing?" John Presler demanded, gripping the lapels of his heavy coat in both hands and tipping his head back to look down at her. "I had no problem with Ivy and thought very highly of Mrs Leach."

"So you don't deny thinking little of Ivy, then!" The Baroness's eyes blazed in the darkness. Her fury was unmistakable. "You've been nothing but trouble since you moved here. The only surprise is that something like this didn't happen long ago."

Everyone could see that Presler was up for the fight. For a moment, I thought he might launch himself at his accuser, but he settled for a verbal riposte. "Prove it."

"I beg your pardon?" The folds of skin on the Baroness's neck wobbled as she replied.

"You heard me, your highness." He spat out these last two words. "Prove that I'm a killer. I know you don't like me. You've told me practically every day since my sweet-hearted wife and I moved here. But it's one thing to throw accusations around, and another to prove them."

Though he was undoubtedly the bête noire of Holly Village, his words had resonated with his fellow residents, and the Baroness struggled for a response.

"We all remember what happened when you first arrived here," she began, but her husband moved closer to interrupt.

"I understand your anger, darling, but there was never any definite evidence to connect what happened back then to Presler." Herbert was a fair man and wouldn't allow untruths, even when they pertained to an enemy. Of course, this left me wondering what had happened shortly after the Preslers had moved to the area.

"Has anyone got any evidence that John Presler was involved in the murders?" I asked when the talk faded.

The Baroness offered no response, as she apparently couldn't think of one. We'd already asked them once to prove that the Preslers were as rotten as they believed and, except for the other couple's poor taste in furnishings, the Wandles had come up short.

The tension held, and I could see that it would take something quite special to calm the frayed nerves. Luckily, there was someone quite special standing next to me.

"Before you say anything you'll regret," Bella began in an authoritative voice, "I think we should avoid any more baseless accusations."

It was the same tone she had used on me ever since we were children: the voice that her mother had passed down to her, which could still make me stand up straighter and check that my shoelaces weren't untied. It was difficult not to feel as if I had done something wrong when she spoke like that, so I can only imagine how our suspects felt.

"We've already informed the police of what we believe happened to my aunt." She held her gaze on the crowd as she said this. "Has anyone called them?"

I was watching the caretaker who, at the very mention of the word *police*, had gone reeling away.

"I sent Carrie to telephone as soon as we realised what was wrong," Miss Haskell explained, and I once again questioned her motives. When we'd first met her, I'd dismissed the self-appointed village administrator as a well-meaning busybody, but seeing her with her fellow residents put darker possibilities in my mind.

"When was the last time any of you saw Ivy alive?"

My question was met with blank stares. John Presler turned to look at his wife, but every other eye lingered on me. Then, quite suddenly, like a chorus line in a theatre, they seemed to launch into action as one.

"She was out and about this morning." Betty was by far the shortest person in the village and had to lean around Silva to be seen. "I saw her walking towards Adele's house."

"Yes, she came to talk to us." Bella bit her lip as she tried to make sense of what we already knew, and the others chattered among themselves.

"She was sitting on that bench over there." Freddy from 7b had returned from slowly ferrying Clive to the gatehouse and actually sounded quite cheerful. Some people are only happy when there's something to make them sad.

"We think she was already dead by then," I replied. "We saw her sitting there at around two o'clock."

There was one person whose voice was absent from the continuing discussion. Ruth Haskell looked strangely guarded. I wasn't the only one who had noticed this. Freddy was watching her, too.

"Ruth, are you quite all right?" he asked, but she clearly didn't wish to respond.

"Now that I think of it," Herbert spoke up when she wouldn't, "I'd say it was around two o'clock when she called at my house. Am I right, Ruth?"

"Miss Haskell?" Bella prompted, and the rather severe woman a few yards away tipped her chin back and looked right at me.

"Was that the time? I really can't say. I've been running back and forth all day like a headless proverbial. I'm sure I saw that troublesome woman on any number of occasions."

"Eh, that's not very nice," Silva Presler objected. I'd come to realise that she did a large part of her communicating through her sizable chest. To show her displeasure at this moment, she folded her arms under her bosom and gave it a mighty heave.

"I didn't mean that..." Miss Haskell could see that she'd said the wrong thing and, still looking at her with some apprehension, Herbie came to her aid.

"Please tell me if I'm wrong," Herbert tried once more. "We were in my sitting room going over the various plans for our Christmas celebrations when Ivy rang the doorbell, wishing to speak to me."

"Yes, yes. That's right." Her voice was oddly hollow. "It was perhaps half past one. I remember now."

"And what did she want?" I put in.

Herbert frowned. "I didn't actually find out. I told her that I was busy with Miss Haskell and that we would be some time. She told me not to worry and that she would return to talk to me later in the afternoon."

"And you didn't see her after that?" I asked to be sure.

Herbert looked once more to Miss Haskell, but eventually shook his head when she wouldn't respond.

Fifty different fireworks went off in my brain as I attempted to account for the final moments of Ivy Frazel's life. Bella, meanwhile, focused on what we most needed to know.

"Did anyone see her again? Can any of you recount Ivy's movements between half past one and two o'clock this afternoon?"

We looked around the group, but no one said a word.

# SEVENTEEN

The villagers' mood was surely not so dissimilar from that of a small child who wakes up on Christmas morning, his heart full of excitement, only to discover that there are no presents, the decorations have been packed away, and the tree has burnt to cinders. After the glee and camaraderie that had been promised by carols and entertainment, sorrow had consumed us. No one smiled, no one spoke in much more than a downbeat whisper, and the only looks exchanged ranged from suspicious to hostile.

I was still most curious about the Preslers. Silva hurried inside as the cold of the evening had truly begun to bite, but her husband stood at his front door, observing his neighbours as though he believed himself the defender of Holly Village. He'd even brought a cricket bat out of his house and not so subtly swung it around a few times to show that he was not a man with whom anyone should trifle. If he hoped this meant we would refrain from considering him a suspect, he was very much mistaken. It only reinforced the impression of him as a potentially violent individual.

The Baroness kept her own watch on the other side of the green, and I got the definite sense that her husband was caught in the middle of these huge personalities, like a rowing boat trapped between icebergs. He stayed at the gatehouse to commiserate with his neighbours, and we couldn't let the opportunity to ask him a few more questions escape us.

"I'm sorry, Herbert," I said as Bella and I approached. "Would you mind telling us a little more about your meeting with Ivy this afternoon?"

"If you'll excuse me, Carrie," he said to his neighbour. "I'll come to see about your sticking door at the first opportunity I find." The old lady nodded gratefully and tottered off to her cottage. Herbert turned back to us with hesitation if not reluctance plain on his face. "Now, you two, what exactly did you wish to know?"

I looked through the window of the gatehouse to see Ruth busily tidying up the hall where the aborted party had taken place. "I was wondering what time Miss Haskell came to your house and how long she stayed."

"Let me think." He put his hand to the back of his head and pulled down his woollen cap. Even bundled up against the freezing temperatures, there was a real flamboyance to his clothes. His thick overcoat had a scrolling design on it that reminded me of a smoking jacket. His silk tie had a large, elaborate knot, and it wouldn't have surprised me at all if he'd pulled out a monocle or donned white cotton gloves. "Well, Ruth arrived at half past twelve. I know that for certain as we made the appointment yesterday, and she is always very punctual. I would say she stayed with me for an hour and a half in all."

He looked at us expectantly, his cheeks sucked in as he awaited the next question. Before we could continue, Sergeant Bulmer and PC Pike strode through the archway into the village. Accompanied by two other constables, they hurried past when they realised who we were. I made sure to glare back to show them what I thought of their presence.

I noticed that Herbert was no happier to see them. Bulmer and Pike were not the type to win many friends.

"And when Ivy came to see you, how did she seem?" Bella asked once Miss Haskell had taken the officers to see the body. "Would you say she was upset?"

He reacted in the manner of someone who had never thought he would be required to answer such a point. "Well... if the truth be told, it was only a few seconds, and I was distracted by the Christmas planning that had kept us busy until then. I can't say Ivy was in tears or what have you."

"And how did she react when you mentioned that you were busy?"

He rubbed his back then, and I thought perhaps he would have preferred to conduct this interview sitting down somewhere away from the elements. "Now *that* I do remember. I told her that I was busy with Ruth, and I would be some time. That was when she started to back away from me. It was rather curious now that I think about it. She hurried along the path, and I called after her to ensure that she wasn't upset."

"And then?" Bella was evidently excited by this revelation.

"And then?" he repeated in much the same tone. "And then I went to make tea, as I had promised to do when Ruth had first arrived. I pride myself on being a good host, but once Miss Haskell gets started on a topic, it can be rather difficult to distract her."

I felt that he would have liked to go into more detail on his excellent hospitality, which we ourselves had already experienced, but that was more than we needed to know.

Bella let no time pass between his answer and her next question. "How long were you in the kitchen after that?"

He almost smiled. "Approximately the length of time needed to make a cup of tea. I put the water to boil, got some Christmas cake from the cupboard and cut two slices. Then, when the time came, I prepared the necessary utensils and took everything through to Miss Haskell."

"And did you communicate in any way with Miss Haskell while you prepared her tea?"

He hesitated then. "Well, no. While I was in the kitchen, she was in the sitting room on the other side of the house."

"Was there anyone else at home?" I asked, as I wondered what his wife had been up to all this time.

"No, no." I could see that just the mention of his wife's name made Herbert Wandle apprehensive. It was hard to tell whether this was because of the Baroness's secretly violent temperament, or she was simply a tough woman who kept him in his place. "Our maid was at the shops, and my beloved Sheena had gone for a walk. She definitely didn't return until three o'clock."

I caught sight of someone just then to whom I wished to speak, and as Bella and I had run out of road on our quest for the truth, the conversation headed towards its conclusion.

"Thank you so much for your help," she told him with a sad smile, but he wasn't quite finished.

"I'm sure you have a clear impression of what sort of person Ivy was, and there were definitely some people here who treated her unkindly, but let me say that she had a heart of gold." A definite note of emotion had entered his voice. "The idea that someone could hurt her is difficult for me to comprehend. That poor—"

His words ran dry and Bella stepped forward to comfort him. "We understand, Herbie."

"I must apologise. I'm a silly sentimental fool, but I've said my piece. If there's anything more you need, you know where I'll be."

It would have been cruel to keep him any longer. We said goodbye, and he thanked us and turned to go.

"Do you sometimes feel that we are asking the wrong questions?" I asked my fellow suspect-botherer.

"No." She was tight-lipped for a few moments as we walked to the entrance. "I *always* feel that we are asking the wrong questions."

She'd drawn a few staccato notes of laughter from me, which was poor timing as we were just passing a group of nervous villagers.

"You got here quickly," I told Inspector Lovebrook as he put his hand out to shake mine. "They only called the station fifteen minutes ago."

"Did they?" He was as affable as ever, and his voice wavered in surprise. "I was wondering what had caused all this excitement."

"You mean to say that you didn't know about the second murder?"

"I didn't until now." With a shake of the head, he showed that he was aware of the dark humour of the situation. "I came to tell you what I discovered at Scotland Yard."

"Well, we've a body to show you either way," Bella told him and, as it was his job to inspect such things, we led him over to the bench and poor Ivy Frazel – briefly detouring to drop off Percy at Adele's cottage.

More officers had arrived, but Sergeant Bulmer looked quite perplexed over what they should do.

"I'm very happy to see you, Detective Inspector Lovebrook," the senior officer told him as he scratched his chin. He looked down at the body as if it were one of those impossible creatures that swindlers tack together in the hope people will believe they've uncovered a mythological beast.

"So, Bulmer. Do you still think there's nothing to Adele Leach's suspicions?" the inspector asked, more than a little provocatively.

The huge, unpleasant officer suddenly looked smaller than he had until then. "It seems that some degree of..." He looked around as though hoping to find the word he needed on a signpost some-where. "... lawlessness has been at play here."

"In which case, I'm glad you'll be able to assist the inves-tigation."

"Sarge," PC Pike moved closer to whisper. "Ask the inspector what it is we're supposed to do."

Bulmer looked deeply uncomfortable for a moment before rounding his shoulders and opening his mouth to speak. Lovebrook wasn't that cruel and answered the constable's question. "I suggest you follow standard procedure."

"Yes, sir. Of course, sir. Standard procedure is exactly what I was telling Pike here that we should follow." The sergeant nodded rather contentedly but remained right where he was.

"Come along then," Lovebrook barked. He could be authoritative when it was required, which didn't always seem likely if you'd glimpsed his softer side. Even his fair hair looked less floppy as he glared at the incompetent subordinates. "Snap to it."

"The only problem," the man contested in a cautious voice, "is that I'm not totally familiar with the procedure in this particular situation. We honestly don't get too many murders around this neck of the woods."

Lovebrook sighed but, rather than embarrass the sergeant in front of his men, he simply answered the question.

"It's simple enough. If the coroner has been called, you must talk to anyone who has been seen here to find out about the victim's final movements."

"That is the very thing, Inspector. The very thing." The tubby sergeant clicked his heels together and marched off to issue orders to his constables. "What did I tell you, men? It's a simple matter of taking statements and the like. A child could do it."

Bella, Lovebrook and I watched the men fluster away, chattering between themselves. Pike made sure to shoot a quick grimace in my direction, so he clearly hadn't forgiven me for getting him in trouble. It felt unnecessary to comment on their ineptitude, so we concentrated on our own job instead.

"Who was the victim?" Lovebrook asked very simply, and I realised how difficult this question was to answer.

"She lived at number one," Bella revealed. "She told us that she inherited the house from her grandmother, and she was very put out when she saw us in Adele's cottage this morning."

"You mean to say she was spying on her neighbours?" Lovebrook raised an eyebrow or two at this.

Bella looked across at me and debated how true this was. "She was clearly the sort of person who was aware of the goings-on around her." As I may have mentioned before, my childhood friend is inordinately polite.

I, on the other hand, don't tend to be. "What Bella isn't saying is that Ivy Frazel was a Nosey Parker of the highest order. You should have seen how she hammered on the door ready to accuse us of housebreaking, robbery and who knows what else."

"So you had a good chance to talk to her?" Lovebrook sat down on the bench, still studying the unfortunate corpse who was preserved by the cold of that winter's night.

"She went into a lot of detail on her long-dead neighbours, was charmed by Bella and then became rather sad. However, I got the sense that she was a capable gossip."

Lovebrook really did smile this time. "They're the best kind of witnesses. Did she confirm any of your friend Adele's theories?"

I took a moment to recall the whirlwind of a woman who had blown in and out of the house that morning. "The truth is that she wasn't the type who responded well to..." I searched for the right word, but Bella was quicker than me.

"We asked about Adele and the Preslers, but she was a prickly woman and rather dominated the conversation," Bella said in a reflective voice.

"She made very nice silk flowers." I realised this made her sound like Eliza Doolittle in *Pygmalion*, so I thought I should add, "It was a hobby more than anything, as she'd inherited her family's fortune."

"A wealthy woman, then?" Lovebrook concluded. "Just like the first victim."

I was distracted by the fact that the posy on Ivy's lapel was missing. The pin that had held it in place was still visible, but the flowers had gone. "You'd better follow me. I have an idea."

"One moment." The inspector approached the body to assess the wounds on Ivy's neck.

"Might the marks there help identify who attacked her?" Bella suggested with hope in her voice.

"If the killer had used his bare hands, perhaps, but that clearly isn't the case. I would say that she was garrotted."

It gave me no pleasure to know that I'd been right in my conclusions. A gunshot to the head would have been over quickly, but garrotting would have taken time and caused significant pain.

Lovebrook looked disturbed by the sight, but he soon moved us on. "What was it that you wished to show me?"

The three of us walked in a line towards number one as I answered. "It was Bella's idea, actually. She wondered whether Ivy was killed some distance away from where she was found."

"It could have happened anywhere," she explained, "but it's unlikely the murderer would have wanted to drag the body too far."

"There would surely have been signs of a struggle," I added. "Her feet could have kicked up the ground, but the problem is that the snow has fallen since and might have covered everything."

We reached Ivy's cottage and began to search the front garden, which was ringed with holly. That most vibrant of festive shrubs had been robbed of its usual cheery connotations. There were so many of them growing around the village that they had come to feel like an invading army that had infiltrated the land while no one was watching. Had they hidden the killer while he despatched Ivy Frazel? However it happened, I had to wonder why he had taken such a risk in broad daylight.

Lovebrook was more methodical than we were and scanned the ground back and forth, his eyes and head turning at regular intervals. I dragged my feet through the snow in the hope I might turn up something, but it was always going to be a difficult task.

"What are you expecting to find?" he asked as the three of us fanned out.

"Confirmation," I called back from behind a bush. "We need to know that our perception of what happened is close to the truth."

We settled in for some hard work, and then, three seconds later, Bella surprised us by shouting, "I've found it!"

She was standing in a sheltered spot beneath an apple tree. The snow still got through the bare branches, but it was not as thick as it was in the middle of the green.

"This is where she died."

The three of us stood in silent vigil for a moment as we peered down at a burst of colour in the twilit snow.

"Miss Frazel's handiwork, I presume?" Lovebrook guessed correctly.

There was a trace of bright red silk poking through the layer of white. It was just enough to identify Ivy's posy of flowers, which must have fallen from her coat as she struggled with the killer.

"What I don't understand," I admitted, thinking out loud, "is why the body was moved."

"How do you mean?"

"Rather than just leaving her here in the bushes, she was dragged out to the bench on the green; that means the killer took the risk of being spotted."

Bella looked puzzled for all of a moment or two. "So then he wanted her to be found."

"Or he didn't want anyone to know she'd been killed here." Lovebrook was suddenly more animated. "We'd best not disturb anything. A despatch from Scotland Yard will soon arrive. I'll have my officers examine the scene."

"And ask them to find out where everyone was between half past one and two o'clock," I suggested. "We know that Herbert Wandle and Ruth Haskell were in his house when Ivy called there. I'd like to know where the Baroness was at the time. Freddy at number 7b definitely didn't like the dead woman – though he doesn't seem to like anyone but Miss Haskell. The Preslers are still something of a mystery, too."

"That sounds like a sensible course of action." Lovebrook gave away nothing as he stalked off through the snow.

Bella and I followed him around the perimeter of Ivy's house. It only took us a minute to find another significant clue on our treasure hunt. As we reached the back door of the Gothic cottage, a broken pane in the window glinted in the light.

"It's another burglary," Bella immediately concluded. "Perhaps Ivy found the killer breaking into her house after she left Herbie's."

The glass that was broken was halfway up the dark brown door. Lovebrook carefully put his hand inside and tried his best to reach the lock.

"No, it's no good." Though he came close to cutting an artery on the jagged shards, it was impossible to undo the latch.

"Which suggests that the attacker either had an unfeasibly long arm, or he never got inside," I thought aloud. "Perhaps he felt that, after he'd killed her, it was too great a risk to pinch a few valuables."

"This is all very odd." Bella's voice was so blank that she might have been talking about the changeable weather or the Surrey cricket team's recent dip in form. "Why wouldn't he just have hidden the body until he'd finished what he'd come to do?"

"You know, it is possible that the killer wasn't from around here." Lovebrook moved his hair from his eyes as he expounded the idea. "Perhaps he doesn't know the area and was worried about someone passing this spot."

"Impossible," I said quite confidently. "There are plenty of expensive houses filled with riches all across London. No self-respecting criminal would enter a fenced-in place like this where the locals are more likely to notice a stranger."

"I'll give you that. And it fits with what I learnt before coming here." He turned around to us to reveal what he clearly considered to be a vital piece of information. "There's a man by the name of Hamish Dumfries who works here. There's a rather thick file on him at the Rosslyn Hill police station that makes for interesting reading. You see, the man is a prolific thief."

# EIGHTEEN

My feet were frozen. My fingers had turned to icicles, and I was more than relieved when Bella suggested that we return to Adele's house to wait for Lovebrook to finish his duties.

"You, my dear Bella, are a very kind woman," I told her as I removed my coat. "I can't wait to settle down in front of the fire and have a nice cup of tea."

"Or cocoa," she said with some glee as she hung up her scarf on the newel post. When she turned back to me, a look of sheer terror had disfigured her features. "Marius, what is that?" She was pointing straight at me, her jaw hanging open.

I looked down at my chest and realised what had induced her fear. "It's not what you think, Bella. I would never..."

I didn't finish that sentence because she was laughing too much to hear. "My goodness, Marius. That is the most hideous jumper I have ever seen."

I raced to explain why I was wearing such a frighteningly horrible creation. "It's not my fault that my mother picked out the knitted monstrosity that my Aunt Clara sent me for Christmas. It's below freezing point out there, and I didn't want to catch pneumonia."

She couldn't reply, she was mesmerised by the design which

featured stars, mountains and a large red blob that was possibly a face, a robin, or something far worse.

"I'm glad you find it funny." I didn't mean a word of this.

She said nothing more, though she did continue to laugh and point.

"Really, Bella. I thought you would be above such a reaction. Aunt Clara may still think I'm a child, be a terrible knitter and have the worst taste of any human being on the planet, but she knows how to keep a man warm."

She had to sit down on the bottom step because the spasms running through her were quite uncontrollable.

"Honestly," I began, feeling self-conscious, "I'm happy that you can find a sliver of light in the darkness."

She finally quietened down a fraction. "As my father often says, Marius, if you don't laugh, you'll have to cry." The smile remained on her lips for a second, but then her breathing became laboured and her whole attitude changed. "I'm sorry. I don't know what's got into me. I'm not normally so..."

She dropped her head into her hands. I didn't know what to do at first, but when I saw several large, plump tears falling onto her dress, I rushed forward to comfort her.

"Bella, there's no need for that," I told her inaccurately. "I can't stand to see you upset. Please continue laughing at me if it helps."

"I'm sorry," she repeated. "I really wish I were stronger, but it's all too much. I've loved our adventuring together, and every crime we've investigated has seemed like a brainteaser for us to crack, but I miss my auntie Addie, and every time I come back to this cottage, her death becomes real again."

I was wrong to say there was no reason to cry; she deserved this release of emotion and so, instead of trying to convince her otherwise, I put my hand on her arm and waited for the sorrow to lessen.

When she finally looked up at me, her sobs turned to laughter once more. "My goodness, Marius. That really is the ugliest thing I've ever seen." She somehow managed to chortle and cry at the same time. "It's actually rather cruel of you to wear it. How am I supposed to be serious now?"

"Perhaps you should hide in the kitchen for a while and make us hot drinks while I get the fire started." I stood up and held my hand out to her.

"Or perhaps we should swap." She poked me in the big red blob as she walked past me to the sitting room.

"Are you sure I can be trusted in the kitchen?" I replied, just to pique her.

"You did a good job with the tea earlier. I think you can handle the increased responsibilities." She paused then and, taking another deep breath, disappeared through the doorway.

I set some milk to boil in a pan, then found a distinctive orange tin of Bournville cocoa to mix into the simmering liquid. I added sugar and found the two largest ceramic cups that Adele had owned to serve our delicious treat. I even frothed it a little with a whisk.

What I didn't do was look for a tray to carry everything, which meant that I nearly scalded my hands on the short journey to Bella. Despite this, I stood marvelling at her in the doorway, as she blew on the already hungry fire. I wasn't her only one admirer. Percy had woken from his nap and was sitting staring at her as if she were a steak and he'd been told to sit.

"It's hard to say which smells better," I said so as not to startle her as I entered.

"What's that?"

"Your fire or my cocoa." I placed the drinks on the low table in front of the sofa and immediately realised I should have brought saucers. They would have saved my fingers, too.

By the time I'd run back to the kitchen to correct this mistake, she'd taken her seat in an armchair and was looking at the display of Adele's diverse artefacts.

"It's amazing," I said when the silence had held for some time and Percy had come to sit on my feet. "You know almost everyone I know, but there are so many people in your life with whom I've never crossed paths. When we were children, your family was forever hosting diplomats, visiting dignitaries and an endless array of aristocrats. I didn't tend to call round at such times."

She looked up at the ceiling, as if I were making a fuss over nothing. "I promise you weren't missing anything. As lovely a fellow as my father certainly is, my brothers and I were barely included in formal occasions. I used to hate having to dress up in stockings and breath-stealing bodices, only to be ignored entirely until it was time to go to bed. That's one of the reasons I used to like coming here so much. Auntie Addie wasn't exorbitantly rich, famous or powerful, which made her all the more special to me."

We glanced around the room then, and I'm certain that, like me, Bella was connecting the unique objects that were on display with the woman who had lived there.

"She used to make me cocoa before bed each night. She always had a tin of the stuff, and I assumed she bought it just for me."

Not for the first time in the last year, I imagined the life we would have had if, instead of panicking before I was shipped off to war, I had asked Bella to be my wife as I'd intended. I thought about the trips we would have made to see Adele and wondered whether she would have treated me just as warmly as she had my friend. I half considered the possibility she wouldn't have died if I'd had my head screwed on tighter.

I suppose we were both caught up in that nostalgic fog. Perhaps it was the glow of the fire, the taste of chocolate on our tongues, the tinsel hanging from the Christmas tree or simply the chance to spend fifteen minutes together without having to run around after a killer. Whatever the reason, when Lovebrook knocked on the door, we both jumped out of our skins.

"Great Scott of the Antarctic!" Bella muttered with her hand on her chest as she calmed herself.

I'd accidentally pushed Percy up to standing when I'd reacted, so he made the most of being on his feet to waddle to the front door. If only I could train him to open the silly thing, my life would be a lot easier.

"We're coming!" I called ahead of me, though I doubted the inspector would hear.

"You know it's really rather cold," he needlessly reminded me when I opened the door.

"I've made cocoa just for you." I pointed him into the drawing room and went to fetch another cup of the stuff.

When I returned, he was already on the sofa stroking Percy, who had plumped himself down on the poor man's lap.

"You're very kind." He accepted the cup and warmed his hands on it.

"Have you found anything useful?" I asked, returning to my seat.

"I was just wondering the same thing." Bella was sitting up to absorb every detail that our friend could share with us.

"And?"

It was Lovebrook's job to answer. "And it looks as though you were right, Lady Bella. Ivy was killed in the spot we found. Beneath the snow, there are signs of the earth having been trampled. I believe her body was dragged behind the treeline, so as to remain hidden, then placed on the bench when the killer could be certain that no one was looking. There are sadly no clear footprints to help us identify who put a length of rope or what have you around Ivy's neck."

"Not rope," I was quick to tell him. "Rope would have burnt her skin in a rougher pattern. Whatever killed her was smoother than that."

"Are your poor subordinates still out there?" Bella asked with no small amount of sympathy for the unknown officers.

"Not for much longer." The inspector savoured the smell of his still hot drink. "The men from Scotland Yard came just after you left. They'll uncover whatever they can and then head off to the station again. It's only getting colder, and even a heavy police cloak can't fend off the snow for long."

"I was wondering whether we should have taken a look inside Miss Frazel's cottage." She turned away as she spoke, though we couldn't see the victim's house from where we were. "Isn't it possible that the killer made it look as if he hadn't been able to get inside in order to throw us off the trail?"

"I had the very same thought." Lovebrook always smiled when he was impressed by one of our hugely speculative ideas. I'm sure it would have been wonderful to have him as a superior, as he was simply so grateful for our contributions. "And that's why I got the spare key to the front door from the gatehouse and had a look."

"And?" I was good at saying this.

"And there was nothing to find. No dirty footprints. No other broken windows. No sign of anything missing."

"Were there any ugly paintings?" Bella asked before I could.

"Not that stood out to me."

I nipped from the room to seize the... what's the opposite of a masterpiece? "This is the one we told you about in the tea room."

He took a moment to look at it, his eyes growing to the size of the saucers under our cups. "I certainly wouldn't hang such a piece in my living room," he affirmed, frowning somewhat. "But then it's hard to concentrate on it when you're wearing that jumper, Marius."

I cursed myself for getting so distracted by the warmth, the cocoa and my graceful companion that I'd forgotten to change my clothes.

Bella was almost over the hilarity of my great aunt's knitting, and it took her a mere thirty seconds to recover this time. "So you didn't see anything similar?"

Lovebrook shook his head.

I was happy that we could concentrate on the case rather than how terrible I looked. "The painting comes from the Caledonian street market. The artist there told us that John Presler is a regular customer."

We'd been so hopeful that this would turn out to be our key to identifying the killer, but it had been eclipsed by the discovery of Ivy's body.

Either way, the inspector was unconvinced by the evidence as we'd presented it. "Don't you think it unlikely that the killer would have intentionally left a clue behind?"

To my surprise, Bella was still keen on the idea. "Not at all. He evidently hoped that no one would notice the painting was missing or he wouldn't have replaced it. And why would he think that we could find the artist? If we hadn't been in the market for a Christmas tree—" She came to a sudden halt and struggled to start up again. "I'm so sorry. I didn't mean to make a pun."

She'd been thrown off track by the unintended wordplay, so I rephrased the point she was trying to make. "If we hadn't gone to the market to buy a Christmas tree, we wouldn't have found the artist. It was serendipity."

Lovebrook crossed and then uncrossed his legs, dislodging an affronted Percy. The inspector sat back in his chair, then sat forward again, and if that wasn't enough to reveal that he was struggling to respond to what we'd just told him, he said, "I'm struggling to respond to what you've just told me. I feel that you're trying to make the evidence fit your theory."

I would have liked to prove him wrong, but that was easier said than done.

"Please understand." He held up one hand in a plea for patience. "I have a very high opinion of your deductive skills... normally. But we seem to have gone a long way from the initial evidence that your friend Mrs Leach uncovered. For example, how is the body you discovered this evening connected to her fears over the way one of her neighbours was treating his wife?"

Bella was quicker with her response than me. "I would say that is fairly obvious."

"Is it?"

"Of course it is. Tell him, Marius."

I couldn't hide my true feelings, and a guilty expression bloomed on my face.

"Not you too!" She was so upset that she had to call Percy over for comfort.

"I'm not saying that Adele was wrong," I began, knowing that whatever I said to defend Lovebrook's point would only fall on deaf ears. "I just think there could be more to the case."

She stood up then and moved to the window to look out at the faintly illuminated snow. "You do remember that she was murdered? There's no doubt that she knew something about one of the men here and was killed because of it."

I waited for a little of her anger to subside before responding. To be perfectly frank, I really did feel guilty for not rushing to back up her ideas.

"I told you before, Bella. I feel as if we've been asking the wrong questions. The notes we found upstairs were talking about a man running around at night without his wife knowing. Perhaps one of the men here was up to no good, but what would Ivy Frazel have had to do with it?"

I suppose the possibility of Ivy being the focus of our killer's romantic attention passed through each of our heads, but even Bella didn't put it forward as a solution.

"What has it got to do with the stolen painting? Or the firework?" I tried again. "Don't you think it's unlikely that a man would have killed his neighbour just to keep his infidelity quiet?"

"No. I would say that was a perfectly common reason for a man to kill." She looked wild and noble as she delivered this answer. "And John Presler is just the slippery sort of character who would do such a thing."

I was tempted to mutter, *Even in a place like this?* but the words never left my mouth, and the silence between us swelled.

"Before you say anything more," Lovebrook intervened to avoid an argument, "I think we should return to the discussion that we put off outside. There is only one man here with a serious criminal record. What have you learnt about Hamish Dumfries?"

"He's the caretaker," I said when Bella landed back in her armchair and wouldn't look at us. "The only other things I know about him are that he's rather grumpy and a wiz with fireworks."

"With *fireworks*?"

"He put on a display for the village tonight. They were still exploding overhead as we found Ivy's body."

"There you go, then. We have a suspect who was previously arrested for violent robberies, *and* he had a stock of fireworks, one of which was surely used in the first killing."

"He hid away in the gatehouse at the first mention of the police, too," I felt I should add.

Bella glared at me before replying. "People deserve second chances. Is it really any wonder that he'd be afraid of getting into trouble if he'd spent time in prison? When was he last arrested?"

Now it was Lovebrook's turn to look cagey. "Over a decade ago," he admitted, and Bella recovered her confidence.

"A decade? Then he's unlikely to have been ransacking London day and night since. And despite your talk of violence, the fact that he did not remain in prison proves that he isn't a murderer."

"You're right about that." Lovebrook was gracious even when losing an argument.

"So what was it?" Bella fought ever so hard to hide her smile. "A brawl in a pub? An argument with a neighbour?"

He pursed his lips before replying, as if trying to keep the answer in for as long as possible. "A guard discovered him in the process of stealing from a workshop. Dumfries coshed him on the head to get away."

"Which was a reprehensible act but not on a par with killing two defenceless women. Mr Dumfries's past shouldn't count against him if he's since made amends for his crimes and chosen the right path in life."

Lovebrook took a last sip of his cocoa and licked his lips. "You are a very persuasive woman, Lady Bella. I would even go so far as to say that you are a greatly superior debater to me. I believe you could win almost any argument against me – unless you wish to claim that there was a better fast bowler than William 'Bumper' Wells during his time at Northants County Cricket Club."

"Why do I feel that, even after you've agreed with me, you're about to disagree with me?" Her confidence had faded, and she sat limply in her chair.

"Because beating a fool like me isn't the same thing as being right." He gave us a few seconds to consider this. "We cannot ignore the caretaker's potential involvement."

"You know, you have a point, Inspector," I conceded. "I for one have a tendency to view certain evidence as if it is set in stone."

"Precisely. And for one thing, if we were to trust Adele Leach's instincts and only look at the men in this village, we would immediately dismiss half of our suspects. I feel that, as a police officer, it is my job to consider every possibility. Is it possible that Adele misunderstood what she thought she saw from her window? Yes, it is. Might it not even be true that she and Ivy Frazel were murdered by another woman and her notes threw us off the right path from the beginning? You tell me."

"I'm not denying that..." Bella began with some vehemence, but it soon ebbed away, and the inspector continued.

"And so, I will leave you now and try to speak to the man who was in charge of the firework which most likely brought about your friend's death. I will ask him whether he has continued his criminal activities and, though I might not have the linguistic dexterity to convince you one way or another, I do have a fairly good sense of whether someone is lying."

He rose from his seat to cross the room but paused in the doorway. "I'm sure I will see you again first thing tomorrow, but if by some strange quirk of fate I end up arresting the killer this evening, I will let you know."

Once the door had shut behind him, and calm had descended over our borrowed house, Bella looked at me, and I looked at her. Percy, meanwhile, just yawned.

# NINETEEN

We decided it was too dark to go out and bother more people, so I made dinner whilst Bella lay on the sofa and stroked my dog's ears. She offered to help, but I could see that she needed to stare hopelessly into space more than I did, so I got to work.

There wasn't a great deal of food in the house, and we should have considered this before settling in for the evening, but I managed to mix a selection of unlikely ingredients into something that was actually quite tasty.

"What..." I said, bursting into the room with a frying pan in my hand and a far too dramatic voice, "... do you think..." I kept pausing as though this would make my creation more delicious. "... about that?"

I brought the pan down to her level and she at least craned her neck a fraction to peer at it. "It looks almost as bizarre as your disconcerting jumper. What have you made?"

I sighed and walked off to the dining table, hoping she would follow. I had already prepared everything for dinner and even found a bottle of wine for us. It was no celebration, but it was still nice to eat together and, both regardless of and due to Bella's glumness, I hoped to make the most of our evening.

"Fried potatoes, fried ham, fried carrots—" I said as she wandered over.

"Fried carrots?" I'd made her laugh at least.

"Dowsed in honey and cinnamon – my own invention... And, to finish it off, I've covered it in strong cheddar cheese from the larder which, you may be able to guess, I fried."

I served her a big helping of the messy dish and awaited her response. "It looks... Well, it looks rather like bubble and squeak that has got dressed up in its Sunday finest."

"I'll take that as a compliment." I sat across from her at the tiny table and poured the wine as she took a tentative first bite.

"All the flavours are very tasty," she said most diplomatically. I noticed that she didn't say whether they were tasty together. "Is this the kind of thing you ate during the war?"

"This?" I'm sure I looked a little shocked. "This would have been considered a royal feast in the trenches. We had biscuits and jam, a little cheese and mustard, and some unholy conglomeration of vegetables. Do you know what I dreamed about most when I was there?"

"Me?" This single word shot through the room like a German bullet. As soon as she said it, I could see that she regretted the joke.

"Yes, of course, my dear." Bella was unequivocally the thing that had consumed my dreams and every waking moment, but I didn't want her to know that, so I said all this with a laugh in my voice. "And after you came good British sausages."

I ate a forkful of crispy potato and tinned ham but still wished I was eating sausages. At the mention of the word, Percy came lolloping into the room. I had a few scrag ends from the dog meat boy to give him, and he looked a little disappointed.

"What would you miss if you were to leave the country?" I asked when Bella fell quiet again.

This at least seemed to distract her a little. As Percy scoffed, she considered the question. "Assuming we're not talking about people, I would miss waking up at dawn and walking through the woods at home as the dew sparkles and rabbits hop about the place.

I'd miss the way the light breaks through the trees to warm the air in springtime. I'm sure there are beautiful forests and jungles all over the world, but none can compare to the Hurtwood."

In that moment, I remembered why I'd first fallen in love with her all those years ago. "You've certainly made me feel stupid for talking about sausages."

She threw her napkin across the table at me and her perfect green eyes shimmered. "Actually, I'll need that back."

I bowed my head as I passed it to her, like a knight returning a favour to a lady after a joust. At least, I hoped that was how I looked. She may well have thought me a fop.

"This meal is tastier with each mouthful," she confessed. "I suppose that you can't go wrong with fried food."

"That is the very philosophy of my cooking – you have neatly arrived at the crux of my culinary endeavours."

"I can see you're quite the artist in the kitchen." The fact that she was willing to make jokes made me feel the meal was a success.

"You should try my bacon sandwiches. A Frenchman I knew described them as almost as tasty as a *tartine de jambon* – which is ham and bread to you or me."

It was hard to say what in this innocuous comment caused her mood to dip but, as she ate, it became clear that jokes were now off the menu.

"I'm sorry, Marius. I know I'm terrible company tonight," she conceded after a minute, when the only sounds were the scrape of cutlery on plates, polite chewing and Percy snoring under the table. "I can't even say that it's just because of Adele's death, as sad as that makes me. I have a feeling of true..." She gripped hold of her fork and brought it down on the table to express her frustration. "Oh, I can't even find the word. I feel as if an explanation for all that has happened is within our reach, but we can't see it."

I considered this for all of five seconds before setting down my glass and standing up. "Come along then. There's something we can still try."

I wiped my mouth on my napkin and went out to the hall to

remove my hideous jumper and put on my coat. Bella followed to peer around the doorframe as though she were afraid I'd lost my mind.

"Marius, what about your lovely ugly dinner?"

"I will re-fry it when we come back and it will taste even better." I realised that my plan was a little half-baked at this moment and returned to the kitchen to choose another bottle of wine.

"Where are we going?" Bella asked even as she pulled on her boots and wrapped a scarf around her neck.

"You are unsatisfied. You don't believe that the caretaker whom no one we have interviewed has mentioned could be to blame for Adele's and Ivy's deaths, and so we must make an excursion to explore another solution."

Aware that this wasn't really an answer, I threw the door open and was immediately astonished by just how cold it was out there. It was lucky we'd found Ivy when we had, as it would have been impossible to turn up any evidence with the snow growing heavier and the drifts mounting around the village.

"Is this really a good idea?" Bella asked, and I pulled her against me to shelter from the blizzard we had chosen to walk through instead of getting warm before the fire.

"Probably not, but when has that stopped us before?"

I think she was smiling then, but she was gritting her teeth against the cold so much that it was impossible to say. Luckily, our arctic trek would be a short one. The path was covered with snow, and it was only visible because there was slightly more of the stuff piled up on either side of us. There was no sign of the police now, or even any of our neighbours. The street lights did what they could to light our way, and there were candles in the window of the Wandles' house that helped a little, but the snowflakes were so large, and the night above so dark, that it felt as if someone had thrown a blanket over the world to smother us.

The house across the green looked quite sinister in the gloom. It was double-gabled and picturesque but, far from being a sanctuary from the harsh conditions, it reminded me of a witch's cottage, lying in wait for a pair of unsuspecting innocents to cross its threshold. Or perhaps that was just the author in me investing meaning when there was none to find.

There was a light above the porch, and I could see that Bella was grateful to arrive at our destination. She tugged the bell-pull, and we continued huddling together, waiting for the door to swing open and the owners of number three to admit us to their home.

# TWENTY

"Silva!" John Presler shouted as soon as he saw us on his doorstep. "Silva, my darling, we have visitors."

"Who's come calling at this time of night and in such weather?" her voice came back to us from upstairs.

"It looks like a couple of snowmen!" He had a good laugh at this and then opened the door wider to usher us inside. "Come in, ya mad things. What were you thinking, setting foot outside in a blizzard?"

I looked at Bella, and I must say that we made a fine pair. As she removed her woollen hat, a heap of snow fell to the floor in front of her. Even her hair, which had been bundled up until now, was flecked white. Her black, ankle-length coat had changed colour too, so you can imagine how I looked alongside her.

As something of a conciliatory gesture, I held out the bottle of wine I'd brought, and Presler put it down on a table near the door.

"Lord Montague? Lady Bella?" Silva asked from the stairs. "It's lovely to see you both, but is something the matter?"

She refrained from asking whether we'd lost our minds, but it was clear that she was wondering it.

"You did say we should call by for a drink," Bella said with great charm. "Well, here we are."

She sneaked a glance in my direction, and I stepped forward to answer their doubts. "We're sorry to come unannounced. We really don't have any excuse." I realised that this did nothing to reassure them we weren't mad, so I tried again. "The truth is that we were alone in Adele's house, and we felt a little uncomfortable."

"So her ghost still walks the place," Silva replied quite authoritatively. "I've 'eard of things like that 'appening. I had a cousin in Broadstairs who swore for the life of her that our great-grandmother Phyllis would appear in her room every morning and tut at her. You can stay with us for as long as you like."

"We didn't have anything to do this evening, did we, darling?" Though he was playing the good host, I could see that our presence there had unsettled John.

"No, of course not – except keeping warm in front of the fire and enjoying the Christmas spirit." Silva winked at her husband and they both giggled.

"We're truly sorry to be a bother." Bella removed her coat, and John took it before awaiting mine. "It's my fault. I told Marius that my mind was running with dark thoughts, and he said that, of all the people we've met today, the two of you were clearly the friendliest, and there was no doubt in his mind that you would welcome a neighbourly call."

John Presler pointed his finger at her and nodded enthusiastically. "That is just the word for us. We always try to be neighbourly sorts. That's probably why the Baronesses and Miss Haskells of this world take exception to our presence here." He paused, and I tried to imagine why this might be the case. "They're jealous of our easy manner. Isn't that right, my darling?"

His wife grimaced a little, as though uncertain how to answer, then motioned to the nearest door. "Won't you come through to the *petit salon?*"

Something about the way she said this suggested that she was trying to impress us. The foreign term was rather out of place in her mouth, and I remembered what her husband had told us of her wealthy father's fishery business. I knew a man in the army who'd come from money but didn't fit in with the toffs with whom he associated, and it split him in two. I had a slightly different problem. While it was true that I'd grown up with a duke's daughter for a friend, I conversely lacked for money, breeding or influence.

Taking the time to examine our surroundings, I noticed that the entrance hall was rather tastefully decorated. Like a lot of what we'd seen at Holly Village, it was as if someone had taken a luxurious parlour from a stately home and reduced the dimensions so that it could fit into a small house near Highgate. There was dark wood panelling running up the stairs and around the room. A few pastoral scenes were hanging in a diagonal line parallel to the staircase, and the only piece of furniture was a small Wellington chest with a bust of Queen Victoria sitting on the top of it.

It was a little old-fashioned, but all in all, I would have been happy to live there myself. That was until we entered the salon, and I saw the artworks on display.

"Not bad, wouldn't you say?" John Presler was clearly proud of the ten or so brightly coloured paintings. "I discovered this young artist a couple of years ago, and I consider myself something of a patron. I 'ave a feeling 'er work will be 'ighly collectible one day."

I don't need to explain that I was looking at a selection of the poorly daubed creations that we'd found in the market that afternoon. It was no wonder the young painter had talked of Presler as if he were a sap; he'd bought enough of her work to keep her dog in steak for a decade.

"They're very..." Although she has the manners of a parish priest and is always sweet-natured around strangers, even Bella couldn't think of a nice word to say about the pieces before us.

"Yes, aren't they!" Presler said enthusiastically, saving her without realising it.

"Do leave those alone, won't you, John, dear?" Standing on the other side of the room, Silva pointed to a decanter of brandy to offer us a libation. I got the definite impression that she did not like the paintings as much as her husband did.

"Not for me, thank you, Silva." Bella closed her eyes in that demure way of hers.

"It's not just brandy I can offer." Our hostess stepped aside to open the cupboard behind her. There were bottles of every description within, and Bella was soon served a small measure of sherry.

I enjoyed the first sip of my drink and was happy to realise that the part of the room that did not contain any landscapes was actually rather pleasing. There was a Christmas tree in the bay window, which itself had church-like glass that was characteristic of the houses there. Chains of golden stars extended from each corner of the room to the crystal chandelier in the centre and, most importantly that night, a fire blazed in the hearth.

"So, your lordship," Presler said, sidling up to me with a certain dubious look about him, "what's your game? Besides being a lord, I mean. Do you 'ave a *vocation?*"

He spoke this word much as his wife had pronounced the room in which we now stood. John Presler was an ordinary man living in a village full of snobs. His need to impress – or at least be accepted – was mirrored in Silva's.

"Marius is an excellent author," Bella informed them. I don't actually think of myself as a great writer – especially since penning the work of hackdom I would soon release. It had taken some time for Bella to get around to reading one of my novels, but I was always happy to know that she liked it when she finally did.

"Books, eh? I didn't know your sort got up to that type of thing. I thought only jobbing fellows like myself entertain the masses with racy stories."

I was afraid he'd already seen through my act as an aristocrat, but I replied in a neutral tone. "I think you'll find that there are plenty of us at it. At one time, the upper classes were the only ones writing. We did all we could to control the knowledge that—"

The look that Bella gave me made it clear that this was not a topic which a lord would normally discuss, and I hastened to talk of something else. "I'm afraid I didn't quite understand what it is that you do, Mr Presler?"

"I told you when we first met, you must call me John. Or Jay, or Jack for that matter. I respond to them all."

He hadn't answered the question but, as we were now used to badgering witnesses, Bella was happy to remind him. "Your job must be something special to have caught the eye of the heir to the Eel King fortune."

He had a smile that curled up his whole face. His cheeks pushed out, his eyes squinted and the skin at the top of his nose became ruffled.

"I don't think it was my profession what attracted 'er." He winked at his wife in a bawdy manner as she took a seat on the sofa beside Bella. This was hardly surprising, as he did everything in a bawdy manner. "As it 'appens, I'm what you might call a *Jack* of all trades. I do whatever my clients need, and I don't complain in the slightest."

I'd gone there with an open mind and been quite willing to believe that the Baroness and a few of her snooty neighbours had taken against the Preslers solely for their working-class accents and poor taste in art. Hearing John's answer to this question changed that. He'd practically confessed to being a criminal and didn't seem ashamed of it in the slightest.

"That must be an interesting existence." Bella tried to draw more from him. "I'm sure you meet some very interesting people."

"Interesting?" He took a quick sip of brandy and rocked his head back as though he were fighting off hiccups. "You don't know the 'alf of it, miss. I 'ave become an intimate acquaintance of people from all walks, runs and even crawls of life. As I've always said, the world is a tapestry and each of us is but one stitch upon it."

This wasn't the least poetic statement I'd ever heard, but he held his hands out and wore a sober expression as he said it to show that he was rather impressed with his own turn of phrase.

Whatever his job was, it did not look as though he wished to reveal it, and so Bella introduced a new matter for discussion. "I'm sorry to darken the mood, but I must ask you about my auntie Adele. Were you particularly close to her?"

"She only lived across the green!" John thought this was very funny, but his laughter was cut short as his wife talked over him. He apparently did not appreciate this and sipped his drink sullenly.

"I loved dear Addie. She was a kind lady and got on well with everyone 'ere."

"That she did," her husband added in a grunt.

"I'm not going to pretend that I thought too highly of some of the company she kept, but I can tell you that she wasn't one to take sides. She was good to us even if the 'igh and mighty *Baroness* wouldn't give me the time o' day."

John's free hand rolled up into a fist at his side and I could see how angry this made him. "If I'd known what kind of people lived around 'ere, I would never 'ave suggested buying the place. My Silva paid good money for this house, but there's plenty what look down on us just 'cos we ain't descended from royalty."

"Oh, come, come," I said in as jovial a tone as I could manage. "You're married to the daughter of a king. Silva is the Eel Princess, which makes you the prince."

He was deadly serious for a moment before that distinctive smile showed once more. "'Ere, I like you! You're not a stuck-up fraud like that woman at number two. I've never seen any evidence that she's a baroness anyway."

"John, there's no need to sink to her level." Silva could be stern with her husband when it was required. "We can disagree with her without casting what-d'-you-call-'ems..."

"Spells?" he guessed.

"No, not spells, my darling. You know what I mean. I don't want you casting..."

"A fishing line?" he tried again.

"Then you clearly don't know what I mean."

"Aspersions?" I suggested, though I was as confused as he was.

"That's the one!" Silva looked askance at her husband. "Why would I be talking about fishing at a time like this?"

"I thought it was a what-d'-you-call-'em..."

"A plea for help?" Bella quickly replied, happy to join in the game.

"No, not that. A... you know!"

"A slip of the tongue." I was unlikely to be right twice in a row, but it was worth a try.

"No, no. None of that." Presler put his hand up to the back of his head, which he was busy shaking. "I thought it was a... a metaphor."

"Oh!" the three of us said as one, before Silva asked, "A metaphor for what?"

"You know, like Jesus Christ." He walked around the sofa, clearly upset that no one had followed his thinking.

I watched him go, now more confounded than before.

"He was a fisher of men!" He threw his hands up in disbelief. "You should know that as the daughter of a fisherman."

Silva tried to soothe him. "Now, now, John. There's nothing to worry about. What were you saying before?"

The misunderstanding had unnerved him, and his simmering anger came to the boil. "I'll tell you what I was saying. I was talking about Ruth Haskell and Baroness Wandle and that miserable bore Freddy What's-'is-name and all of them who treat us like they're farmers and we're pigs." I'd expected him to steer clear of metaphors after the last time, but evidently I was wrong.

"There's no need to raise your voice, John," Silva tried to pacify him once more, but I could see that it would do no good. "It's not Lord and Lady Montague's fault that the world ain't fair."

"When did I say it was?" He took a step closer to her. "All I'm saying is that this was supposed to be a friendly place. Everyone said it when we first visited, but they're really just—"

"Which side did Ivy prefer?" Bella, perhaps wisely, interrupted. "We met her before she was killed, but I can't say that I had any sense of where she fitted into your community."

She made no effort to hide the fact that we were trying to uncover the truth of what had happened. I was worried this approach had already fallen short, as John stared at the carpet, and neither of them looked as if they wished to reply.

"We don't mean to pry," my friend continued more cautiously. "I only wished to—"

"We thought she was our friend at first," John spoke in a more vulnerable voice, but that note of fury was always present. "We thought she was our kind of person. In the end, she was as bad as the others."

The schism in the village seemed like little more than a playground feud. I needed to find out whether it went any further. "Ivy pretended to like you, then talked about you behind your back to the Baroness. Is that what happened?"

John wouldn't look at us again, and so Silva answered. "It might sound like nothing, but we had a terrible year when we first arrived here. Adele was the only one of them who really tried to be our friend. She was brave, and I believe that she even stood up to Ruth Haskell once. It caused quite the disagreement."

"And what of Miss Haskell?" Bella was capable of asking blunt questions that would have normally put people on guard. "She evidently considers herself the leader and unifier of the village. Didn't she play devil's advocate at least?"

John still wouldn't answer. Holding her unsipped glass of sherry, Silva looked uncertain whether she should.

"The problem in a place like this," she said, pausing occasionally to pick the right words, "is that people say one thing in public and another elsewhere. Ruth was always on our side when it was just the three of us, and she still maintains a civil façade when the village comes together, like at the fireworks and what 'ave you."

"But...?" I said to urge the gory details from her.

"But we heard from Adele that, ever since Freddy Ponting from 7b started paying her Sunday visits – if you know what I mean – her whole attitude changed. Apparently, she said the most terrible things about us."

"She liked to tell everyone 'ow common we are." John let out a snort and took a few seconds to continue. "Freddy Ponting is a crabstick, but spending time with him wasn't the only reason his sweetheart turned against us."

Silva attempted to talk over him again. "When I invited Lord and Lady Montague here, this wasn't what I had in—"

"Haskell and the Baroness and the whole lot of them became a lot worse when—"

"John, don't."

He delivered his response straight at his wife, even though it was for our benefit. "Things got really bad after everyone accused me of being a thief."

# TWENTY-ONE

"John!" Silva spoke to fill the inevitable silence that followed this revelation. "Can't you forget all that? Can't we move on with our lives?"

"'Ave they forgotten it?" His rage had reached a whole new level. "'Ave they given us even 'alf a second chance?" When she didn't answer, Presler continued with his explanation. "They all said that I'd stolen a sculpture from old Mrs Anderson's 'ouse, and I want it on record that no one proved a thing against me."

I can't say I regretted going out in the cold anymore. This was exactly what we needed to hear. The one thing I found strange was that John Presler was so happy to incriminate himself. We'd only been in his house for fifteen minutes and he'd given us any number of useful titbits that would count against him should he ever be hauled up on charges.

"We've heard Mrs Anderson's name before," I said to myself as much as the others. "I believe it was Ivy who first mentioned her. She said that they were close, and Mrs Anderson died a couple of years after she arrived. Did the theft have anything to do with her death?"

"No, that were months later." John leaned away from me as I said this, as though he wished to be far from any such suggestion.

"And go easy! It was bad enough that I were blamed for a burglary that was right on my doorstep. I mean, I'd 'ave to be a special kind of dolt to go burgling my neighbours. Either way, the statue or what have you went missing, and 'cos I don't talk nothing like them, I was the one what they pinned the crime on."

I was fairly confident he was exaggerating his East London speech patterns to make his point.

"Was the sculpture really worth so much that it created all this fuss?" Bella sounded surprised that this would be the case, but after all the treasures we'd spotted in the houses we'd visited, it seemed quite possible.

"I'll say," John continued, and I noticed that his wife hadn't uttered a word in some time. "I don't know 'ow much you know about the work of Frederic Leighton..." He seemed to know rather a lot. "... but his sculptures are particularly highly regarded. *An Athlete Wrestling with a Python* is p'r'aps his most famous piece."

"And if I'm not mistaken, it's displayed at the National Gallery of British Art," I thought it worth mentioning.

"Yes, but Mrs Anderson 'ad a smaller bronze cast of it. It wasn't tiny, mind you. It stood in 'er hallway, and she used to wrap 'er scarves round it. From what Herbie could tell, looking through old auction catalogues and the like, it was worth upwards o' five thousand pounds. That's more than we paid for this house."

"So, what happened?" Bella placed her empty glass on the table beside her. "They accused you of stealing it, and what did you say?"

"I told the truth, didn't I? I told them I was innocent. As she's the self-appointed guv'noress of the village, Miss Haskell called the police. Down came Sergeant Bulmer shouting his arrogant mouth off as ever, and he said he would ransack every 'ouse if it weren't returned by the following day."

"John had nothing to do with any theft," Silva quietly informed us before her husband continued.

"No, I did not, but what do you think 'appened? The bronze strongman fighting off a snake appeared on Mrs Anderson's front doorstep the next morning, and the police weren't involved after that. You can imagine what the Baroness and her ilk thought though: I still got the blame."

When he mentioned the Baroness, I realised that she had come close to telling us all this herself that afternoon. Even if they believed the Preslers were responsible for its disappearance, Herbie and his wife had kept the story to themselves. I suppose they were trying to be fair, but Presler had told us everything regardless.

The room fell still for the first time in a while, and I asked another question. "What sort of person was she? Mrs Anderson, I mean."

"The typical sort you get around 'ere." Everything John said might just as well have been accompanied by gritted teeth.

"She wasn't the one accusing my husband of being a thief, if that's what you're wondering. She was a bit like you two: you know, 'igh-class. She was the daughter of a peer of some description, and 'er 'ouse were like a treasure chest. It was full to bursting with precious paintings and bits of pottery and the like. She used to give tours of the place to anyone interested. And despite all that, she didn't look down on us. Even if, in 'er heart, she might have thought that John was to blame for robbing her, she never said nothing about it."

"Did she have any close family?" Bella asked, though I couldn't see what difference this would make.

John looked too angry to answer and deferred to his wife.

"No one from outside the village came to the funeral. Us locals were all there, though, and I must say we managed to maintain our civility. It was a solemn occasion, as Mrs Anderson was very much admired in these parts." She shook her head mournfully. "A few days later a man with a wagon came to clear the 'ouse."

"That's right," John said, going to help himself to another drink. "Mrs Anderson's heir had arranged it. 'E was some undeserving distant cousin 'oo'd never actually met the old lady what left him a fortune."

This all seemed quite inconsequential to more recent events. "Did Ivy or Adele have any enemies?" I asked to correct this.

"'Ow do you mean?" John replied, as though he'd never before heard this word.

"I mean, can you think of anyone here who would have been angry enough to hurt them?"

The couple took their time to answer, looking across the room at one another to decide who should speak. It fell to Silva this time. "Ivy was a little flighty, if you take my meaning. She was always upset about one thing or another. She'd been good friends with Agatha at number four."

"Agatha?" Bella was on this comment like a tiger on a chicken. "I thought the lady who lived at number four was Betty."

"That's right, Betty's there now, but she only moved in a couple of years ago. Before that there were old Agatha. She was very frail, even when we moved 'ere. When she died, Ivy took it badly. The two of them used to spend a lot of time together and, to be quite honest, it loosened the screws in Ivy's 'ead even more. She essentially went into mourning for a year. It was the same with Mrs Anderson before that, now that I think about it."

Silva paused to recall her most recently slain neighbour. "She was a high-strung woman, Ivy Frazel was. For a while after her friends died, you could say nothing to her without causing offence. I suppose that was one of the reasons she threw 'er lot in with the other lot." I took this to mean Ruth Haskell, the Baroness and their associates. "'Er friends kept getting old and shuffling off, so she had to look for new ones. It was easy enough to blame us for everything and win favour with the nobs."

"Why did you move here in the first place?" I asked, as they would have stood out even if no crimes had been committed.

John went to sit down in the chair next to his wife and took her hand in his. "This isn't the first place what treated us poorly, but we 'eard about Holly Village, and it sounded like a real haven. It might not look that way, but we're all misfits here, and we thought it would suit us to the ground. When Miss Haskell showed us about, she promised that it was the most welcoming place in London." They looked out of the window at the snowstorm, and it was clear that neither of them agreed with this.

I realised then that we were not about to identify the killer after all. There had been various moments when it seemed that John Presler's angry nature could account for the violence. But the atmosphere in the room had fallen flat, and all I saw before me was a pair of question marks. Was Presler as tough an individual as he seemed? Was Silva as well-meaning as she made out?

Bella must have come to see the futility of our task, too, as she suddenly said, "It's Christmas. We should talk of happy things. Tell us the story of how you met. Marius and I have known one another since we were tiny, so I'm always interested in other people's stories."

John apparently wasn't prepared for this change in mood and looked at her distrustfully.

Silva answered the question for them both. "I hired John to do some work for me, and he never left. Isn't that right, my darling?" Her plump cheeks swelled with affection for her husband, but his eyes were cold. "I'd been married once before. I'm no spring chicken as anyone can see, but my Johnny doesn't see age, do you, darling?"

Their eyes met, and I could tell just how much Silva loved her husband. Did the thirty years between them matter? If it had been the other way around, and John Presler had married a woman half his age, no one would have thought twice about it. Was this the real reason that the people of Holly Village had taken against them?

I was trying to keep an open mind, but there was a nagging doubt that Presler had only married his bride for her money. Sometimes it's hard to tell the difference between logical conclusions and prejudices. The fact that two people with a large gap in their ages can fall in love does not rule out the possibility that one is taking advantage of the other. And as I was thinking all this, the conversation moved on.

"Yes, that's a lovely idea," Bella cooed. She was so believable in her sweetness I'd quite forgotten that she considered John Presler the likely killer. We'd only gone there because of her, and yet she acted as though they were now her best friends. "In my family, we always read funny stories on Christmas Eve, but a poem could be even better."

"Go on, John," Silva encouraged him. "Get your book. You read so beautifully."

In that occasionally shy manner of his, he hesitated and then pushed himself up to standing, much as if his body were weary after a long day. "Oh, very well. It's normally only you I read to, Silva. You know that. But I appreciate our new friends coming to visit, so I'll make an exception."

There was a small bookshelf behind the Christmas tree. It held no great selection, but John ran his finger along their green and blue spines, like a librarian consulting a vast trove of tomes.

"'Ere we are," he said, selecting the right volume. "I often read Rosetti's 'In the Bleak Midwinter' at this time of year, but everyone knows it, so 'ow about something different?"

"Read Sir Walter Scott," Silva suggested. "I love that one of his about the olden times. What's it called?"

"Don't be daft, Silva. I'd be 'ere 'alf the night reading that." He'd opened the slim book and was flicking through the pages to find something that appealed. "I've got it. This is a lovely little poem. You'll all like this one."

The cold light bounced off the snow and in through the window, but it was instantly beaten back by the glow of the fire as John Presler prepared to read.

"'Mistletoe' by Walter de la Mare." He reminded me of a child standing before his class to recite his homework. He even adopted a posher voice and stopped dropping his Hs. "Here I go then...

> "*Sitting under the mistletoe*
> *(Pale-green, fairy mistletoe),*
> *One last candle burning low,*
> *All the sleepy dancers gone,*

*Just one candle burning on,*
*Shadows lurking everywhere:*
*Someone came, and kissed me there."*

Something about the way he spoke this final line told me that he knew he'd chosen the wrong poem. On the surface, it described a pretty little scene full of the mystery and nostalgia of a good Christmas, and yet there was something uncanny about it. I happened to remember that Walter de la Mare was a master of tales of the supernatural, and the thought of this unknown presence, lurking in the shadows to steal a kiss, sent a tingle through my body.

*"Tired I was; my head would go*
*Nodding under the mistletoe*
*(Pale-green, fairy mistletoe),"*

Presler came to an unexpected halt before the two final couplets. His eyes strayed around the room, his face was grave, and I believe that he looked across the village to the bench where we'd found Ivy's body. He had to clear his throat before delivering the last lines of the poem more hesitantly.

*"No footsteps came, no voice, but only,*
*Just as I sat there, sleepy, lonely,*
*Stooped in the still and shadowy air*
*Lips unseen – and kissed me there."*

Silva applauded her beloved husband, and Bella joined in with *aahs* of appreciation, but I could tell from that haunted look on John Presler's face that he felt just the same as I did. The week that two innocent people had been murdered was not the time to open the door to ghostly visitors.

The evening never truly recovered from this chilling moment. Christmas had long since been associated with ghost stories, but they were not my idea of a good time. I found the everyday world frightening enough without having to worry about spirits stealing me away to the land of the dead.

Bella was wonderful, of course. She kept the conversation going and was bright and cheery till the end. John, meanwhile, would not be reanimated, and I was not much better company. Silva talked of frivolities, and Bella cast us back twenty years to our childhood in the Hurtwood. She remembered countless details, which I had forgotten, of desperately longed-for Christmas presents that now resided in long-closed cupboards. She talked of her brothers' troublemaking on Christmas morning, and the tricks they would play on their father.

"Imagine growin' up with a duke for a daddy!" Silva marvelled, and I was glad that no one had asked me what title my fictional parents had as, though I do that very job for a living, I'm not the best at making up stories on the spot.

"A duke comes below a king," I reminded her, and the two ladies laughed politely at a joke I'd already made once that night.

"If you'll excuse me..." I didn't think this sentence needed finishing, but John was a blunt man and made sure of my intentions.

"Toilet, is it?" His eyebrows rose, though he did not. "Upstairs on the right, just like in Adele's 'ouse."

I looked at him for a moment, then moved across the room and through the door. I didn't really need to use the lavatory, but I thought that, if I was going to have the opportunity to poke around in their house, this would be it. I listened at the door for a few seconds and could tell that the conversation had continued much as I'd left it. I had to hope that Bella would guess what I was planning and keep them busy.

I decided to go upstairs first and, yes, perhaps I felt a twinge of guilt for abusing the hospitality of two potentially innocent people who had given us shelter from the storm, but I had a job to do. If it weren't for unscrupulous people like me, far more murders would go unsolved.

The first floor of the house was decorated in a more modern style, which I felt reflected John's tastes more than his wife's. Every room was painted in a different shade of pale pastel. The colours matched the prominently displayed painting in each room. Sadly, none of them was the missing Manet from Adele's house. Equally disappointingly, all of them were the creations of the chancer we'd met at the Caledonian Market. It was impressive how talented she (and her dog) were at taking real life and making it look far uglier.

I needed to find the room where the Preslers kept their secrets. Aside from a bathroom, which had a painting of a ship being tossed about in a poorly painted sea, there was nothing particularly personal up there. I should probably mention that I drew the line at rifling through their wardrobes. I'm a mystery writer, not a parlour-jumper.

I left the upper floor behind and went down the curving staircase to what, seeing as Bella and the others were in the *petit* one, I could only assume was the *grand salon*. It was not. It was a study of some description, and I wished that I'd started there. It was all dark wood, like the entrance hall, and there was a bookshelf covering one wall that had nothing but glass figurines on it.

On the desk, there was a sombre photograph of the Preslers on their wedding day. John wore the expression of a man who had just been sentenced to ten years' hard labour, and Silva somehow looked even more miserable. A lazy detective would take this as a sign that the marriage was a sham but, if the truth be known, I'd seen far worse examples. My parents' own wedding picture – one of the few photos that I can remember seeing of them – makes them look as if they'd never met before and are confused as to why anyone has approached them with a camera.

Far more interesting was the linen-bound notebook just next to the silver frame. I opened the cover to discover marbled endpapers, which I was fairly sure wouldn't tell me who had killed Ivy and Adele, so I kept flipping. The first relatively blank page said, "Engagements 1928", and I at last hoped to find out what John did for a living.

The paper within was covered in neatly ruled columns with the same titles on each page. They read, *Client, Date, Time, Total Due, Paid*. Whatever his job, the sums charged were impressive. I calculated that, over the course of most weeks, he was making anything up to fifteen pounds. That was four times the average working man's wage, but not unheard of for bankers, stockbrokers or competent criminals.

I didn't recognise any of the names and only an initial was given in most cases. I saw that P. Henson was listed most often, closely followed by L. Lipstiff and E. Pritt. These names still didn't mean anything to me, but it was interesting to see that he had regular customers. If he were an art thief, were these the clients who commissioned the loot he stole? Was there a more innocent explanation that a crime-riddled brain like mine was incapable of summoning?

There was a brown leather chair tucked under the desk, and so I wheeled it out of the way to access the drawers there. The first contained nothing but writing equipment – a fountain pen, a blotting pad and two bottles of black ink. The second was empty, and the third (I had to hope) would contain the reason I had come to the house in the first place.

It stuck a little as I pulled it out. Wood screeching against wood made me pause in case someone had heard. When I finally had the courage to move again, I looked down to see a bundle of papers not so dissimilar to the ones I have in a drawer in my flat in St James's. On the top was a demobilisation certificate stamped 1919. I didn't need to read the heading to know what it was. I recognised the layout instantly from my own matching document. I was unlikely ever to need it again, but it was not the kind of thing that one could throw away.

There were a few photographs of a platoon of soldiers. The first showed the men arranged in rows, their faces stony. I decided that either their captain was shouting at them to concentrate, or it was taken just before they headed into battle. I spotted John Presler fairly easily. He'd had scruffier hair back then, but the same gap-toothed, slightly oafish look to him.

The next was less formal. There was a line of five friends, each with their arms over one another's shoulders and a beaming smile on their faces. Their uniforms were dirty and the man on either end was using his rifle like a crutch. The joyfulness of their expressions made me wonder whether it was taken after the armistice had been signed. Only John was looking at the camera. The others were peering at one another, mid conversation, and a big fellow on the left of the image had his mouth open as if he were calling out in celebration.

It was a single moment that had been burnt onto a negative and frozen in time. There are probably similar photos of me somewhere in my old friends' homes, but I don't have any – I don't need any. Being an ex-Tommy means that you live your life with constantly firing memories of a short period that dominated everything around it. I was only called up for the last year of the war, and yet a photograph like that can send me shooting back there in an instant.

It was frankly unsettling, and I was about to close the drawer and slink sheepishly back to the petit salon to see the others when I noticed something underneath. It was an identity card and the name at the top of it wasn't *Presler* but *Jones*. I shuffled back to the demobilisation certificate and saw the same thing. It didn't say *Private John Presler*, but *Private Preston Jones*.

Ten different explanations entered my mind, but before I could choose a favourite, I heard the sound of a door opening in the entrance hall. I stuffed everything back in the drawer and said a silent prayer that it wouldn't squeak again.

"I love these figurines," I said without looking around as someone came into the room.

"What are you doing in here?" my host's voice came back to me.

"Sorry, old thing. I was just having a nose about the place. And I must say, I admire the playfulness of the decoration here. We don't have anything like..." I sought a description for the unappealing figures before me. "... glass clowns in our house, but they really brighten up the place, and I say bravo."

For the first time that day, I was grateful that I was acting like a toff. It's far easier to pretend that everything is tickety-boo when you can throw a few "old things" and "by Joves" into the conversation.

Sadly, he didn't appear to trust me even then. "Yes... well, that's Silva's business, not mine. Like I told you, I'm more into landscapes."

He wasn't looking at me as he said this. His gaze had come to a stop on the chair that I had failed to tuck back under the desk.

In the hope I might distract him from it, I walked over and put my hand on his shoulder. "John, old thing, I mean this most sincerely; you have a lovely home here, and I fully understand why you would move to a place like this. It's just a shame that your neighbours didn't welcome you as they should have."

He was less than forthcoming with his reply but shrugged and seemed to accept my sincerity. "That's very nice of you to say so, Lord Montague."

"Please, call me Marius," I told him with my most charming smile. "My mother does."

I patted him on the back, and we returned to the *petit salon*, where I encouraged him to tell me more about his art collection.

# TWENTY-THREE

By the time we left the Preslers' house that night, my cheeks ached from having to smile so much. I never felt that John had forgotten what he'd seen. Whenever the conversation got a little friendlier, or Silva diverted it towards a new topic, he would look in my direction, perhaps still trying to figure out why I would have entered the study without permission.

The evening passed fairly painlessly, and a natural moment to leave eventually arrived. Thankfully, it was not a long walk home. The snow descending outside had lessened a little, but the night felt even more hostile. The temperature must have fallen another five degrees, and the wind had picked up, so we fought our way back to Adele's cottage as much as walked.

We couldn't even share our thoughts on what we'd just experienced, as the wind was too loud to think, let alone speak. But when we got back to the house, and Percy came padding out from the sitting room to see us, I closed the door and felt quite wonderful. My body seemed to fizz as it warmed up from the outside in. The warmth of the still-glowing embers in the grate penetrated my every atom, and I felt as you should feel just before Christmas. I felt somehow at home.

"That wasn't the evening I'd been expecting," Bella revealed when we'd shed our external layers, brushed the snow from places it had no right to be, and removed our icy boots. "I have to admit that I might have been wrong about them."

"Do you really mean it?" I replied, quite amazed. "There was nothing you saw there that made you think your aunt was right and John Presler is the murderous cheat that her notes suggest?"

We stood at the bottom of the stairs, uncertain whether to take the discussion into one of the more comfortable areas of the house or be done with the day and go to bed.

She opened her mouth to respond in the same breezy manner, then stopped herself. "Why? Is there something I didn't notice?"

"I found him to be every bit the thuggish disruptor that we'd imagined," I told her vaguely. "He couldn't hide just how much he disliked the other villagers."

"That is true, but I found myself thinking they were more to blame than him. If there'd been any evidence that he'd stolen the statue from Mrs Anderson, someone would have told us about it, don't you think?"

We would clearly need time to discuss all this, so I led her to the kitchen and lit the hob once more. As soon as I smelt the aromas of my hodgepodge dinner, I realised how hungry I was.

I kept talking as I heated up the leftover food. "I'm not surprised that Presler has a temper. Nor was I amazed that a work of art had gone missing here before – even if it was eventually returned. Someone – possibly John or even Silva – stole the bronze figure, then became frightened of being caught with it so gave it back before he could get into trouble. What I don't understand is why the police so readily gave up their search for the thief."

She took her place at the table. "I'm not denying any of that. All I'm saying is we've seen nothing to prove that the Preslers are criminals. Don't forget that John was the one who told us about the theft. Why would he have done so if he was responsible for it?"

"To make you ask that very question, perhaps."

She tilted her head to look at me, and I could see that she

appreciated the chance to discuss matters, even if it wouldn't get us any closer to the truth.

"That sounds like a risky scheme. Criminals incriminating themselves to seem innocent surely only works in theory – and books like yours. It's not a true contradiction of their involvement, and it provides further reason to suspect them."

"Yes, but that wasn't all. How many of his questions did he leave his wife to answer? Personally, I took it as evidence of a guilty conscience."

Percy now staggered into the room with a look on his face that suggested I'd been terribly cruel to wake him from his slumber. To make up for it, he would simply have to go to sleep on Bella's feet.

"That's not evidence, Marius," she insisted as the friendly beast got comfortable. She sounded like Inspector L'Estrange, the detective from my first three books (and one cancelled stage play). "It's just another theory."

"Then what about Presler's job?"

"What about Presler's job?"

"We've asked him twice what he does, and twice he's been evasive."

"Perhaps he does something horrible and is embarrassed," she suggested a little coyly.

"Perhaps he's a murderer who steals precious artworks from his victims."

She wrinkled her nose then, and it was clear she had almost entirely reversed her opinion of the man. I had to wonder whether this was because of the time we'd spent with our neighbours across the green, or she simply enjoyed disagreeing with me.

"A few hours ago," I continued, "you tried to persuade a serving police inspector of Presler's guilt. All it took to convince you otherwise was a nice glass of sherry and a friendly chat."

"It's not my fault." She looked perplexed for a few moments as she tried to account for her inconsistency. "I trusted my auntie Addie more than I can say. That was always the case, and it didn't change as I became an adult. Adele was smarter than anyone else I knew…" As though afraid I wouldn't take this personally, she made it clear that it was personal. "Including you, Marius. She had seen and done so much. She understood human behaviour and had learnt the lessons that life taught her."

"How does that explain why you no longer believe that Presler is the likely killer?"

"Because… well… maybe I've taken it to an extreme. Maybe, as wise as she was, she was wrong about the Preslers. I keep going over the evidence we've accumulated, and there's really nothing that connects them to Adele's or Ivy's death."

I wondered if she would still feel the same way in thirty seconds' time. "There's something I haven't told you. When I went off to look for the lavatory, that was just a clever ruse."

"How clever." She didn't sound sarcastic, but I knew that she was.

"Thank you. I thought so. Anyway, I used that time to have a good poke about, and do you know what I found?"

"More ugly paintings?"

"Oh, definitely. There were numerous examples, and several practically identical ones, but that isn't what I have to report."

"So?" she prompted me when I took too long.

I was excited by what I was about to reveal. "So John Presler's name isn't John Presler."

She sat bolt upright. "No!"

"I found some of his papers from the war, and they were made out in the name of Preston Jones."

From her expression, I could tell that she immediately doubted my conclusion. "Couldn't they belong to a friend of his? Someone who died fighting alongside him, perhaps?"

"That's impossible. His demobilisation certificate, issued one year after the end of the war, was right there in the drawer of his desk. Dead men don't get the chance to leave the army. Besides, I could imagine him keeping the dog tags of a fallen friend, but not dry-as-dust papers that don't even have photographs attached. And don't forget the name."

"What about it?"

"Preston Jones is not a million miles away from John Presler. You must admit that's more than a coincidence."

She looked about the kitchen before answering. "Then maybe it's for his job. Actors and the like often adopt aliases. Some of them have multiple different ones."

The food was now warm enough, and I scooped it onto two plates once more. "Then why wouldn't he just tell us if that were the case? If he were the amazing, acrobatic Preston Jones, or Preston the fire-eating ventriloquist, why would he keep it to himself? It might have led to more interesting conversations this evening than all that talk about what we did for our holidays and which beach in Hastings is the best."

Bella fell to contemplation. She chewed her food and presumably considered this new mystery, which we would add to the fifteen or so others we had failed to answer. For my part, I kept thinking that it was the questions themselves that we were getting wrong; how could we go about solving a pair of murders if we didn't know what we should be asking?

"Perhaps dear Inspector Lovebrook is right after all," she said after a few minutes of comparative silence – Percy's snoring made sure that it was never too quiet. "Perhaps the person here with the criminal record will be the killer. We know nothing about the caretaker, and if I weren't such an emotional..."

Her words caught in her throat, and her eyes dropped to the tabletop. I wanted to comfort her, but there was nothing more to say. We were both exhausted after a day that had lasted a week. So when we'd finished eating, I put her dirty plate on top of mine and carried them to the sink.

"I think it's time you went to bed."

"I should help." Her voice was still fragile. Perhaps it was the thought of going to sleep in Adele's house without her friend. "You've done everything."

"It's fine," I replied, already filling a bowl with water. "You should go up already, though if you could check there are sheets for me to use, I'd appreciate it."

She didn't say anything more. She just nodded and looked back with unmistakable sadness in her eyes. How I wanted to hold her then. My brain and body screamed to run across to her; if I were a compass, she was due north. But I wouldn't give in. I was used to her withdrawing whenever she remembered the sorrow she'd endured. It had been happening for months, and perhaps the strangest thing was how quickly we'd both got used to it.

"Goodnight, Bella."

She mouthed her reply, and I waited for her to leave before clearing the table and putting the wine in the larder. I can honestly say I have never included a scene in any of my books in which my detective takes time away from a case to wash the dishes, but that is what I did that night. I stood at the sink in front of the kitchen window, and the lights were just dim enough for me to see the practically Siberian scene outside.

I doubt I thought about the beauty of the falling flakes for long. I half hoped that the distraction of washing plates and cutlery would turn off the part of my brain which deals with the present and leave me free to unlock some significant element of the case. The problem with having such an intelligent assistant – if "assistant" is the right word for Bella – is that she never has wildly unrealistic theories which then kindle my own ideas and help us on to otherwise unreachable conclusions. I hope she can make the same complaint about me.

There was another reason I wasn't paying attention to the weather outside or the water in the sink. I knew that, in a few minutes' time, with the dishes cleaned and dried, I would have to go up to a cold bedroom. I would put on my ill-fitting pyjamas that, for some inexplicable reason, my mother had selected from the very bottom of the drawer in my bedroom, and I would climb into bed and take an hour to fall asleep.

By the time I got upstairs, Bella was dead to the world in one of the spare bedrooms. Her door was open just a crack and I could hear her soft breathing. I turned off the electric light on the landing and stood by her room, listening for a moment and wondering for the millionth time what would have happened if the war had never ripped us apart. I stood there, acting like the romantic lead in a book that no one will ever bother writing, before remembering that lingering outside a sleeping woman's bedroom was more like the behaviour of a creeping killer than a dashing hero.

I got ready to go to sleep and found a bed in the room next door to Bella's. We were separated by three inches of brick and a couple of headboards. I lay on my back wishing for sleep, but it refused to come. It was the first time I'd slept so close to her since before the war, when we'd left our houses after midnight without telling our parents. We spent the night in her treehouse staring into one another's eyes. Sleep had been slow to come then, too. Bella drifted off first, but for a few sweet minutes, I'd watched her in the semi-darkness until I followed her into that mist-bound and mysterious realm.

Percy must have realised that he was alone downstairs, as he eventually wandered into my room, clambered onto an ottoman and from there onto the bed, where he quickly fell asleep on my feet.

# TWENTY-FOUR

Exhaustion overtook me at some point, but I woke early the next morning. I could tell that Bella was still asleep when I left my bedroom. There was light peeking through the closed curtains around the house, and I wondered how much of that was the snow magnifying the dawn. Percy followed me back to his spot in the sitting room, where he instantly curled up before the long-starved fire. Why are dogs so good at sleeping when I'm not?

I had nothing else to do, and I couldn't imagine that any of our suspects would be keen for me to knock on their doors at such an hour. So I took the box of decorations that we had bought for the tree and hung some leftover garlands from room to room in diagonal lines. There were still any number of stars, baubles and chains of tinsel left even then, so I got dressed, put on my shoes and coat and ducked outside to decorate the pair of rounded holly trees in front of the cottage.

They looked rather like sugared lollipops with their white coating, and I brightened them further with splashes of red and gold. The snow had stopped falling, but the sun, as it peeked over the trees that bordered the village, sent a pleasant shiver through me. I was just finishing my task when I heard a noise on the far side of the green and hid behind the tree. This obviously sounds like the action of a hardened detective, but I think it was more my fear that people would think me childish for getting up with the sun to decorate bushes in the freezing cold.

From my hiding place, I could see the Preslers' door open and John step out. Silva was just behind him, and he gave her an enormous kiss on the lips and dipped her backwards like a tango dancer. I couldn't hear what they said, but her loud giggles carried across to me. She looked at him with such love as he skipped along the snowy patch where the path normally was that I felt a twinge of jealousy.

Silva watched her husband all the way to the gatehouse and then slipped back inside. The moment she was gone, another instinct fired, and I went racing after him. Though thicker than many December snowfalls I'd known, the dramatic weather from the night before hadn't left the high drifts I had expected.

There was still no ice underfoot and I could make good ground on him. It was also lucky that I had my essential effects in my coat pocket, as I was quite uncertain where this unplanned pursuit might take me. The sky was blue for the first time in days and, if I'd had more time, I might have enjoyed the spectacle of the glittering white world around me.

By the time I got through the gatehouse, making sure that he wouldn't spy me as I emerged from the arch, Presler was at his Morgan Runabout. He had already cleared his windscreen of snow and was cranking the engine. It was so cold that it took him a few attempts to get the vehicle started, but then he jumped inside and was away.

I immediately ran to my Invicta, feeling doubly thankful that she was blessed with a reliable ignition. The snow was so fresh and powdery that I could push it straight off the car and out from the wheels, and I gave chase just twenty seconds after my quarry had left. It was slow going along Swain's Lane but, thirty yards in front of me, the Morgan Runabout was struggling even more. Once we got to Highgate Lane, it was a different story. Countless cars and carriages had already navigated the busy road, and I spotted a team of hardworking individuals with salt carts.

Presler took the road all the way to Kentish Town. Even in the inclement conditions, the area was lively. It was nearly Christmas, and London wasn't going to rest just because there was a bit of snow about. Families were already bustling towards the tube station to head to the city for festive entertainment. A group of smartly dressed men in half-melon bowler hats were strolling along together, and Presler was going to... a florist?

He stopped the Morgan beside a clear bit of pavement in front of the Oxford Vaults pub. Right next door was a small shop with a display of flowers, wreaths and mistletoe in the window. Presler was hurrying towards it before I could pick a spot to park my car on the other side of the road. He looked particularly chipper and was dressed in a far flashier suit than the ones he'd worn the day before. He looked as if he were stepping out to the opera, and his hair was as slick as could be.

He knocked on the door of the closed shop, then a man looked out and waved him inside. I wondered what kind of criminality this surreptitious behaviour might have indicated before remembering what day it was: Sunday trading is prohibited by the Factory and Workshop Act, even in the days before Christmas.

A bus hooted at me, so I eventually picked a space to park. I sat watching the shop over my shoulder. Two minutes after we arrived, Presler reappeared with five bouquets of mistletoe, winter roses and dried gypsophila in his arms. They were huge great things wrapped in red paper cones, and he placed them carefully inside the car before cranking the engine and getting back into the driver's seat.

He waited for a break in the traffic, then turned back on himself. I was worried he might see me when the nose of his car came swinging in my direction, but he gave no sign of recognition and sped back up the hill. It was just at that moment that a knacker's cart came crawling past to block me, and I had to wait. By the time the road was clear, Presler had disappeared. Furious at myself for not being ready to give chase, I followed the road for a while, but there was no sign of him ahead of me.

I drove slowly, peering along each road I passed until I spotted a flash of royal blue on Lady Somerset Road. It was just enough to tell me that I'd driven too far, and so I turned back at the next junction and got there just in time to see Presler approaching a modest stock-brick house with one of the bouquets in his arms. I drove past but didn't see who opened the door and, when I stopped the car, they'd both gone inside.

I sat there in the cold for twenty minutes. Even with the roof up on the Invicta, it's no furnace, and I rather wished I'd taken Percy with me to warm the air. By the time Presler reappeared, I was weighing up the choices I'd made in my life. I was a writer who hated the last book I'd written. I was in love with a woman who couldn't return my feelings, and instead of spending time with my loved ones that Christmas, I was driving about London, spying on a man for no other reason than the fact he got up early... and lived very close to the site of two recent murders... and had a false name... and was a shifty fellow at the best of times. Actually, I considered this last decision to be fairly sound, especially when he emerged from the mid-terrace house with his arm wrapped around an old lady and the flowers now gone.

"It's probably his mother," I said aloud for no reason, before seeing what they were up to. "No, that's not his mother."

The two stood together on the doorstep, wrapped in a tight embrace. Now, I'm not saying that sons shouldn't show affection to their parents. Indeed, if anyone deserves a hug, it's dear old Mum and Dad, but let me tell you that I have never hugged my mother with the passion that John Presler displayed.

They turned, and I could see the lady's face. Around seventy years old and not so very different in appearance from the man's wife, she seemed most content with her morning visit. Her mascaraed eyelashes batted as she pulled away from him, but then she leaned in again for one last cuddle.

Backing away down the steps, Presler waved goodbye. He

thankfully didn't turn the car around this time, but drove past me, off to the next stop on his despicable itinerary. By the time he left the subsequent building at number two Dartford Park Road, I was convinced he was a bigamist.

"Adele Leach was right!" I declared. In my defence, I wasn't used to investigating cases on my own; there was normally a dog with me, at the very least. "That dear lady was right all along. Presler's been carrying on with other women behind Silva's back. What did she say? He went weaselling about the place? Well that's definitely true."

The second woman he visited was evidently richer than the first. She looked more like the Baroness, in a long black Victorian dress with a jewelled lace bodice and elaborate clips of marcasite and pearl in her hair. If anything, she held on to John Presler more passionately than the previous lady had and looked as if she might cry when the time came for them to part.

The polychrome house was impressive even by the standards of that refined area of the city. It had a loggia at the front with four columns and elegant white pointing all around the façade. It was at this point that I gave him the benefit of the doubt and accepted that he might be an embezzler or a confidence trickster. And if that was the case, had Adele realised it? I was struggling to think of any other reason he would keep a string of wealthy women about the place.

"I will miss you every moment we're apart, my dear Nancy," I could hear him shout to her as he got into his car. "I can only wish you a very Merry Christmas, and you need not doubt that I will see you before the New Year."

He was actually far more charming than I had imagined. With his broad shoulders and that sparkle in his eyes, it was easy to understand why his victims had overlooked his other failings. Victim number two stood on the step with her hands to her breast like a young maid in love for the first time. I was immediately put in mind of the way that Silva had looked at her husband as he skipped out of Holly Village an hour earlier. It was almost enough to make me give up my pursuit. I was sure that there would be more lonely women who had put their faith in that rotter John Presler, just like the two I'd already seen.

Sure enough, there were three more stops that morning and, for each, he delivered his flowers and nearly got eaten in return. The final visit was to Caen Wood Towers, which was as extravagant as it sounds. It was located on a quiet lane beside Hampstead Heath, and I could only peer in through the gates as Presler went about his business. I instantly began to wonder about the people who lived within the vast stately home. It was hard to imagine how a lickspittling character like John Presler could have gained access to the owner, but there he was, tiptoeing through the snow up to another grande dame's door.

I found it maddening to think of the Christmas presents they must have lavished upon him – the orders to their bank managers to deposit sizeable sums in his account. I can't stand injustice of any kind, but the thought of these trusting ladies falling for his tricks made my blood boil, my skin crawl and my scalp itch all at the same time – though that last condition was due to a ridiculously cheap homburg that I'd recently bought on the Old Kent Road. I knew it was a poor investment when I saw it.

As with the previous stops on this seedy journey, he was inside the house for almost half an hour, and his hostess looked terribly fond of him as she saw him outside. I could only hope that, now the fifth bouquet had been delivered, Presler's errands were complete. When I saw him on his way back down the path, I ran to the Invicta, which I had parked a little way off the road.

As I sat there waiting for him to pass, I heard his car sputter into life and growl along the road. I was about to start my own engine when the Morgan came to a stop just behind me.

"So you're 'ere too, are you?" he shouted through his window. "Get out of the car and show your face. I know you've been following me."

# TWENTY-FIVE

For a moment, I considered how I might wriggle out of this tight spot but knew it was impossible. I was parked in front of a large pile of snow that had been cleared from the lane, no doubt by some hardworking servant from the big house. There was no way forward, no way back, and if I'd tried to make a run for it, he would have recognised me.

Reluctantly, I opened my door and stepped outside. It was either that or wait for him to come to me. "I'm sorry, John. I can assure you it's nothing personal."

"Lord Montague?" He left his mouth open after muttering my name in disbelief and I realised that, for him, this was the big revelation at the end of the novel when we find out that the person we really thought was on our side is actually the villain.

"I mean it. I'm not here to cause you any trouble." I'd started in a far too apologetic manner and had to change my tone. "However, I've rumbled your little game, and you can't play the innocent."

"My little game?" He smirked at me then. I hadn't expected such a reaction, but it spoke to the nature of the man. "I'll 'ave you know that this is no game, your lordship. I'm a professional, not that it's any business of yours anyway."

"A professional? What would your wife think of that?"

"My wife?" Yes, we both kept repeating expressions in questioning tones. It was his turn this time. "I'll 'ave you know that Silva is very supportive of my occupation. I'm glad to say that she's not a snob like some people I could mention."

You'll be happy to know that I did not respond with the phrase, *Some people you could mention?* Instead, I slowed things down and tried to take stock of the situation. "Come along now, Presler. We know that Adele had worked out what you were up to." I walked a little closer to him and realised that the snow was deeper there than I'd predicted. "Whether you're playing a game or not, it's over – your luck has run out."

The rage plain on his face, he practically kicked his door open and came out to deliver a rebuke.

"Now listen 'ere, you toff. I don't give a fig's end what you think of me, but don't you start talking about my dear, kind wife, or poor Adele for that matter."

There was a brief standoff during which I said nothing, and he presumably realised it wasn't a good idea to pick a fight with me. Instead, he fumbled in his pocket for a tin of tobacco and a pipe. He would probably have looked more intimidating if he were a cigarette smoker. The flare of a match, a drag on the fiery tube – that would have left more of an impression on me than the emptying, filling, prodding, tapping and careful lighting that followed.

"I don't know what you think was 'appenin' with Adele," he continued, "but I've already told you: she was our friend. If you've got it into your 'ead that I 'urt 'er in some way, then you couldn't be further from the truth." He pointed at me with his free hand, and I could almost feel the poke in the guts he wished to give me. "You've got more imagination than sense, my friend."

"Evidently, I'm not your friend, Presler. When we arrived at Holly Village yesterday, we found notes in Adele's spare room detailing the movements of a man on the estate who she believed was deceiving his wife. The last time I saw her alive, she told me that this suspicious sort went walking about at night even when there was snow on the ground. And here you are this morning, sneaking out with the dawn to pay calls on your harem."

"Harem?" he muttered, and I thought, *Oh no, we're back to that again!* "If I knew what that word meant, I might take the time to be offended."

He took some pride in his ignorance, and I would have put my accusations to him again, but I could see there was little sense in continuing the discussion. "Just move your car out of the way and let me go home. You'll hear everything I have to say on the matter when the police come banging on your door."

"Now, now, matey." Clearly frustrated, he pulled his lips into his mouth as though trying to work out the best plan of action. "There's no need to involve the police. What I do is for the benefit of my clients. Just because I'm not an alderman or a judge, that doesn't mean I'm 'urting anyone."

I snorted a little as this was the most bare-faced self-exculpation I'd ever heard. "That's some impressive reasoning. I've never come across a person who could explain away his criminality like that."

He leaned back against his car and puffed on his pipe. In his poorly chosen dinner jacket he looked a cross between the flamboyant owner of a West End bordello and a wizened lighthouse keeper.

"I'm sorry if that's 'ow you feel, but let me say my piece. I'm not a bad fellow. That's why I like to visit my ladies before Christmas. The poor dears are all alone, and I bring them flowers every year to tell them that someone is thinking of them. It's the least I can do."

"Don't I know it!" I couldn't stifle a cynical laugh this time. The man was deluded.

That familiar note of anger entered his voice. "All right, Mr Pious, what is it about my spending time with these ladies that so offends you? I offer all the kindness and attention that they require from another human being."

I really couldn't reply at first. It took me five seconds to make a sound. "We were in your home last night. We sat making conversation with your sweet-hearted, generous wife, and you're asking me why I would take exception to your behaviour?"

Something must have clicked for him at this moment as he held both hands out and the pipe went flying through the air. There was a slight hiss as its contents fell into the snow. "You've got it all wrong, your lordship. I'm no sneak. Silva knows what I do."

"How could she—" I began, but he hadn't finished.

"That was 'ow we met in the first place." He was smiling as he bent to retrieve the pipe. "She was one of my clients. Course, I was much younger then. Not so sophisticated as I am now, but she took a chance on me, and we've never looked back."

It was harder to reply to each thing he said, because each thing he said was more difficult to understand. "Presler, what exactly do you do for these women?"

He blushed then. It was even more noticeable because of the snowy trees just behind him and the whiteness all around. "Well, I don't like to put a name on it. There are names, of course, but none of them suit my thinking on the matter."

He could see that I was becoming impatient and hurried to explain himself. "Let me put it like this... if a lady of some means is looking for someone to listen to her woes and give 'er a shoulder to lean on – an 'and to 'old..." He was phrasing all this ever so carefully, his eyes scanning the ground in search of the phrases that could explain his trade. "If a lady requires an escort to the theatre or out for dinner, or any kind of companionship really, I am 'appy to say that I provide such a service."

"My word." I'm sure I sounded quite flustered. "You're a renter, aren't you?"

He folded his arms and poked the empty pipe into his breast pocket. "It's not what you're thinking. And I'll 'ave you know that I prefer the term gigolo!"

## TWENTY-SIX

"In the past, they'd have called me a petticoat pensioner, which sounds a lot more respectful, if you ask me."

I had to sit down on the back of the Invicta, as I couldn't quite fathom what he was saying. "But Silva is rich, isn't she? What was that you said about inheriting the Eel King's fortune?"

"That was all true, but I don't want to rely on a woman for my upkeep."

"That is literally what you do for a living!" A hint of my disbelief may have emerged just then.

"You're twisting my words now. You know what I mean, I couldn't bear the thought of being a leech on my dear Silva, and so I continued in my profession."

"Surely it would be better to share in your spouse's wealth than shop yourself around the city to be pawed and..." I didn't finish this sentence as I didn't feel I needed to provide any more details.

"You've got the wrong end of the stick, chum. My activities with these women are strictly platonic. There's certainly nothing that goes on under the jumper, if you will."

Even if this were true, it seemed to contradict his previous assertions. "Then why were you afraid when I mentioned the police?"

He curled one lip. "'Ave you ever met the bobbies in this city? They're not the most understanding chaps. And as for the local lot, that Sergeant Bulmer 'as been bothering me ever since I moved to the area. If 'e knew what I do, 'e'd instantly think the worst, just as you did. It's difficult for an honest man to make a living these days."

I could respond with nothing more than a blank look. I was truly bowled over by what he was saying. It wasn't simply the idea of this rough individual making a living from chastely cuddling old ladies around Hampstead Heath. I was considering what, if true, this would mean for the case.

"Silva knows about all of this?" I asked to be certain. "You swear that she accepts what you do for your clients?"

"You can ask 'er yourself. I told you; she was my first ever customer." Even as I sought the final word on the matter, he spoke as if he might hit me at any moment. "I was only young, and she were lonely after 'er first 'usband died. I 'elped get 'er back on 'er feet, but in that one and only instance, things developed beyond the professional."

"And what about Adele?"

He looked outraged again. "She was never one of my clients."

"No, man. I'm asking whether she knew about what your work entailed."

"Oh, I see... Then, no, she didn't. As I've already tried to explain; mine isn't the kind of job that most people would consider respectable. I thought you understood all this last night." A strange thing happened then. A single tear appeared in his eye. "I love my Silva so much it almost kills me. She's like no other woman on earth. She's the pearl in an ugly grey oyster."

He stepped forward to slump onto me so that his head rested on my shoulder. How was I supposed to suspect the man of murder when he was sobbing like that?

"Now, now. There's no need to cry. I can see that you... love her."

I thought this half-hearted response would do little good, but he gripped hold of my arm and pulled back again. "Thank you, your lordship. Thank you so much. I will never forget your kind words."

I could see that he was trying to control his emotions, and so I simply responded, "You're very welcome, John. I'm sorry if I've upset you." His lip started shaking once more, and I was about to help him to his car when I remembered something important. "There is one thing I still have to ask you, though. Your name isn't Presler, is it?"

"No, but..." He looked shocked again, then presumably worked out what I'd discovered in his study and admitted the truth. "I changed it to get a 'ouse at Holly Village. If Miss Haskell had found out what I do for a living, you can imagine what would 'ave happened."

"I do understand." My tone was a touch more accepting than before. "And as it happens, I'm not a lord. Ivy Frazel assumed that, just because I was with Lady Bella, I had to be her husband and I was therefore an aristocrat. My dear friend was happy to maintain the façade in the hope we might discover the truth about Adele."

He was already on his way back to the car but stopped halfway. "Are you saying you're not even married?"

"That's right. You see, I'm actually a private detective and Bella is—"

"My goodness." In a moment, his whole attitude changed. "You come into our 'ouse under false pretences and then accuse me of being a fraud and a killer. You really are a nasty piece of work. I take back every nice thing I said about you. We don't want your sort moving into our lovely village."

With this said, he spat on the ground and climbed back into the Morgan. He'd forgotten that the engine was turned off and had to get back out again to crank it. He watched me the whole time, perhaps afraid I would jump into the car as soon as he'd got it started and make off with it.

"Good riddance, *Mr* Montague... if that is your real name!"

He slammed the driver's door, and I just managed to send an

"Obviously it isn't," after him before he could get too far away. "Really, Percy," I lamented, "some people's behaviour is truly impossible to predict." I looked back at my car and remembered that my dog wasn't there. I doubt he'd have had much to say on the matter either way.

I went back to the Invicta and climbed inside. I turned the ignition, put the car into reverse and pressed the accelerator, but the tyres just spun. I thought I could roll forward half a yard and try again, but that only got me stuck faster, and I knew I would have to get out and push.

When I finally got back to Holly Village, my trousers were soaked, and my forehead was bleeding after I'd slipped and smashed it against the car radiator. All I wanted was to have a steaming hot bath. I should have known that this was never going to happen.

I spent the mile-long yet fifteen-minute journey thinking over the numerous mistakes we'd made on the case so far. I came to realise that we'd set out to investigate Adele's murder as if it had happened in a stately home, as if the suspects were all heads of state or minor royals, and the killer was a criminal mastermind who had narrowly evaded us because of his superior intellect. I had the creeping sensation, as I shook my soaking feet in the footwell whenever I had to stop at a crossroads, that a pair of murders in a curious little village was a very different proposition, and we had failed to make the necessary adjustments.

Even before I could park the car in front of the gatehouse, I caught sight of my dog walking along the road. He was not alone, you'll be happy to know, but it did come as something of a surprise. Bella was with him, and she was acting like a detective. I know what this looks like as I'd done the exact same thing that morning when spying on the Preslers. There is an almost irrepressible instinct that I'm sure most people possess which forces us to impersonate the clever fellows we've seen chasing after rogues on the silver screen. The fact was that, if whomever Bella was following had turned around, her proximity to the bushes would have done little to hide her, but she hugged them, none-theless.

"Would you care for a lift, madam?" I asked as I brought the car to a halt beside her without stopping the engine.

She was concentrating and waved me away at first, then realised what I was suggesting and hurried over.

"It's the caretaker," she whispered, her tone just as a furtive as her previous stance had been. "I think he's up to no good."

She climbed into the car and that four-stone beast scrambled in on top of her. I sometimes forget just what a whopper Percy is until I see him with another person or, even more so, another dog.

Bella leaned forward in her seat to clear the misty glass with her glove. "Make sure you keep your distance."

"Yes, ma'am." Once the door had closed behind my faithful hound, I moved slowly away from the village. The snow was far slushier than it had been a few hours earlier. After a period of silence, I posed a question. "Do you have any reason to believe that Mr Dumfries is up to no good?"

I'm not sure she had actually looked at me yet. Her gaze was off through the window, directed at the huddled figure in the distance as he wandered up the road.

"Lovebrook telephoned the house this morning to tell me that the caretaker's wife claims she was with him yesterday at the time at which Ivy Frazel was murdered. He'd apparently gone home for lunch and fallen asleep. None of the other villagers could prove where they were at the time, though the Baroness said she was walking on the heath."

I tried to recall when I'd seen Dumfries the day before but couldn't immediately disprove his alibi. "So you're saying that, now you've been told he can't be the killer, you're more willing to accept that he's to blame?"

She rolled her eyes but still didn't look at me. "Not at all, but if he insists on skulking about the place, what does he expect me to do?"

I would have liked to point out the limitation of this approach, but as I'd adopted much the same reasoning that very morning, I could hardly complain.

"Has he done anything to suggest he isn't simply off to the butchers to purchase the Christmas goose?"

"Well, for one thing, he's walking in the opposite direction to the city and away from the nearest shops, but more than that, when he left the gatehouse, he looked around as though he were afraid someone might follow him."

I would once again have liked to criticise the simplicity of her thinking, but she had relied on more evidence than I'd had when haring after John Presler.

All I could think to say in reply was, "Very well."

"Is that it?" She finally turned her dubious gaze upon me. "Don't you wish to tell me that I've got it all wrong and the real killer is off somewhere plotting his next crime? Don't you have some great revelation to deliver after your excursion this morning?"

I cleared my throat. "No. No, I don't. If you'd like me to look for a silver lining, I could say that I've done my best to rule out a major suspect, but to put it another way, a theory to which I had become attached can now be dismissed."

"Then let's hope this current escapade reaps better results." Her eyebrows flicked higher before she turned back to her vigil.

"I should probably tell you what I discovered, seeing as it might well undermine our whole—"

"Wait one moment, Marius," she interrupted, pointing at Dumfries. "He's crossed the road. I think he's going into the cemetery."

I slowed the car even more, and was glad there was still snow about, as it gave me an excuse for creeping along the road.

"He's gone through the gate," I said, though Bella could see this for herself. "Shall I stop here?"

There were a few spaces in front of the large, unmistakably Victorian gatehouse that, like a lot of the architecture we'd seen over the last day, looked as though it had been modelled on a church.

"Drive past and park just after. Then we'll see which way he's gone without drawing attention to ourselves."

It was comical just how similarly we'd come to think. This was another of my brilliant tactics from that morning. I accelerated a little to be sure we didn't lose sight of him and brought the car to a stop short of another pile of snow into which I had no intention of driving.

Bella jumped out without saying anything, then Percy issued a bark and fell from the vehicle. By the time I'd shut my door, they'd both disappeared through the wide-open gates, and I followed their footprints through the snow. There was not nearly as much footfall through the cemetery as there had been around town that morning. I saw no one laying flowers or tending to graves, which made the place even creepier than normal.

When I'd first moved to London, and I still considered myself a serious writer, I would spend my weekends exploring places like this in search of inspiration. Highgate Cemetery does not just look old; it looks as if it came crashing to earth from a different world. The whole place is overgrown, much like Sleeping Beauty's castle. The trees, ivy and unusual foliage push through the tombs, graves and grand mausoleums as if to say, *We were here first!*

A few yards in front of me, Bella kept her eyes on Dumfries, Percy kept his eyes on Bella, and I was distracted by the sights all around us. With the snow coating every flat and nearly flat surface, the whole place was transformed, which made it look even more alien than usual. Gravestones, crosses and pyramid-topped obelisks peeked out from the white covering as though they had been planted there. The Victorians knew how to deal with death – architecturally at least – and the place is a work of art.

Having looped around the bottom of the west cemetery, we passed the grave of Christina Rossetti. I looked out for the Dickens family plot, where old Charlie's wife and daughter are buried, but it must have been hidden by the snow. Soon after, the caretaker seemed to go back on himself and cross to the far side of the cemetery through which we'd entered. This did give us the opportunity to spy the scientist Michael Faraday's final resting place, but it also made me wonder what Dumfries was up to.

"Perhaps he realises he's being followed," I told Bella in as low a voice as possible as I caught up with her.

"I would think just that if he'd turned around even once. He might have heard our footsteps, but he can't have seen us, and he looks in no hurry to run away."

Still keeping our distance, we curved back to the centre of the cemetery and came to the Egyptian Avenue with its two great stone needles, which might have been stolen from Cleopatra herself. Egyptianate columns topped with stone lotus leaves framed the entrance to the long walkway. This area contained any number of rich families' tombs, but I couldn't imagine that was why the caretaker of Holly Village had trekked there on a frozen morning two days before Christmas.

Dumfries stopped in the middle of the ornate corridor as two crows flew overhead, cawing as though we were trespassing in their home, which I suppose we were. I was certain that he would turn around and see us, but he looked at the cast-iron doors to the catacombs on either side of him and pressed on towards the Circle of Lebanon. I can't say I felt entirely comfortable chasing a man through a graveyard in the snow, but if Bella shared my feelings on the matter, she kept them to herself.

I looked at the twenty or so doors and took in the names of the families who had owned them. I had to wonder how many were still visited, or whether they remained locked all year round. When we emerged back into the light, Dumfries followed the now curving path to a set of steps in the shadow of the towering Lebanon cedar that gave the circular plot its name. He walked with great purpose, but it was hard to imagine why anyone would take such a circuitous route if he hadn't simply come to appreciate the history or design of the place.

Bella really sprinted up the steps after him, and Percy made a good attempt at lolloping, but they had to stop at the top as, I could only conclude, Bella was afraid of being seen.

"What were ye thinking making me meet ye here?" the Scotsman complained before I was high enough to see him or the person he addressed. "I've spent ages walking around this here place no' finding ye."

"Where's your sense of adventure, man?" a familiar voice responded.

"I left it at hame! Which is where we should ha' met rather than coming out to this blessed place of a morning."

"Calm down, Dumfries."

I crouched on the steps where Bella was hiding but could just see Herbert Wandle in his long black overcoat. Standing before a large, pillared tomb, he looked like a sombre guardsman.

Dumfries had not obeyed his companion's command. "I'll be calm when I'm home wi' ma wife wi' ma pipe and slippers. I dinna like all this nonsense."

Herbert laughed, but it wasn't his usual fluted tone. It was deeper and more confident. It almost sounded as though he'd adopted a new character and had adapted his manner and mannerisms to match it.

"You know that I couldn't have anyone in the village seeing us together. I don't want them to be suspicious."

"As I say, that's a load of old nonsense, but here ye go." Dumfries had his back to us, and I couldn't see what he handed over, but I heard the unmistakable sound of jangling keys.

"And is everything arranged as I asked?"

"Of course it is. And I expect ye to make all this worth ma while. I'm not yer servant, though most in the village seem to mak' the same mistake. Miss Haskell is forever sending me off tae places I dinna wish tae go."

Herbie stepped around him and leaned closer. It was hard to say whether the gesture was one of affection or intimidation. "Don't I always pay you well for the little services you provide? Isn't that why you came out here to see me?"

Dumfries gave no reply, but he crossed his arms against the

cold and stamped his feet. This served to remind me just how cold (and still wet) my own footsicles were.

"And besides," Herbert continued, glancing about in a contented manner, "I like coming here. As an antiquarian, I appreciate this beautiful folly far more than any building some forward-thinking architect might tack together today."

"Well, I prefer sitting in front o' the fire in ma living room!"

The Scotsman stamped his right foot one last time and huffed out a steamy breath as he turned to head back in our direction. Funnily enough, Percy was the first to react. He scampered away down the steps, and I was worried that he would stumble, but he just about maintained his balance. The more pressing danger was that the men we'd just followed would find us there, but we were lucky on that score.

"Remember, Dumfries," Herbert's booming voice travelled over us. "You mustn't tell anyone!"

We were hiding out of sight by this point and couldn't see how the caretaker reacted, but he didn't sound particularly impressed by the reminder. "I know that, ya glaikit ouf. Ye dinna have to tell me twice."

"Not a soul, do you hear me?" Herbert's voice carried down to us, but Dumfries didn't react. He turned away at the bottom of the steps and Bella and I (though probably not so much Percy) could breathe again.

# TWENTY-SEVEN

For the first time since we'd arrived in the area, I felt that we were finally making progress.

"If you stay with Herbert," Bella suggested once we were sure that the caretaker was out of earshot, "I'll follow Dumfries in the car."

My dog subtly moved a little closer to her at this moment so as not to be forgotten.

"You take Percy. That way, you can say you're out for a walk if you're spotted." Bella didn't wait for my agreement but picked my key from my pocket and rushed off on her own. This was fine by me as, setting aside my wet shoes, socks and trousers, and my bloodied forehead, I could think of nothing more pleasant than a walk around that magnificent site with my hound at my side.

It wasn't long before Herbie appeared at the bottom of the steps and (fortunately) turned away from me to walk around the circular path. I waited fifteen seconds before following him and rather liked the way he explored the graveyard. He followed a twisting route without clear direction and, whenever something caught his eye, he would stop to examine it. In this manner, he looked at several stone angels, their wings extended, and an elegant tomb topped with a life-size lion, slumbering with its eyes closed and paws together.

On we marched, picking up the pace a little, then slowing down once more. We followed the serpentine walkways and when we reached the gatehouse, next to which my car was no longer parked, he crossed the road to the eastern cemetery. This section was less ramshackle than the older one, and it felt less inhabited, with wider, park-like areas and graves dotted here and there. Herbert once more took us to all four corners of the space, stopping first to pay his respects at the grave of George Eliot and Mary Ann Cross (two names, but only one person), with its granite obelisk standing proud from the snow.

I had to stop a few times in case Herbert realised my dog and I had been matching his speed for the previous twenty minutes. However, he seemed quite content to take his time and was apparently unaware of our presence as he meandered back to the entrance before finally leaving the cemetery in the direction of Holly Village.

I couldn't imagine what Bella was thinking at that moment. She'd initially held on to the idea that Presler was the killer before coming to like him and then switching her hopes to the caretaker with the criminal past. Exposing Herbert Wandle as the culprit would surely be too much for her to bear, though she'd shown no great torment when we realised who it was that Dumfries was meeting.

If Herbie was the puppet-master behind the theft and murders, he was remarkably relaxed about it. It takes great arrogance to believe that you can get away with such a scheme, so perhaps he thought himself above suspicion. Although I had enjoyed his company and many in the village had told us what a generous, community-minded person he was, he would not be the first suspect we'd encountered who wore two faces.

Occasionally, as he walked down the road, he would feel in his pocket for the keys Dumfries had given him or take them out and swing them around his finger contentedly. My mind was already full of ideas for what they would open. Perhaps Adele's painting had been locked away somewhere, and he would lead us straight to it. I doubted we would be that lucky, but stranger things do happen.

We'd been walking so long that Percy was getting tired. He swayed more noticeably whenever he was exhausted. Bassets aren't really built for exertion. It's hard to know what they were built for, but it's certainly not an excess of athleticism. To give him his dues, he didn't complain. Once he realised we were almost home, he positively cantered to the village gatehouse, clouds of hot breath coming from his open mouth as we went.

We waited around the corner for Herbie to pass through the archway, and he stopped for a moment to look over his shoulder. It was a good thing we'd had the time to hide, or he would have been on to us, and we'd never have found out the purpose of his clandestine rendezvous.

As I walked through after him, I noticed Dumfries in the gatehouse, but there was no sign of Bella. I was about to follow Herbie along the path when he stopped once more and peered around the village. He was afraid of being discovered – that was as plain as day. It made me more cautious and so, instead of immediately pressing on, I waited to see where he would go.

"What have I missed?" Bella asked a moment later, running up behind me from the street.

"Where's my car?" I found myself demanding, as I hadn't seen it outside or heard her approaching.

"I parked it out of view in case Dumfries saw me."

I saw some flaws in her approach but answered her question as Percy settled down on the dry ground under the arch. "Herbie just arrived, but he's not heading towards his own house."

I pointed along the path that led past the Preslers' cottage. Even before he reached his destination, I had a sense of where he might be going.

"The empty house," Bella correctly predicted. "Perhaps he..."

She didn't finish her thought, but we both had enough theories in our heads to keep us going for months.

Herbie looked around one last time before putting the key in the lock of number five then swiftly passing through the door and into the house. There was something quite dramatic about that moment. We exchanged a glance as though asking one another, *Is this it? Have we reached the end?*

"Percy, stay here in the warmth," I said to announce our departure, and he made a noise which seemed to say, *I'll be right here if you need anything.* Or perhaps he was just a bit sleepy.

There really is no way to cross an open space surreptitiously, especially when it's covered in snow. The path was well worn with footprints by now, and the bright sun overhead had gone some way to melting it, so we moved fast enough, but it was frankly idiotic of us to round our shoulders and duck our heads in the hope that would make a difference. What were we afraid of? Snipers? It would have made more sense to walk calmly over there. For all anyone knew, we were making a call on Ruth Haskell at 6a.

We made it to number five with our lives, if not our dignity, and then we crept up to the front window to peer inside. There was no sign of Herbert, so we continued around the building to try the next room. Sure enough, there he was, rubbing his hands in front of an easel with a painting under a covering. There was a pile of boxes around him on the floor, but Bella didn't wait to see anything more. She shot back to the front door and threw it open.

I suppose she was lucky it didn't have a night latch, as she was able to walk right through. I arrived just in time to hear her rebuking him. "You monster, Herbert Wandle. To think that my aunt trusted you – I trusted you – and you killed her for the sake of—"

"My dear girl," he interrupted, his voice rising in indignation, "I don't know what you think I'm doing here, but I can solemnly swear that I had nothing to do with your aunt's death. You know full well that I was at home with my wife when the firework exploded."

Bella stood in the doorway of the small sitting room, which was empty of any personal effects. I could see the uncertainty running through her at that moment, but she wouldn't give up.

"What's under the sheet, Herbie? Adele's painting went missing, and here you are."

He sighed, begrudgingly yet compliantly, and stepped forward to pull the thin grey cloth from the easel. "There, my dear. Do you believe me now?"

Looking back at us from inside the gilded frame was the image of the Baroness. She was just as haughty as in real life, but there was something not quite natural about her. Painted in a very modern style, there was an elegant simplicity to the portrait. It was colourful, but not childish like the examples hanging in the Preslers' house. One interesting feature of it was that, standing just behind the Baroness, half out of the frame, we could see Herbie himself peeping over her shoulder. It was quite unlike anything I'd seen before, and I appreciated the playfulness of the composition, despite the more traditional focus of its main subject.

"It's a Christmas present for my darling Sheena," he said, replacing the cloth. "The Lord knows she's put up with a lot from me over the decades we've been married. I wanted her to have something truly special this year, and so I contacted an Italian artist I have long admired by the name of Gino Severini. He is well known for his earlier, more experimental style of painting but, as you can see, he has moved in a different direction recently. Don't you think it's rather wonderful?"

I actually did, but it wasn't my place to say anything.

"Why did you drag Dumfries out to the graveyard in the snow if this is all so very innocent?" The doubt was already present in Bella's strained voice. "You could have picked up the key from the gatehouse and no one would have been any the wiser."

"I dragged him out there, as you so deftly put it, because the man is a pain in the neck. He spends his whole life complaining and, just because I wanted him to pick up the painting from Victoria Station this morning, he made a big fuss about it. I'm very generous in my compensation whenever he is called upon to provide a service, but he likes nothing better than to whine and moan. I simply gave him another reason to indulge in his favourite pastime. And besides, I wanted a walk."

This was a truly petty thing to do, and I'm fairly certain that I would have done much the same in his position. For her part, Bella just stared at the painting. She had clearly put much stock in the possibility that Herbie's sneaky behaviour had presented. After all she'd suffered the day before, I couldn't blame her for clutching at straws.

"What about the other parcels?" I asked, mainly so that she wouldn't have to put more points to him that he could dismiss.

The smile that appeared on Herbie's lips then was both sad and sympathetic. He clearly looked at us as silly children who had taken a game too far. "My dears, these are presents for my fellow villagers. I bought a leather wallet for Freddy, even though, much like Dumfries, I've never known the man to crack a smile. There's perfume for Betty, a book for Carrie and a rather pretty antique necklace for Ruth Haskell. You know the sort of thing."

"Yes, of course," Bella's voice was hollow. "You've always been very generous, Herbie, and I'm sorry for wasting your time."

She turned to leave, and I thought that would be that.

From the anguished expression on Herbie's face, I could tell it pained him to let her go in such a state. "My dear Bella, please don't look so sad. I know how you must feel. We all loved Adele, and I will miss Ivy despite her eccentricities. It's hard to express just how much the village will struggle to get over their deaths, but that's why I ordered these extra gifts yesterday. I sent Dumfries to pick them up from my shop on his way back from the station this morning. I was certain that Sheena would notice if I came into the village laden with boxes and what have you."

"As I said, I'm terribly sorry, Herbie." She tried to leave once more, but he hadn't finished.

"No, wait. Please wait." He breathed out rather despondently and then went searching through the pile for a particular gift.

"This one is for you. I was planning to leave it on your doorstep on Tuesday morning like Father Christmas, but I think it might do you more good now."

She was a shadow of herself as she accepted the present, and it rested in her open palm. The box itself was fairly flat, as though it might contain a slim volume of poetry, but when she opened it, there was a silver picture frame inside, with a simple pencil sketch of Bella as a child and her auntie Adele.

"Now, my dear, that is just a temporary picture, as I didn't have a photograph of either of you. You can throw that away and find something worthy of displaying."

This was all he would say before Bella threw her arms around him and began to cry. "I'm sorry, Herbie."

He patted her on the back. "There really is no need to be."

"I'm so ashamed that... I love the drawing, and I will treasure it."

He pulled away to look her in the eye. "You can do whatever you like with it. I just wanted you to have something to remember our beloved Adele, and I thought this might help."

She rested her head on the old man's shoulder again.

"Come along, Bella," I eventually told her, placing a hand on her shoulder to help her from the ownerless house. "I think it's time we went home."

## TWENTY-EIGHT

I collected Percy, and Bella hugged her photo frame all the way to the cottage. She looked so sad that I thought she might want to go back to bed, but that wasn't her way. She sat down on the sofa in the sitting room and swapped the frame for Percy, who was only too happy to receive such attention.

I wanted to say something to make her feel better, but I couldn't imagine what. I thought we'd hit our low the night before, and we'd clearly both woken up that morning determined to get a grip on the elusive killer, at least metaphorically. All we could do now was sit lamenting our misfortune, but that wouldn't fix anything.

"There's something you should know," I decided to tell her. "When I followed John Presler this morning, I discovered a piece of information that could explain your aunt's view of things." This wasn't easy to say, so I sat down on the arm of the sofa and tried to get my thoughts straight in my head. "I believe that he was the person who Adele suspected, but I don't think he's the killer after all."

"How can that be?"

This mess of a case was too much for her. I hated to make it any worse, but there was no going back.

"She must have seen him coming and going from his house at strange hours, and perhaps she even spotted him with another woman, but that doesn't mean he murdered anyone."

She pursed her lips and, though she didn't say a word, I knew she was thinking, *Explain, yourself, Marius!*

"You see, that's what I saw. I followed him to five different addresses within a fifteen-minute drive from here, and in each of them there was a woman who was very fond of him." I hurried on so that she didn't fall into the same trap that I had. "As far as I can tell, he's not a bigamist though, or an embezzler."

"So what is he?" At least her curiosity had overcome her sorrow somewhat.

"He's a…" I sought a better term for it than *fully-clothed gentleman of the night* and settled for the one that Presler himself had used. "He's a gigolo: a paid platonic companion. From what I've seen, he keeps rich, elderly women company, takes them out to the theatre and buys them flowers. I don't think he had anything to do with Adele or Ivy's death. He's a rough sort with a definite chip on his shoulder, but we simply haven't found enough to connect him to the crime."

She still wouldn't give up entirely. "But that doesn't mean he isn't to blame."

"You're concentrating on the wrong thing, Bella. That's what we've both been doing since we got here. What if Adele's notes and what she said to me at the ball have nothing to do with her death? She evidently didn't tell anyone in the village of her suspicions or we'd have heard about it."

She could no longer look at me. She hugged Percy even tighter and tucked her legs beneath her.

"It's just as we saw with Herbie. We thought that catching him in an apparently compromising act meant that he was connected to the murders. It's clear now just how naïve we were. People do odd things, but that doesn't mean that they're capable of killing – just as there are thieves, burglars and swindlers around who would never physically hurt another person. We got it wrong, Bella."

"I don't know anymore." She shook her head then relented. "Maybe you're right. Maybe we've made a hash of this entire case. Let's be honest, it was always going to happen one day. We were fooling ourselves that we could beat the police at solving crimes and spotting criminals. Perhaps our adventuring should finally come to an end."

As silence fell between us, I knew that this was the worst possible outcome. Although it had required some persuading on her part for me to take our detective work seriously, I hated the idea of abandoning it. I hadn't considered until now that it was the main reason we still saw one another.

I tried my best to lighten the mood, nonetheless. "My goodness, I know you've been through a lot, but I didn't think it would get so bad that you'd ever give up on making me poke around in other people's business."

I'd drawn at least a suggestion of a smile from her, but it was a melancholy one at best.

"Bella, there is nothing you enjoy more than getting involved in matters that have little or nothing to do with us. Just because you're actually connected to the goings-on this time around, that doesn't mean we should give up."

She looked away again to hide whatever emotion her expression would have betrayed. I knew then that it would take something drastic. "Stay right where you are," I told her, before running upstairs and straight back down.

"Not the jumper, Marius," she said, her cheeks still glistening even as the unmistakable sound of joy escaped her throat. "I told you yesterday, it's really not fair to subject me to that."

I sat down on the sofa so that I was that little bit closer to her, and Percy started frantically licking her hand as her laughter continued.

"Look at me, Bella," I spoke very seriously and kept a straight face, but I was wearing the ugliest jumper known to man, so I knew what effect this would have. "Together, we can find the killer."

She tipped her head back and groaned in a mix of frustration, amusement and perhaps relief. "Fine! But only if you take off that jumper and promise to lose it on a lonely moor somewhere."

I was already shedding the indecipherable woollen monstrosity. "Lose it? But then it might turn up again. Don't you think it would be safer if I sent it to Australia or Mexico with no return address?"

She put her hand to her mouth as a final laugh escaped her lips. "I really do."

"Poor Auntie Clara will be heartbroken, but very well." I put my hand out for her to shake. I don't honestly know why I did this other than to feel her fine, silken fingers in my thick, rough ones. I held her gaze for a few seconds, and it might well have lasted longer if there hadn't been a knock at the door.

"I'll go," I told her, still in that same stern tone. "I've been a very good boy this year, and it may be Father Christmas."

It was not the big man in red, carollers, or wise men from the East. It was our friend Detective Inspector Lovebrook, but at least he came bearing gifts.

"I've got two things for you," he announced, clearly uncomfortable with the weight of the sackcloth bag he was carrying. "I've brought lunch and an important piece of information."

"You've outdone yourself," Bella told him. "I would have been happy just with the food."

"How did you know we hadn't eaten?" I felt it was my duty to ask as he came inside and emptied out our provisions on the dining table.

"I told you, we spoke on the telephone," Bella explained, but we were both distracted by the boxes of food which Lovebrook had brought. In our defence, there had not been much in the house for breakfast, nor had I found time to eat what little there was.

There were quails' eggs from Harrods, Continental pastries from Selfridges, pies and pastries from Fortnum and Mason and, at the bottom of it all, a hamper full of everything we could want for lunch, from West Country cheddar cheese to an apparently home-made Christmas pudding.

"I mean this with great respect, but... who are you?" I put to him. Although we'd known each other for very nearly a year, there was still a fog of mystery around the inspector that we were yet to clear.

"I know it's nothing too substantial," he, for some reason, apologised, "but I'm sure it will be tasty. My mother generally has good taste and, as she was in town, I asked her to select a few things for us."

This did not explain... One) how he could afford to patronise some of the most expensive shops in London. Two) why he would choose to share such delicious goods with us and, Three) who his mother was that she had developed a taste for fine food. On another occasion, I might have raised these points, but I was rather busy tucking into a chicken and mushroom pie with the most delicious gravy I can remember eating.

"I'm sure you've kept yourselves busy whilst I was exploring various possible avenues of investigation," he continued. "I take it Bella told you about Mr Dumfries's alibi, Marius?"

I could only nod and murmur, but he understood me well enough. We sat around the table, with a plate in front of each of us and piles of exquisite food in small portions. It was enough to distract a man from murder.

"You may be surprised to know that Bella and I have decided to close our detective agency," I said once my mouth was empty. "We've finally been beaten by a case."

Bella tried to kick me under the table and ended up poking Percy instead. He was busy and didn't notice. Lovebrook (or perhaps his mother) had thought of everything and included a raw pork chop in the package.

"We're not giving up on anything," she insisted, and I was glad to hear the determination back in her voice. "The only problem is that we've been through the obvious suspects, examined the evidence, and come to approximately zero useful conclusions."

Oddly enough, this made us both smile, and I realised something important, if not particularly helpful. "You know, it's actually quite liberating to admit defeat. We are not geniuses, nor did we ever claim to be. We have simply met our match."

"I don't believe you." Lovebrook looked a little bemused. "Perhaps all you need is a third person who has made limited progress over the last day. We can only hope that, together, our abilities will be magnified – as opposed to cancelling one another out."

I was opening a bottle of champagne by this point and poured three glasses to toast his fine proposal. "To making the most of limited resources."

"To competence, if not outright mediocrity!" Lovebrook joined in.

"To still finding some way to solve this case." Bella brought us back down to earth – though the bubbles would soon alleviate that minor hindrance.

"Now I may be able to help in that area." He held up one hand to get our attention. "You see, I've discovered an important piece of information."

"Yes, you said that at the door."

Lovebrook ignored me and continued in just as suspenseful a tone as before. "What I found out is a real turn-up for the books, even for an old hand like me." The inspector couldn't have been more than thirty, and while he had a youthful air about him, he occasionally spoke as though he were a hundred years old. "You see... someone living in Holly Village is here under a false identity."

He had built up the tension so effectively that this anticlimax was more than a little disappointing.

"Yes, we know. We found out last night."

"You did?" It was his turn to be disappointed, and he clicked his fingers accordingly. "How did you manage that? It took me a morning of sifting through old papers to uncover the truth."

Having previously dismissed our abilities, I was rather proud to talk up this minor success. "We invited ourselves to his house last night, and I poked about in his office until I found his real name."

"What do you mean, *his* real name?" He paused to give me time not to answer. "I'm talking about the Baroness."

# TWENTY-NINE

It turns out that it's actually quite difficult to discuss the finer points of a case whilst enjoying finger food and drinking fizz, so we allowed ourselves ten minutes to eat, and then took our drinks into the sitting room to continue the discussion.

"Let's make this clear," Bella suggested. "What you're saying is that Baroness Sheena Wandle isn't actually a baroness?"

"That's right. And the strangest thing is that she's not putting on airs. In fact, you might say she's taken some off."

"You've lost me now," I had to confess, as I built up the fire to warm the house once more. "Who is she really?"

Lovebrook's whole face was a smile at that moment. It was abundantly clear that he enjoyed telling a good story. "She's not a baroness; she's the daughter of an earl."

"And an earl is worth more than a baron, isn't that right?" I thought it best to confirm.

"No one is worth more than anyone else," Bella said with a hint of vexation. "We're discussing people, not chess pieces."

"Though both a chess piece and an earl can be knights!" Lovebrook quipped and waited for the laughter that would never come.

"Very droll, I'm sure." Bella wasn't impressed, and I wasn't as posh as either of them, so I wasn't the audience for such humour.

"But, yes, Marius. In terms of rank, the daughter of an earl would generally be considered of higher status than a baroness, though the daughter herself would have no specific title other than Lady."

"How fascinating." For some reason I've never been able to define, this sort of discussion made me terribly sleepy.

"I'm glad you agree." Lovebrook failed to realise that I'd only said this to pique my friend, and he continued in a cheery voice. "From what I discovered with the help of a studious constable at Scotland Yard by the name of Simpkin, Lady Sheena Wandle, née Henderson, was the daughter of the Earl of Selhurst. He lost his entire fortune and had to sell his estate after the Paris Bourse crisis of 1882. The family had most of their wealth invested in France and, when things headed south, they were ruined."

"That doesn't explain why she would pretend to be someone she's not," Bella surmised. "What could she gain from it?"

"That is the very question I asked when I called at her house on the way to see you."

"And?" it fell on me to enquire.

"And she was terribly helpful and really very sincere."

"Well, she would be," I said, but no one listened.

"She told me that, when her world fell apart and she saw how bleak the future could be without the luxury to which she was accustomed, she thought it would be better to be an impoverished baroness with an actual title than a non-specific lady. She also thought it less shameful. Her father had been one of the richest men in Europe, and he had died of a broken heart – her words, not a coroner's, I imagine – after his fall from grace."

"The poor woman." Bella excelled at finding sympathy for our suspects. "This does explain some of her more eccentric behaviour. Was her husband there when you interviewed the Baroness?"

"No, she believed he was off collecting a last-minute Christmas present, as he'd left the house before she rose. Do you have any reason to suspect him?"

"We suspect everyone!" I once more uttered and was once more ignored as I added a log to the now blazing pyre.

"No, but he's very protective of his wife," Bella replied in a tone that made us both listen. "I could imagine him stopping the interview if he were worried about how it might affect her."

Lovebrook took a sip of his champagne and, I dare guess, thought about his response. "As I said, she was most forthright. She admitted that it was vanity on her part that had made her adopt a false name, but she was fairly young when it happened, and she blamed her naïveté."

This was all very well, but I couldn't see what impact it would have on the case. "So another non-starter? How many more will there be before we back a winner?"

Lovebrook even looked encouraged by this gloomy comment. "Perhaps not every dead end is quite so terminal."

"I doubt you would say that if you'd had the morning we've had." Bella slumped back on the sofa in an uncharacteristically informal manner. In was not particularly *Ladylike*, in the aristocratic sense of the word.

"Perhaps if you go over all that happened, we'll be able to spot something which might at first have seemed irrelevant."

So then we told the inspector about John the gigolo and Herbie the caretaker-teasing, present-giving, graveyard lurker, and he replied, "You're right. That really isn't too promising, is it?"

"What a great help you've been, dear friend." I doubt that even he could have failed to notice the sarcasm in my voice this time. "If you have any more ideas, please do call again."

"Marius, you old cynic. I'm not saying that we can't yet extract anything from this peculiarly complicated affair." He walked over to the window with real purpose, as though he had a significant plan in mind. "We must go back to the very beginning and sift through the evidence. That often works for me, and I once saw the famous detective—"

"You know, you're right!" I said, remembering a particular occasion when I met that master sleuth Lord Edgington. "I performed a similar trick myself with a bar of soap. Wait there for just one moment."

I ran off to the bathroom, leaving Lovebrook looking oddly frustrated for some reason. Two minutes later, I was back with a bar of Yardley Old English Lavender Soap and the free-standing mirror from my bedroom.

"It works like this," I began once I was in place beside the fire. "We mention every single detail that comes to mind – every last theory and piece of evidence, no matter how unrelated they might seem. Let's start with the notes from Adele and the comments she made at the party."

I wrote them as neatly as I could on the mirror with one corner of the soap while Bella asked her first question. "So you don't think we can ignore them after all?"

"I'm not saying that. I just think we have to bear everything in mind if we're to find the killer."

"The firework that killed her," Lovebrook suggested, and I immediately added it to the list. "I spoke to the coroner who dealt with Adele Leach's body, and he thinks it could have caused her heart attack. Not only did she already have problems with her health, he's recently heard of a condition which weakens the heart muscles to leave sufferers susceptible to sudden shocks."

"We mustn't ignore the fact that it was the caretaker, Mr Dumfries, who was in charge of the fireworks."

Bella raised this point before Lovebrook politely raised his hand to speak. "Dumfries told me that the fireworks were kept in the gatehouse. Anyone here could have helped themselves to one. There is a spare key hidden in a flowerpot on the windowsill there. I still say it was an incredibly arrogant act to risk using the rocket to scare her senseless. The whole village could have woken up."

"However, this house is away from the others, and I do not wish to make generalisations, but some of the residents' hearing may not be as strong as it once was." I was writing continuously. Soap really isn't the easiest quill to employ. "And then there's what the killer did once Adele was dead. He gained access to the house—"

"Adele rarely locked her door," Bella explained. "She said that if anyone wanted to break in, they'd find a way and do more damage in the process."

"Yes, but once he was inside, he didn't take any of her treasures." I pointed around the room at the various pieces on the shelves. "Nor did he go through her jewellery up in the bedroom. He merely swapped one painting for a far less valuable one."

"So that means he expected to get away with it," Lovebrook concluded before I could. "He didn't want to draw attention to his crime and focused on the most valuable item in the house, hoping that no one would know the difference."

"And the maid didn't notice because there was no proof of any crime until we came here and Bella realised what was missing."

I was worried that this specific trail of evidence had gone cold, but Bella was quick with another point. "Even if she were mistaken, we know that Adele thought poorly of John Presler and believed that he was carrying on behind Silva's back."

I merely wrote *Presler secret gigolo* on the mirror and hoped this would suffice.

"Then there's Herbert Wandle's job," she continued. "The fact he is an antiquarian would make it easy for him to sell the painting."

I had been thinking about this since we'd seen Herbie with his stash of presents. "But perhaps that's altogether too obvious. We know that he's a clever man. If he is the thief and thus the killer, he must realise that the police would suspect him."

"That's a valid point," the inspector conceded. "His occupation certainly stood out to me and my colleagues when we were reviewing records back at the station. For now, I think we should move on to discussing Ivy Frazel." Lovebrook already had three fingers raised to list various points. "First, it seems from all I've heard that she was the village gossip, and quite the eccentric. I haven't spoken to anyone who considered her a close friend."

Bella's voice became a touch more hesitant than normal. "She mentioned missing the residents who had died since she moved here."

The soap dropped from my hand to the carpet. "That's right!" I was quite excited by what I'd realised. I also had slippery fingers. "She said that she associated snow with death, because so many of her old friends were taken by the cold weather."

"She became quite upset by it," Bella added. "I remember her turning morbid, but then we changed the subject, and she seemed to forget about it for a while. What else do we know about her?"

We both looked at the inspector, who had done far more general investigating than either of us. "Very little, actually. She was never married. She had no children or family to speak of. Her grandfather had been wealthy, and she could well afford to live in a place like this, but apart from her hobby making silk flowers, I don't believe she ever had a job."

"One thing we can say is that it's unlikely she was killed for her valuables," Bella replied. "The house was locked, and the killer made no real attempt to enter. If he'd wanted to get inside, he could have broken another window. Instead, he only made it look as if that were his intention. So why was she killed?"

The room fell still. The only noise was the crackling fire and my dog's not so gentle breathing in the hall.

"She wanted to talk to Herbie before she died." Bella looked out of the window at the neighbouring house. "Perhaps she'd realised something about Adele. He was busy with Ruth Haskell at the time. The killer might have killed Ivy to prevent her from sharing what she knew."

"Why would she have told Mr Wandle?" Lovebrook murmured, and Bella was suddenly more animated.

"Because he's the grandfather of the village. He goes out of his way for everyone here. Ivy told us how much she liked him, and Ruth Haskell was full of praise when she spoke to us."

"In other words, he's far too good to be true." Lovebrook wasn't the kind of person you'd want at a funeral. He was far too sunny for that.

"He's also the only person with at least partial alibis for both killings," I thought it best to mention. "And when we got it into our heads that he was plotting something, it turned out that he's even more generous than we'd previously realised."

Bella returned to the previous point. "We didn't tell Ivy that we were detectives, so she had no reason to come to us. Herbie would have been the obvious person with whom to share her suspicions."

"Suspicions of what?" The inspector rounded his shoulders as he listened.

"The first snows of winter." I paused to consider what I was saying. "We may have been the last people to talk to Ivy before she went to Herbie's house. She had looked so distraught when she mentioned the friends she'd lost, and I've come to wonder whether perhaps she'd realised that they'd died of some not quite natural causes. In a place like this, with elderly people making up the majority of the population, there's nothing to say that a coroner would have taken the time to consider foul play. It's the perfect location for a killer to pick off wealthy victims, steal one or two priceless items and go undetected."

There was one thing in all this which Bella didn't grasp. "What's that got to do with winter?"

"He used the falling snow to cover any sign that he'd been in the houses before the people died." I was only half sure of this, but it sounded like the arrogant affectation a killer might adopt. "Imagine this: he went to the house of Mrs Anderson and..." I tried to remember the names of other departed residents.

Bella came to my aid. "I believe there was an Agatha and a Mr Parsons who also died in the last five years or so. Ruth Haskell talked about them in her speech last night."

This set at least one bell ringing in my head, but I was thinking about another more pressing issue. "That's right. In addition to Adele and Ivy, we know of three people who have died since the Preslers moved here. We discussed it with them last night. So let's imagine the killer went to each of their houses, then used a method to despatch them which wouldn't attract too much attention. If he were a resident here, he'd know which of his neighbours had close families who would notice the absence of a valuable artwork."

"It's an interesting theory." Lovebrook put one leg across the other and looked wistful. "I don't suppose you happen to have any proof that it happened?"

"The sculpture!" Bella and I said at the same moment, and I motioned for her to explain.

"There was a sculpture stolen from Mrs Anderson's house which reappeared soon after the police were called." The idea ran through her mind like a flash, lighting her features as it went. "It seems quite possible that whoever was responsible realised that they could be caught and looked for a better method to pick the purses of the other residents."

"So that puts the caretaker back in the picture," Lovebrook suggested. "He was a professional thief for years. He may claim to have escaped that lifestyle in order to settle down with his family. But the only thing ruling him out is the alibi his wife had provided, and that's far from impartial."

"But John Presler, or Preston Jones or whatever his name is, was the man accused at the time." Bella stood up to take the soap from my hand in order to connect a few of the points on our map of evidence. "He is an angry man who bears a grudge, and I believe all that makes him the obvious suspect."

"I hate to disagree with you, Bella," I began before realising this wasn't true, "but we've been through these arguments before. Thieves aren't automatically killers, and nor are gigolos. Presler was accused of the crime because he was the newcomer, is considerably younger than anyone else who lives here and was born without a silver spoon in his cutlery drawer, let alone his mouth."

She would not relent. "The crimes didn't begin until he and Silva moved here. What's more, you told us yourself how he has done what was necessary to stay on an even footing financially with his wealthy wife."

"That's circumstantial evidence at best!" I barked like the

barrister I sometimes pretend to be when writing court scenes for my books.

"I appreciate your position, Marius," Lovebrook intervened to play peacemaker. "But nothing you discovered this morning rules out the possibility Presler is to blame. You saw him visiting his clients. Even if his wife knows about his unusual job, that's hardly proof he's not the killer."

"I'm not denying that the notes Adele wrote apply to him." With everyone talking over one another, and a pleasant cacophony in the sitting room, I needed a moment to be sure of my theory. "What I can't come to terms with is the idea that he would have killed her as a result of what she'd discovered. What would he gain from it?"

"Perhaps it wasn't just his night-time excursions she had noticed." Lovebrook scratched one short sideburn as he suggested this. "Perhaps there was something more."

"To echo a point you recently put to me, Inspector, I don't suppose you happen to have any proof?"

He laughed and looked ready to accept defeat when Bella changed the topic.

"We'll put Presler to one side for the moment. The advantage of finally knowing what Adele's notes mean is that we can ignore them." She stepped back to the mirror with the soap still under her control. "By which I mean that we must also consider the possibility that the murderer isn't a man, as we assumed, but one of the women who live here."

"Have we really been through all the male suspects, though?" Lovebrook asked. "We've mentioned Presler, Wandle and Dumfries, but what about the others?"

I was curious to hear what Bella thought about our female suspects, so I gave a quick answer. "Although he may well be the grumpiest man in London, Freddy Ponting walks inordinately slowly and requires a cane at all times. I believe this would make it hard for him to corner and garotte Ivy. Even carrying the painting across the green would have been an ordeal for him."

I took the soap back to write the words *The bad painting –
Presler* on the mirror as we'd forgotten to mention the coincidence
of the replacement artwork in Adele's house matching the collection the Preslers had shown us.

Bella had one more detail to add. "Someone mentioned that
Freddy and Miss Haskell see a lot of each other. There's nothing to
say that the killer didn't have an accomplice."

I was happy to have a new hypothesis and wrote it on the
mirror as Bella continued.

"There's also the old soldier, Clive, in 6b. He was very
welcoming when we visited him but told us that he keeps to
himself and that his real friends are the characters in the books on
his shelves."

Lovebrook pulled a pad out of the inside pocket of his suit
jacket at this point. "My constables inform me that Clive Whitworth was visiting family in Basingstoke on the night Adele was
murdered."

There was a troubling noise outside the room then, and I
attempted to identify it.

"Wait just one moment," I said, walking closer to the door.

The sound was getting louder and louder. It was a nasty sort of
scraping, scratching, tearing noise, and it set my teeth on edge. I
put my hand on the door, but didn't open it, as I was afraid what I
might find out there. I turned the handle and, when I looked into
the hall, it was just as I feared.

## THIRTY

"Really, Percy. How many times have I told you?" I asked the disobedient creature. "You mustn't scratch the carpet whether you're in our own house or someone else's. You're lucky you haven't torn a hole straight through it."

He cocked his head and pretended to look remorseful. I knew he was only putting it on. Within fifteen minutes, he'd have forgotten what I'd said and be back at it. Giving up on changing him, for the time being at least, I ushered him into the sitting room.

"I'm terribly sorry about that," I told the others. "Go on, Bella. We'll leave the men aside as you suggested. What about the women? I'm particularly interested in Silva Presler, Ruth Haskell and the Baroness, who is not actually a baroness."

She'd gone to perch on the wide windowsill and, with the light spilling in behind her, she looked like the little girl she'd once been. Her legs swung as she spoke, kicking her long black skirt so that it billowed outwards.

"Well, for a start, almost everything we've said about John Presler could apply to his wife."

I found one small hole to pick in her argument. "Except that she's the one with money. If the victims were murdered for their artworks, that would seemingly rule her out."

"Unless the thefts were designed to hide the real motive," she replied brightly. I could see that such reasoning would go spiralling on for ever, so I didn't interrupt her again. "As for the Baroness, money is more likely to be a motive, seeing as she told Lovebrook of her change in fortune. Living in a cottage is quite a step down from the stately home in which she was surely born."

"Her father went bankrupt nearly fifty years ago," the inspector was right to point out. "She didn't describe her plunge in status as though it were particularly painful anymore. She really only mentioned it to explain why she had changed her name."

"And you skipped Ruth Haskell," I told Bella once Lovebrook had finished talking.

"No, I didn't. I left her until the end." She was evidently anticipating what she was about to say, and so Lovebrook and I just waited.

"It occurs to me that of everyone in this village, she holds the most sway. She sees herself as the chief organiser and was the person to arrange the carol concert last night. Judging by how little interest Hamish Dumfries takes in anything, I would imagine she was the person to order the fireworks, so she would have known where they were stored. If she is the killer and was up to no good when Adele spotted her, she may have taken drastic measures."

"When you say 'up to no good'...?" Lovebrook asked without actually forming a question.

"I mean that the first snow of the year had started to fall. She was presumably planning to kill again and steal whichever item had taken her fancy when Adele, who until then had been spying on John Presler, saw her creeping off somewhere. Don't forget that hers is the only house we haven't entered. She may still have the painting there."

"You said that she'd taken an interest in Freddy at 7b," Lovebrook reminded her.

"Exactly. And when we were in his house yesterday, I noticed some silverware on display that was remarkably old and no doubt very valuable. Maybe her original plan fell apart when Adele saw her after the party. Instead of killing and robbing Freddy, whom she befriended, she stole the painting from Adele, but she hadn't taken the time to plan the crime in quite the same way. She hadn't known that I would come here and realise what was missing. And then, when Ivy spoke to us, she noticed the pattern of deaths here."

I didn't interrupt because I found the tale she was weaving so engaging.

"Ivy told us that the first snow of the year always brings death, and that realisation sealed her fate. She went to tell Herbie what she'd discovered, but Ruth was already there in the house. She became frightened or wished to avoid confrontation, so they arranged to meet later instead. But while Herbie was making the tea, Ruth was alone and could have hurried after Ivy with a cord from the curtains or a belt or some such. That would explain why Ivy was murdered just outside her house."

"That is all quite..." Lovebrook began, turning this sentence over in his head before choosing the right conclusion. "... feasible. But what about the bench where Ivy was found? Why didn't Ruth leave her where she lay?"

"The timing." Bella was as quick as lightning now. "Ruth moved the body and placed her on the bench as though she were sitting there watching the snow fall because she wanted people to think that Ivy died sometime later."

"So, by putting her on the bench, it made it seem as though she were still alive when she wasn't, thus confusing the time of death." I was essentially just repeating what she'd said.

"Well, yes." Bella smiled, and it lightened my heart a little. "Ruth Haskell was very conspicuous for the rest of the afternoon, dealing with the carol concert where everyone could see her. I'm sure she wanted to distance herself from her crime."

"You know, that's really rather clever," Lovebrook declared, rubbing his hands together before the fire.

When I said nothing, a look of uncertainty came over their faces. I took my time, not because I'm such a ham (normally at least), but for the simple reason that I wanted to be certain of what

Bella had said. I tried to adopt a different perspective from hers — to tear into the hypothesis with all my force, but it was surprisingly resilient.

"Come along, Marius. You must see it," she insisted. "Ruth Haskell's the killer. Think about the way she's spoken to us ever since we arrived here. There's something so practised and precise about her. It's as if she rehearses every word before speaking. You can't deny that she's our strongest suspect yet."

"I don't..." I almost launched into a full-throated exclamation of support, but something held me back. "I believe you're right. I can think of no reason to rule out Miss Haskell, but nor can I be sure that it's her."

Having held their breath for some seconds, they breathed out dispiritedly.

"I'm not saying it's impossible. I'm not saying you're wrong. I just think that we're lacking the key piece of evidence that could prove everything else."

Bella had heard enough and turned away from me. Lovebrook had heard enough and rose from the sofa to walk across to the window and stare outside. Percy hadn't been listening in the first place and was tearing at the carpet again.

"My dear friends," I began most sincerely, "I'm sorry to be so demanding, but I'm certain that you can feel it just as tangibly as I can." I paused, and the two of them glanced back at me. "We may not have deciphered the precise series of events which led to the murders, but we are ten steps closer to the truth."

# THIRTY-ONE

To save the soft furnishings if nothing else, I decided that it was time to take Percy for another walk. Luckily, the perfect spot was just a short trip from Holly Village. Bella was understandably distracted, but I memorised our list on the mirror before wrapping up for the cold, and I knew that the exercise would do us good.

The buffoons from the local police station were patrolling the village. Sergeant Bulmer normally vacillated between furious and smug. The look he sent in my direction was a mixture of the two, but he soon changed when he noticed the inspector close behind me. Lovebrook made his excuses and went to talk to him, and we continued on our way.

Even in the lingering winter sunshine, the air was frosty, and I half wished I'd worn my hideous jumper – though the thought of solving the case in such attire was enough to prevent disaster.

The pavements around the neighbourhood had cleared and, at the edges, the snow had been compacted, ready to be shovelled away by road cleaners. In intermittent patches, there was ice underfoot, so Bella held on to me, but she rarely met my gaze as we walked towards Hampstead Heath with only Percy's panting as an accompaniment.

We crossed Highgate Road and found ourselves in nature.

Once upon a time, not so very long ago, that part of England was a byword for the countryside. If you watch a Restoration comedy, men from Hampstead were considered country bumpkins. Over the centuries, the city had spread and eaten up the landscape, so that only the heath now revealed the neighbourhood's former bucolic identity.

I'd only ever been there in the summer before, when the trees were in leaf and the grass was a luscious green, but even dressed in white it felt as if we'd travelled a thousand miles in the space of a minute. Behind us was the expensive neighbourhood where Adele had made her home, in front of us, the wide vista that made up Parliament Hill.

And what life was there! There were children rolling down the snowy heath on their sides so that, by the time they reached the bottom, their clothes were as white as the ground beneath them. Others descended on toboggans – yet more had found the lids of tea crates and were pushing one another back and forth. There were snowmen lining the well-trodden paths and a group of girls were enjoying a snowball fight, much to their nanny's horror.

"Girls, girls, girls," she shouted, and they happily ignored her, "that is not how nice young ladies should behave."

I remember Bella's short-lived governess saying much the same thing when we were seven. On another day, I could have imagined our joining in with the fun. Instead, Bella walked with her head down, presumably picking over every moment of the last few days.

She only stopped to look around when we got to the top of the hill. Between two patches of bare trees, we could see all the way to St Paul's Cathedral and the Houses of Parliament, five miles south in the centre of the city. When I'd been there in the past, I'd considered that London seemed to have been built for that hill. It was as if whichever Roman general who founded the place had decided to build something pretty for people up here to admire. And in the two thousand years since, the city had grown and changed, but the historic centre was still where it had always been.

"Do you remember when we tried to climb the tallest tree in

the Hurtwood when we were children?" Bella asked me out of the blue.

"No," was the only honest answer I could give.

"Of course you do," she insisted with every ounce of self-assurance with which she was born. "We wanted to see my house from high up, and so we spent an eternity trying to throw a rope over a branch so that we could climb up it and then work our way higher."

"None of that rings a bell."

She frowned with her eyebrows. "I'm sure it will in a moment. You were the first to climb up, mainly because you were trying to impress me."

"I was not trying to impress you," I objected.

"I thought you didn't remember any of this?" Her manner had changed, and she was suddenly brighter than she had been.

"I don't remember that specific day, but I do remember not trying to impress you... in general." I smiled, well aware that she would disagree.

"You went up first to impress me, and then you tried to keep the rope steady as I came after."

For a moment, I thought I remembered the time she was describing. "Wait a moment. Did you fall back down again?"

"No, I didn't fall back down again," she said in much the same voice she would have used back then, and I realised just how much my perception of her was shaped by those first years we shared together. "I put my feet on the trunk of the tree and worked my way, hand over hand, up the rope."

She had to stop then, as a yelling boy on a bin lid came shooting down the hill and nearly crashed into us.

"Hooligan!" I shouted, certain before the word was out of my mouth that I'd done far worse at his age.

The interruption hadn't broken Bella's concentration for a second. "I got to the first branch, and we both realised that it wasn't nearly as high up as it had looked. I must have felt pretty stupid for thinking we'd be able to see much more up there than we had from the ground."

"And so you kept climbing."

"You remember!"

"No, I just know you well."

She looked disgruntled again, but in an oddly happy way. "Yes, I kept climbing. It was your turn to be the sensible one that day, and so you were the voice of reason. You told me it was too high, and I wouldn't listen. I doubt I got more than a few branches up, but it seemed a lot higher at the time, and then all of a sudden, I was stuck."

In a flash or perhaps a flicker, the memories appeared in my brain. I hadn't thought of that moment for years – perhaps since it happened. But then, as if I had pressed a button to call the image forth, I could see Bella in the tree above me.

"I remember," I said in little more than a whisper as I came to appreciate the magic trick she had performed.

"You told me to come back, but it was too late for that. I started to cry, and you must have realised that there was no way I could get down on my own, so you called for the rope and tied it around your waist to make your way up to me."

She stopped and looked across the whole of London in three seconds. I was hoping that I had gallantly saved her that day, but there was more to the story, and I left her to tell it.

"The problem was that, even with you up there, I didn't have the courage to climb back down."

"Which was a great relief to me," I had to admit, as this was the part of the story I remembered best. "When I looked down at the ground, I realised that I was just as scared as you were."

"Well, you seemed perfectly calm. You sat on the branch and tied the rope around me so that it would break my fall... or cut me in two. It's hard to know what would have happened, and I'm glad to say that we didn't find out."

The wind picked up, and a brief blizzard blew off the trees in our direction, but Bella kept going. "You talked to me. I don't remember what you said, but you found a way to help me forget that we were a thousand feet off the ground. You managed to calm me down so much that I wasn't scared anymore, and I finally took the time to look across the tops of the trees to my house in the distance. I couldn't believe it, but we'd achieved what we'd set out to do."

"That was a rare thing," I confessed when she fell quiet. "I wonder how many of the countless plans we made together were ever completed."

Her cheeks became even rounder, and her sea-green eyes shifted back to me. "Marius, the reason I'm thinking of this now is because the way I felt up there with you – that sense of safety you gave me despite the danger I was in – that was how I always felt with Auntie Addie. She was the most wonderfully comforting person. Whatever my problems were, she knew how to make them seem smaller. I went to stay with her after you left for the war, and she put me back together again. She was my guardian angel, and that's why I owe it to her to solve this case."

I would have liked to tell her that I understood completely, but she spoke so sweetly, I didn't dare interrupt.

"I know I haven't been much use since I turned up at your house yesterday morning. I know that I've been crying half the time and asking stupid questions for much of the rest, but maybe what I've just told you helps explain my behaviour."

Percy, who had been ineffectually yet optimistically running after any sledge that came near now gave up and sat on Bella's feet.

"We'll find the killer," I promised. "We're only feeling so much pressure because we know that it's almost Christmas and we want to get home to our families." I imagined this was the case but couldn't say for certain. "I hate the thought of the savage responsible for Adele's and Ivy's and perhaps all those other villagers' deaths being free to enjoy his Christmas, thinking he's got away with it yet again. No matter what happens, we'll get him." I had to add, "... or her," as I'd remembered that our current top suspect was a woman.

She didn't reply. She just reached into her pocket and pulled out a folded piece of paper. I didn't recognise it at first, but then I saw what it was. Bella had brought the notes that Adele had made in her tower.

"It's like I said last night. I want to believe that John Presler is to blame because that's what Adele thought. I want to do right by her, but I don't know how."

She held up the page in her leather-gloved hands, and we both read it for the fifth, tenth or twentieth time. The notes were clearly a log of the comings and goings of John Presler as he went off to charm his clients. Now that we knew what he did for a living, I struggled to extract anything particularly sinister from them. I suppose Bella realised this, as every breath she took made it sound as if she were reprimanding herself.

It was hard to ignore the possibility that we were looking for hidden meanings when there were none to find. And it was as I had this very thought that one of the phrases stood out to me.

"Bella, look," I said, but she was already reading it aloud.

"*Wednesday 7.15 p.m. He's weaselling off in darkness while She's out till late.*"

# THIRTY-TWO

We never quite decided which of us was the first to solve the case, but it didn't really matter.

We discussed the finer points all the way back to the village and, when we arrived, Bella went up to the first constable we saw. Making sure to use her full title, and reminding him of our close friendship with his superior, she told him of our theory and how urgent it was to apprehend the killer. He did not argue but ran off with a colleague to do just that. And then we went looking for Lovebrook to explain why.

We found him in Ruth Haskell's house. He was sipping tea and had apparently just hauled the last person we'd identified as our main suspect over the coals.

"We're sorry to interrupt," I said, though I really wasn't, and this was no time for pleasantries. "We've worked out what happened."

He almost spilt his tea. "Who? How? And when? And for that matter, where?"

"We both did... at the same time." Bella sounded proud of herself and maybe of me too. I really can't say. "We were up on Parliament Hill. Perhaps the air is cleaner up there, or the walk did us good, but the pieces finally fell into place."

Percy had followed us into the house and stood in the middle of the chintzy living room, panting and looking out of place. I took a moment to look at our surroundings and I noticed that the furnishings were not quite as luxurious as in other houses we'd visited.

"Would you like some tea, too?" Miss Haskell asked, and looking down at my dog, added, "Though perhaps he'd prefer a bowl of water?"

Bella studied the nervy woman before responding. "Actually, yes. That sounds like a good idea."

Our hostess nodded and stepped from the largely beige sitting room.

"Did you get anything of use from her?" I asked as soon as she had gone.

Lovebrook kept looking at the door through which she'd just passed and, when he answered, it was with a certain reluctance. "She says she knows nothing about any kind of criminality and that the killings came as a great shock to her."

This didn't surprise me, but I had more on my mind than Ruth Haskell.

"Come along," Lovebrook said, sitting straighter in his armchair beside the fireplace so as to listen all the better. "What have you got to tell me?"

Before we could answer, the door opened once more, and in walked Sergeant Bulmer. "Is this where the killer lives then? I heard a rumour that you've identified the culprit."

Lovebrook adopted his authoritative attitude to address the incompetent fellow. "Marius and Bella here were just about to reveal their thinking."

I thought that Bella would want to explain everything, but shyness or perhaps the emotion of the day overtook her, and she gave me the floor. That's not quite true, as she chose to kneel down on the floor to give Percy a good scratch behind the ears, but she did let me talk.

"I can't deny that it's a complicated story we have to tell you," I began, and Lovebrook immediately interrupted with a quip.

"I would expect nothing less. I've read your novels, after all."

"Hilarious, Inspector. With a comic turn like that, you should be on the stage." For someone who did not consider his own books to be masterpieces, I was surprisingly protective of them. "Now, listen. I believe that we got half of the story right earlier, but we missed several key points. Bella and I are convinced that Adele was not the first victim. We believe that Adele and Ivy were murdered because they realised that there was a killer living here in the village, which forced him to change his modus operandi. Before that, he followed a slow, steady approach to the crimes and spaced them out over the years. He presumably got to know his targets well to make certain that no one was close enough to them to realise anything had been stolen."

"We will, of course, have to confirm all this." Lovebrook had enjoyed the last of his tea and now moved on to a Pat-A-Cake biscuit.

"Jolly good. You can order the exhumation of the bodies to check which poisons killed them. My guess would be thallium, as it could be mistaken for many other illnesses and can be administered over a length of time."

"I can't promise I'll get the permission to dig up any graves," he replied, setting down his half-eaten biscuit on a saucer, as it was not compatible with the discussion. "You believe that someone was killing the other residents of the village in order to steal from them. But is there anything more to the motive?"

"Yes, like a lot of things here, it was a matter of keeping up appearances."

"And keeping up with the Joneses," Bella was right to point out.

"If there is one thing we noticed as soon as we arrived, it was the rivalry between the two sides of the green. Though a certain peace has held, there was something we couldn't quite define: a frostiness that had nothing to do with the cold weather."

Perhaps it was in response to this rather workmanlike turn of phrase, but Bella found her voice and took over. "The fact is that, with such a concentration of wealth in this otherwise fairly humble setting, it is fertile ground for a person without scruples. The killer had got away with murder for so long that he presumably became over-confident. Adele spotted something from her tower one night last week. She believed that one of her neighbours was capable of murder and tried to tell the police."

Bulmer raised his hand to defend himself, but Lovebrook silenced him. "Let them speak, Sergeant."

Bella did just that. "The culprit must have realised he was being watched and put the firework through her letter box literally to scare her to death. Perhaps he changed his plans as a result and stole her painting instead of a valuable from whomever he had intended to target."

"I believe it was Betty in number four." This idea had only just come to me, but it made a lot of sense. "She had been ill recently but recovered this week. I think the killer had been slowly poisoning her, but when Adele noticed what he was up to, he had to stop. A gradual decline like that would have been less suspicious than Betty's sudden death."

"And you say that Ivy was killed for a similar reason?" Lovebrook prompted us.

"That's right," Bella replied. "Something she mentioned when she came to see us helped her, and subsequently us, to see what had been happening."

"It was the snow," I clarified, though Lovebrook had already heard as much an hour or so before. "She realised that each of the people who had died since the Preslers moved to the area did so around the time of the first snow. At first, I assumed this was chosen so that any footprints would be covered as soon as they were made, but there was a simpler explanation."

"You're getting ahead of yourself." Bella wouldn't allow any such thing. "You didn't finish explaining what happened to Ivy. She became aware of the horrors that had taken place here and decided to discuss them with Herbie before going to the police, but he was busy with Ruth Haskell, and no one saw her alive again."

"Yes, I understand the timetable of events quite well." Lovebrook was eager to discover the parts of the story we were yet to reveal. "What I don't know is who committed this terrible run of crimes that went undetected for so long."

"And I am ready to arrest them when the moment comes," Bulmer put in most officiously. The man was a useless lump of lard, and this was his only real purpose there.

I looked at Bella, but she was happy to let me say it. "The killer will be here at any moment."

We all turned to look and, as if we'd planned it in advance, the door to the sitting room swung open and in walked Ruth Haskell.

"My apologies," I was quick to say. "Not Miss Haskell..." I waited for a few seconds and heard the front door open and the constables pushing the culprit inside.

"This is a travesty," Herbert Wandle complained as he was led into the room. "I'm as innocent as a lamb."

# THIRTY-THREE

I was curious to see Miss Haskell's reaction to the killer arriving in her house with a police escort. It was hard to imagine what she was thinking. She simply froze where she stood, a tray held tightly in her hands. We never did get that cup of tea.

Bella was the opposite of our hostess. "You terrible man. You killed innocent people for your own petty greed." The emotion rushed to the surface, and she couldn't hide her feelings any longer. "You killed your own friends and pretended all along that you were the moral centre of the village."

"Him?" Bulmer pointed, and how I wished he would shut his mouth. "But Mr Wandle is a pillar of the local community! I can't tell you how much he's contributed to the policemen's widows' fund."

"How interesting," I replied in the hope he might stop talking.

Herbert used the interruption to argue his cause. "You've got it all wrong, my dear," he said in as kindly a voice as ever, raising his hands to reason with Bella. "I'm no killer. You know me. You know I would never do such a thing."

"Prove it," I said, well aware that the task I'd presented was impossible. "Prove that you're not a killer."

"Well..." he prevaricated. "For one thing, I was at home with my guest when Ivy was murdered. You said it yourself, and Ruth here can confirm it."

"Do you remember exactly what happened, Miss Haskell?" Lovebrook asked the terrified woman, who was now standing with her back to the wall.

"I..." She looked at the prisoner and was obviously a little afraid. "I remember Ivy knocking at the front door. She whispered something to Herbert, and he tried to reassure her. He said that they would speak again very soon, and that she wasn't to worry."

"You see!" Herbert took this as vindication. "I would have liked to help the poor frightened woman, and yet I was busy with Ruth and couldn't leave my home."

He'd already contradicted himself, though I doubt he realised it. "We talked to you after we found her body, and you told us that you didn't know what she wanted. Now you're saying that she was frightened. Surely if she was so frightened, you should have paused your meeting to help her."

"I don't now remember the exact words we exchanged," he replied directly. "I don't know if you've ever been accused of murder, but it is not conducive to recalling precise details."

Herbert was a slippery one and wouldn't give in as easily as I had expected. I'd pictured him breaking down in tears as soon as the police came banging at his door.

I ignored his performance to ask another question. "What happened next, Miss Haskell?"

"Next?" She was a box of nerves.

"After Ivy Frazel left the Wandles' house, what did Herbert do?"

"After that..." She could no longer look at him. She stared at the inspector instead, as though to reassure herself that no one could hurt her. "After that, Herbert suggested that he make tea. He went straight to the kitchen."

"And as their house is similar to all the others I've visited, the kitchen presumably had a back door?"

When neither of them answered, Lovebrook directed my question to the accused man. "Mr Wandle, is that true?"

"I'm not going to deny having a back door to my house, but that doesn't make me a killer." He couldn't resist the urge to smooth down his tie beneath his paisley waistcoat, and it gave me another idea.

"No, but the fact you crept outside to strangle Ivy to death with your tie does. She came to discuss her suspicions regarding the earlier deaths and so you killed her."

Unable to answer this point, he appealed to men in charge. "Inspector Lovebrook, Sergeant Bulmer, this man is evidently some kind of lunatic. You mustn't take his unhinged assertions seriously?"

As I was apparently unfit to accuse him, Bella continued the tale. "I believe it was Mrs Anderson – a woman you murdered four years ago – who gave you away. Ivy told us that she associated the first snow of the year with death, and that's when you killed each time, wasn't it?"

"Tell the truth now, Wandle," Bulmer said, to feel more important than he was.

An arrogant impulse now shaped the culprit's features. I could tell he considered himself above such questions. "No, my dearest Bella. None of that is true. I am a carpenter and an antiquarian, not a heartless killer. I make my money finding new homes for previously unwanted items that I believe are worth more than people ask for them."

"Which put you in a perfect position to sell the objects you stole from your victims. I saw a number of French items in your shop in the high street, and your wife mentioned your trips to the Continent. You couldn't have got away with selling stolen artworks here; I imagine that you took them abroad and got a good price for them."

"So what has the snow got to do with anything?" Lovebrook was an expert at ensuring that our evidence was correct and fair.

"It was merely the time of year, not the snow that was important," I replied. "Isn't that right, Herbie?"

"Do you really expect me to agree?"

"You were replenishing your bank account, as you know just how expensive Christmas can be. I'm sure that the painting you commissioned from a famous Italian artist must have cost a pretty penny, and from what I've seen of your shop on the high street, it's not exactly packed full of customers."

"You did all this to buy Christmas presents?" Even Lovebrook sounded appalled now.

"No, I..." Herbert came very close to confirming my theory then, but he held his response back. He stared at Bulmer, who could do nothing to help him.

"It wasn't just to purchase presents, though you made sure to win over everyone in the village by giving them each a little something." I took a step closer to drive the point home. "You bought their trust so that you could murder and rob more of them in the future. I can only assume you were trying to meet your aristocratic wife's expectations. A woman who is so disgraced by her fallen status that she would demote herself from lady to baroness surely has expensive tastes. You did this for her, didn't you?"

"You have no evidence." All his charm had disappeared, and he protested with a snarl. "This is a fine story, Mr Mystery Novelist, but where's your proof?"

I wouldn't answer. I wanted Bella to do that. I wanted her to look that monster in the eye as she read out the most important note that Adele had written.

"You must already know that my aunt was watching your comings and goings. That's why you scared her to death, after all. She must have seen you coming out of Betty's or one of the other ladies' houses. You realised you'd been rumbled when she returned from my party last week, so you waited for her to settle down for the night, then took a firework from the gatehouse and put it through her front door. At first, we thought that this noisy method was born of arrogance, but it served another purpose. You could return home once the deed was done and wake your wife to ask her whether she'd heard an explosion. She remembered the moment but must have been half asleep and wouldn't have realised the discrepancy in time."

"Proof," he shouted again. "You need proof, not conjecture!"

"Very well." She took a deep breath. "You almost thought of everything, but what you didn't know was that my aunt had made notes about what she'd seen."

Herbert was past trying to convince her of his innocence, but his truncated response gave a hint of the anger within him. "She wasn't even your aunt, you pretentious—"

"We thought they were about John Presler, as his job..." She paused to choose her words. "... his job takes him away from home a lot. You were happy to promote him as the culprit. You told us of your suspicions of Presler. You even bought a painting like the ones you'd seen in his house to replace Adele's, and you were fortunate that much of what she wrote could apply to either of you. We understood that she told Marius her suspicions that someone here was taking advantage of another woman for her money. That description might have fitted you or John. But over the last day, regardless of your faults, I've seen that you both worship your wives."

I thought I could fill in one element of the story here. "Adele must have thought that you were running around with other women and that was why you were visiting your neighbours late at night when your wife was out."

"I believe in community spirit." He looked away as though none of this bore any relevance to him. "I like to help out those who need it. Ask anyone."

I could see the fire in Bella's eyes glow brighter at this moment, and she held up the paper that would seal his fate. "It says here, '*Wednesday, 7.15 p.m. He's weaselling off in darkness while She's out till late.*'"

He just stared back at her in contempt, as if to say, *And?*

"I read that sentence so many times before realising its importance." She waited to see if he could unlock it, but it had taken us more than a day. "Your wife goes to the opera on Wednesday nights. Isn't that correct?"

He still didn't say anything, but a touch of fear was visible in his troubled gaze. He lowered his hands to hide the fact they were trembling.

"Every note on this sheet of paper begins *She* or *He*, and I instantly wished that my dear Adele had simply included the names of the people she was watching from her tower, but I now see that she did. They were there all along; she wrote *He* for Herbert and *She* for Sheena. She even used capital letters in the middle of sentences."

He searched the room for a friendly face, but even Ruth Haskell, who had told us how much she admired her fellow villager, returned a look of revulsion.

"You're quite mad. I'm no killer. I cherish my neighbours – cherish them!"

It's hard to say whether Herbert Wandle would have continued to feign innocence had a newcomer not joined us at this point.

"That's enough, Herbert," the Baroness proclaimed, appearing in the doorway like the apparition of a long-dead noblewoman. "It's time to admit the truth."

He didn't turn to see his wife but, in an instant, fell to his knees.

Two quiet, desperate words emerged from his lips. "You knew?"

"No, my darling. Not until I spoke to the constables outside." She placed her hand on his cheek to force him to look up at her. "I would never have suspected anything, and yet as soon as I understood the charges against you, I realised how everything fitted together. Adele came to see me last week. She said that she couldn't understand why you spent so much time visiting Betty, and I insisted that you were just doing your neighbourly duty to a sick woman."

She peered down at him with love in her eyes, and it was painful to watch. She was looking at her husband, the murderer, and she still found it in her heart to show tenderness. I suppose that must be what true love is – an undying emotion that can't be cut short no matter what. Perhaps the Baroness couldn't approve of the man kneeling before her, but her companion of the last fifty years would be treasured forevermore.

"I'm sorry, my angel." Now it was his voice that trembled. "I know it might not sound like it, but I did all this for us. I wanted to be enough for you. I've only ever wanted to be enough. You deserve so much more than I could give you, so I—"

She put one finger to his lips, and he immediately stopped talking.

"That's something you never understood about me, Herbert." She was a strong woman and resisted the tears that would surely fall in time. "You see, I already had the thing I needed most in the world: I had you."

# THIRTY-FOUR

Silence surrounded us, and I certainly didn't wish to be the one to shoo it away again. Bella was quite pale. She closed her eyes and wept for her aunt, and I finally wrapped my arms around her and held her close to me.

Still staring at the killer, Detective Inspector Lovebrook shook his head in disgust and finally issued the necessary order. "Take him away, Bulmer."

"Wait one minute," I said to pause the process. "Something doesn't make sense."

"You're not going to tell me that this was all a ruse, and the killer is really out in the courtyard somewhere, celebrating his escape?"

"You really have read my books, haven't you?" I was frankly impressed.

"What's the matter, Marius?" Bella asked, pulling away from me.

I hadn't connected the pieces myself yet, but I would do my very best. "Well, think about it: Adele already suspected Herbert on Thursday morning, which is why she went to the police. When she came home that night, Herbert knew he had to kill her."

I noticed a slight spasm in the prisoner's neck. His head jerked to the side and back, and I knew I was on the right path.

"Someone told him of her suspicions." Bella looked first at Ruth Haskell, then the Baroness.

"There's more than that." I leaned back against the wall as the reality of the situation sank in. "Just how large a contribution to the policemen's widows' fund did Herbert Wandle make, Sergeant?"

The odious man's jowls wobbled. He turned left and right and clearly couldn't believe that his luck had run out. "Now, now, we'll have none of that. You've got the killer fair and square. I wouldn't... I mean, I didn't..."

I had more to say. "You're something far worse than a useless officer, aren't you, Bulmer? You're corrupt. When we went to talk to you at the station, you told us that Adele had mentioned John Presler's name, but you only said that to distract us from the real killer. The same thing happened when you investigated the scene of her death. You told her maid that there was nothing suspicious about the disturbance there and evidently convinced the inspector from Scotland Yard of the same thing."

"This is madness." He was shaking with impotent rage, but he couldn't find an explanation for any of it. "Why would I get involved in any such thing? What would I gain from it?"

"I would say that was quite simple. When the very first item went missing here in the village – I believe it was a Frederic Leighton sculpture – you were called here to find the thief. Instead, you said that if it turned up, there would be no further action taken. This struck me as a bizarre approach, as there would have been very few suspects who were capable of moving such a heavy bronze sculpture, and I would have thought that you could have identified the culprit quite easily – especially as he was the local antiquarian."

He clamped his mouth shut this time. It was something he would have to get used to in prison.

"You came to an arrangement with Mr Wandle here to protect

him from prosecution in exchange for a percentage of the profits. Those poor widows need all the help they can get, I suppose."

"But Sarge," the spotty young constable we'd met at the station spoke up, "you told us that money was going towards the New Year's Eve party."

"Shut your mouth, you stupid boy!" The immense sergeant shook his finger at his subordinate. He'd turned so red, I thought he might explode.

"He forced me to do it." Herbert tried to shift the blame now that his accomplice had been revealed. "The sergeant made me steal from my neighbours in order to—"

"I've heard enough from both of you." Lovebrook looked uncertain what to do next. Under normal circumstances, he would have asked one of the constables to arrest the suspect, but as it was difficult to say whether they were just as bad as their superior, he did the job himself. "Sergeant Bulmer, I'm arresting you for being an accessory after the fact to murder. Not to mention perverting the course of justice, bribery and misconduct in public office. In fact, you've totted up so many offences, I think I'll take you down to Scotland Yard myself."

He borrowed Pike's handcuffs and took great pleasure in shackling the sergeant.

"This is a travesty!" the soon-to-be-former officer complained. "Avenge me, Pike! Avenge this injustice!"

Pausing in the doorway as Bulmer was escorted outside, Inspector Lovebrook had a promise to make.

"Lady Bella, we will get your aunt's painting back. I have no doubt about that. I won't give up until this toe-rag reveals what he did with it." He looked at Herbie for a moment, but the man wouldn't raise his eyes from the floor.

"I hope you do," Bella replied, smiling despite a hint of tears in her eyes. "But even if it has been sold and we never see it again, I have a thousand mementos of Adele that can't be stolen."

The dear inspector nodded and prodded the prisoner through the door ahead of him.

After the excitement died down, and we'd given one of the constables from Scotland Yard a statement on everything we'd learnt, I stood in the centre of the village, looking up at Adele Leach's tower.

"You know, we're really not very clever," I told Bella.

"Thank you very much." Her lips curved upwards. This was not a sad or conflicted smile; it was the one I knew and loved best. "Do you have any particular reason to say this, or is it just our general incompetence you felt you had to mention?"

I pointed up to the tower to see if she would notice what I had. "There are windows on each side," I told her when she failed to respond. "When we first went up there, I turned the telescope around to look at John Presler on his doorstep. It would have been pointing through the other window at Herbert's house until then."

"So what you really mean is that *you're* not very clever." She winked at me.

"That's the ticket."

We started the walk back to Adele's house. There was an unspoken doubt lingering between us, and so I decided to resolve it. "You can call Caxton to pick you up," I said to avoid having to hope for anything else. The idea of spending Christmas with her had been quietly simmering in my mind since we'd arrived in Holly Village, but I was a fool to hope for any such thing.

"Yes..." She was still looking up at the tower. "Yes, that's a good idea."

Percy waddled ahead of us, and that was that: my fate decided. Bella would go home to Hurtwood to be with her family, and I would remain in London with Mother. It would take Caxton some time to arrive, but when we got to the cottage, Bella didn't want to reminisce on old times or sing carols. She sat on the sofa in front of the Christmas tree and stared at the thoughtful gift that a murderer had given her.

I packed my things and, when I came back downstairs, she was sitting in the exact same spot, still looking at the drawing of herself and her aunt in its elegant silver frame.

"I think it's time to go," I told her, and Percy instantly howled in disappointment. He doesn't know a lot of English, but he understands departures, meals and walks implicitly.

For five long seconds, she didn't look up at me, but then she wrenched the frame open, pulled the picture out and went to throw it in the fire. She watched it burn and, when she turned around, it was as if nothing had happened.

"Thank you for staying here with me, Marius," she said in a restrained voice, much as if I'd watered her plants while she went away for the weekend. "And for everything else you've done."

I wanted to hug her goodbye. No, that's a lie. I wanted to kiss her and never let go, but I fought my instincts with every muscle in my body. "You're welcome, Lady Isabella. I hope to be of service again very soon."

"I dare say our paths will cross before long."

A feeling of utter loneliness shot through me, and I tried to delay my leaving after all. "Are you sure you wouldn't prefer me to wait until your chauffeur arrives? I really don't mind."

She looked around the sitting room and then nodded. "I'd like to spend some time here alone. I have to say goodbye to a very dear friend."

I hid my disappointment and put on my hat. Percy wasn't nearly such an accomplished poker player as I was and ran over to Bella for one last scratch behind the ears. He liked it so much that he tried to lick her hands as she did it, which he soon discovered was impossible.

When he heard me open the front door, he came bundling after, and we followed the path around the rectangular green. I wanted to believe that Bella was watching us from the window, but I didn't look back to find out. Sometimes it's better to live with our pleasant misconceptions than to challenge them. I was happy to imagine that she was still hopelessly in love with me, just as she had been at seventeen, but I wasn't going to ask her and ruin the fantasy.

We got to my car, and I put my case in the luggage compartment as Percy climbed into Bella's seat. The snow had melted across much of the city, but there would be more falling before long. The winter was just beginning, after all.

Percy sat beside me watching the capital flash past the window, and we made it through busy old London town and back to St James's just in time for tea.

# THIRTY-FIVE

Whatever came after the events at Holly Village was only ever going to feel dissatisfying. Mother was out with friends from her church that night, and so I wrapped the few presents I would be giving and tried not to think about how lifeless my flat was. On Christmas Eve, my aunt and uncle came to visit, and my editor Bertie called in with his family, but I wasn't in the mood to celebrate. I was quiet and taciturn and had quite forgotten how to hold an interesting conversation. I told myself that all I wanted was a peaceful Yuletide. I didn't care for presents or singing around a piano. Even the promise of Mother's roast dinner could not cheer me and, when everyone went home that night, I told myself it was for the best.

When I woke up the next morning, it didn't feel like Christmas Day. The house was too quiet for that, and I knew that I'd made a terrible mistake. The smell of bacon cooking in the kitchen wasn't enough to rouse my spirits, and so I decided to do something about it.

"I'm sorry, Mother. I know I said that I wanted to stay here for Christmas, but I was wrong."

"That's wonderful," she said to interrupt my apparently not so dramatic announcement. "I told your uncle to buy extra food just in case you changed your mind." She turned off the cooker, took off her apron and walked to the door before pausing there. "I take it we're going to Hurtwood?"

To say that I was amazed would be an understatement.

"You clever thing." I kissed her on the top of the head. "You always know what I'm thinking before I do."

It would have been just like her to have her bags packed and ready to go, but we both needed a short time to prepare. Percy ran back and forth in excitement at the unplanned journey. I whipped up some bacon sandwiches and, ten minutes later, we were on the road. Though there'd been no more snow in London overnight, the way was icy, and I couldn't be sure whether the single-lane country road into the village would be passable, but I drove like the clappers nonetheless.

I can remember winters from my childhood when the whole village was cut off by a blizzard, but I had faith we would make it. What a terrible Christmas Day would it be for a well-meaning mystery novelist and his long-suffering mother to drive hours in the snow to see our loved ones only to have to head back home again with our mission incomplete.

When we passed into Surrey, all thoughts of the city were abandoned. The snow drifts were deeper in the fields and hills alongside us, but the roads remained clear. I admittedly almost missed the turning I had taken so many times because the world looked different from the one I knew, but the joy was steadily building within me as we entered the tunnel of trees into Hurtwood Village.

Five minutes later, we pulled up in front of my childhood home and I don't think I'd ever felt so happy to be back there. My uncle had evidently taken the news of our visit to heart, as he was stringing up extra decorations on the front of the house, and I knew where that particular instinct had originated.

"Welcome, both!" he bellowed down to us from atop a ladder. He was so happy I'm surprised he didn't topple from it. "The fatted beast is ready to be opened, the presents are on the fire, and there's a log in the oven. I'm just so glad you decided to come."

"It's nice to see you too, Stan," I told him as Percy launched himself from the Invicta with uncharacteristic athleticism to go running up the steps to see his dear friend.

Mother couldn't contain her happiness either and stood breathing in the scene as if it were an expensive perfume. Whereas Auntie Elle must have heard the commotion, as she wheeled herself to the door and peeked out to see us.

"My lovely boy! You're here!" Sadly, this comment was not for me, but my dog.

Whether Percy grasps the concept of Christmas is very hard to determine, but he clearly felt the thrill of the moment as almost all of his favourite people (and I) converged on the same spot. He went haring into the house, and my body seemed to buzz with anticipation for the day ahead. My throat developed a definite lump, my stomach tied itself in knots and my scalp itched from that blasted hat again.

And just when I thought I couldn't feel any greater contentment, a 1914 camel-brown Sunbeam motorcar pulled up alongside the Invicta and out stepped *my* favourite person in the world.

Dressed all in white, Bella looked more angelic than I can describe. "Marius, what are you doing here?"

"I could ask you the same thing."

We stood there for a few moments looking as though we were posing for a photograph. Neither of us knew who should answer first, but I eventually did the honours. "Mother missed my aunt and uncle too much, and so I offered to drive her up here."

"He's lying, Bella," my dear mater called down to us from the steps up to the front door. "My boy is far more sentimental than he would ever admit. He was the one who wanted to come."

Bella's shoulders pulled forwards for a moment as she produced a silent laugh.

"I never doubted it, Mary," she called back and, a second later, my family had vanished into the house.

"Now that you know my secret," I began, "will you tell me why you are here?"

She rocked backwards a short way before relenting. "It's perfectly simple. You left your present at my house after the party. As my brothers were being perfectly tiresome at home, and I needed a break from them, I thought I would leave the gift with your aunt and uncle."

She handed me a slim parcel that was not very different in size from the one Herbert had given her.

"You were insistent that I open it on Christmas Day. Now you can make sure that I do." As I finished what I was saying, I bent to extract something from under the driver's seat of my car. It was only a tiny package, but I handed it over to her.

"What is this, Marius? You already gave me such a practical present the other day. I will think of you every time I use those bath salts."

"Which is exactly why I bought you something better."

I'd somehow jumped the queue, and she was the first to open her present.

"How did you..."

Bella removed the cameo I'd gone back to buy in secret at the market three days earlier. She watched it dangling on its chain as it gently spun in the frozen air. Her black hair contrasted against her white woollen coat and the matching snow, and I struggled to imagine any other human looking more beautiful. A few flakes fell lazily to the ground around us, and it made me think of an article I'd once read about a man in America who has spent his life looking at snowflakes through a microscope. He says that each one is unique, but I'm sure they can't compare to my Isabella.

Her voice fell quieter. "The moment I saw it on that antiques stall, it reminded me of Adele."

"I know." I took a deep breath to force myself to slow down and not say anything I'd regret. "That's why I bought it for you."

She opened the clasp and held the ends up to her neck, then turned around so that I could connect them. When she looked back at me, a few tiny frozen crystals had settled in her hair, like pearls on a wedding dress.

"It's perfect, Marius."

I could have stood watching her for hours and not grown bored, but she picked up the present that she'd put down on the bonnet of my car and held it out to me. "I hope you like it."

I had to pull off my gloves to open the flat box and remove whatever was inside. When I realised what it was, I had to laugh.

"A silver cigarette case. It's just what I've always wanted." I decided not to remind her that I don't smoke, on the off-chance this wasn't a joke.

Thankfully, she quickly explained. "I'm so sorry. I'm a terribly indecisive shopper. I was at Gamages, and it won't surprise you to hear that the assistant assured me that any man would be thrilled with a cigarette case. I wasn't myself that day, and she was so pushful that I went along with her suggestion."

"Bella," I whispered to interrupt her chatter. "It is lovely. I will use it to store my pens on my desk at home."

Her eyes looked into mine and I could see twenty different emotions there. "Do you mean it?"

"No, I'll take it back to the shop next week and get something more useful."

She smiled and punched me on the arm. "Merry Christmas, Marius Quin."

"Merry Christmas, Lady Bella. Would you care to come inside so that my family can convince you to eat more food than any one person needs?"

"That sounds strangely pleasant. I would love to."

I could hear my uncle singing "The Holly and the Ivy" at the top of his voice. The snow continued falling, my heart beat to a rhythm of its own choosing, and I offered Bella my arm to walk into my childhood home. Despite everything, Christmas had come after all.

# A LETTER FROM THE AUTHOR

Many thanks for reading *The Holly Village Murders*, I hope you were glued to the book as Marius and Bella raced to unmask the killer. Should you wish to join other readers in accessing free novellas and hearing all about my new releases, you can sign up to my readers' club!

benedictbrown.net/benedict-brown-readers-club

If you enjoyed this book and could spare a few moments to leave a review, that would be hugely appreciated. Even a short comment can make all the difference in encouraging a reader to discover my books for the first time.

Becoming a writer was my dream for two decades as I scribbled away without an audience, so to finally be able to do this as my job for the last few years is out of this world. One of my favourite things about my work is hearing from you lovely people who all approach my books in different ways, so feel free to get in touch via my website.

Thanks again for being part of my story – Marius, Bella and I have so many more adventures still to come.

Benedict

benedictbrown.net

# ABOUT THIS BOOK

I normally like to cram in as much historical information about the settings of my book as I can manage in the plot itself, but I neglected to mention one very significant fact about Holly Village, which is a real place in the north of London. The person who commissioned the building of the village was one of the most significant figures of the Victorian age.

In 1837, aged just twenty-three, Angela Burdett-Coutts became the second richest woman in Britain (can you guess who was number one?). In fact, Edward VII said she was the most remarkable woman in Britain after his mother, Queen Victoria. But what would the heiress to a banking fortune do with all that money during that cold-hearted era when poverty was rampant? Well, somewhat surprisingly, she didn't keep it to herself and dismiss the poor as feckless wastrels, she became a major philanthropist.

She was close friends with Charles Dickens, who dedicated his novel *Martin Chuzzlewit* to her and was instrumental in planning Holly Village with her. They also embarked on her first philanthropic venture together by founding a house for women who had fallen into crime and prostitution. Dickens was very much involved with the daily running of the facility and their approach to reforming the inmates sounds comparatively modern to a lot of charities of the day.

Angela did not stop there, of course. She built schools and churches, co-founded the National Society for the Prevention of Cruelty to Children, which is still a vital charity today, and helped transform a London neighbourhood, establishing a fairly priced food market and promoting social housing in an innovative new manner. She was also president of (in order of strangeness) the Royal Society for the Prevention of Cruelty to Animals, the British Beekeepers' Association, and the British Goat Society. She was clearly an animal lover and invested money in installing one of the world's most elaborate drinking fountains in Victoria Park, London, which was designed for both humans and canines to enjoy. Percy would have approved. She left an incredible legacy behind and, on a personal note, I'm grateful that she helped finance the building of the Royal Marsden in London – a specialist cancer hospital through which my brother has been receiving his care for the last two years.

She sounds like a formidable person – more about that in a minute – and, though she didn't marry until she was sixty-seven, she proposed to her close friend the Duke of Wellington, who was forty-five years older than her. He said no, and so, some thirty-four years later, she married her American secretary, William, who was thirty-eight years younger than her. She was clearly a woman of diverse tastes!

William took Angela's surname and continued her charitable work after her death in 1906. Rather amazingly, by marrying him, Coutts lost three-fifths of her fortune, as there was a provision in her step-grandmother's will which dictated that the next heir in line would get the bulk of the inheritance if she married a foreigner. It must really have been a love match – or perhaps she decided that the resultant two-fifths of an unspendable fortune was plenty either way. Incidentally, the woman who left her all that money was also an interesting character. Harriet Melon was an

Irish actress born into poverty who went on to marry the banker Thomas Coutts, who was fifty-one years older than her. Why she objected so much to her step-granddaughter marrying a foreigner, I cannot say. Well, I can guess, but that wouldn't be very historically accurate of me.

I did not discover a great deal about the thinking behind Holly Village, but it was built on a small section of Holly Lodge Estate, where Angela Burdett-Coutts' family seat was. It seems likely that she built the eight-building (but twelve-dwelling) village to house her former workers, but it's unclear whether that ever came to pass. What's certain is that great thought was invested in the look of the place. Each building is unique, with gargoyles, towers and turrets. They also included an under-floor dust removal system, and the woodwork throughout was carved by visiting Italian craftsmen. It is sadly not open to the public, but you can see the gatehouse and peer through to spot Adele's tower-like house.

I only found out about the place because I spend too long looking at pretty old houses that come on sale online. I think I saw an advert for Adele Leach's cottage on the website of *Country Life* magazine. You'll be disappointed to know that this (more or less) bestselling author can't afford the £3 million price tag for the three-bedroom, $140m^2$ property. But if everyone reading this tells a thousand other people to buy my books, I might just manage it one day.

As so often happens with my writing, the setting dictated almost everything else. Holly Village is right next door to the immense and majestic Highgate Cemetery. What's particularly remarkable about the place is the combination of grandiose and oddly ethereal Victorian architecture with the untamed nature that threads itself through the tombs and headstones. I would say it is the closest thing in London to visiting a wild and ancient temple like Cambodia's Angkor Wat, with ferns, bushes and creepers pushing through everywhere you look – though don't trust me on that. I haven't set foot in Asia and, as I hail from south of the river, I haven't actually spent that much time in north London!

By the end of the Second World War, the cemetery was almost

totally overgrown and there weren't even clear paths to walk around it. It was owned at the time by a private company, who decided that there was nothing they could do to make it a profitable concern and wished to sell the land. Luckily, a bunch of plucky underdogs (well, I assume that's what they were) banded together to form the Friends of Highgate Cemetery Trust. They volunteered to tend to and tame the cemetery and eventually secured the freehold of the site and saved it for all Londoners. You can now take guided tours, which even go into one of the tombs in the Egyptian Avenue.

Some of the most famous people interred there include George Eliot, Christina Rossetti (both previously mentioned), Karl Marx, Beryl Bainbridge, Lucian Freud, Stella Gibbons, John Galsworthy, Ian Holm, George Michael and Douglas Adams. As you might be able to tell from several of those names only having died this century, it is still used for new burials. Highgate is considered one of the Magnificent Seven of the Victorian cemeteries in London, though it is really more like two in one, with Swain's Lane (where you will find Holly Village) running through the middle. The western cemetery opened in 1839, as church graveyards were full to bursting, and the eastern extension came into being twenty-one years later.

Charles Dickens is buried in Poet's Corner in Westminster Abbey, but several people from his family have their graves at Highgate. His estranged wife Catherine, daughter Dora, who died at just eight months old, his parents and his older sister Fanny (whose sickly son Henry is believed to be the inspiration for Tiny Tim in *A Christmas Carol*) are all in the family plot. I'll go into the life of Catherine in the next chapter, but I was happy that this famously spurned woman popped up a few times in my research. It turned out that she was the reason that Angela Burdett-Coutts ended her long friendship and collaboration with the famous author. He is said to have treated his wife so poorly that the philanthropist would have no more to do with him.

Another important setting in the book is Caledonian Market,

which is a short drive south from Highgate. If you go there today, you'll find a park and sports fields, but the immense clock tower still stands and is a testament to how grand the place must have been. It was once the biggest livestock market in London and was built to avoid the need to bring animals to Smithfield in the centre of the city. Opened as the Metropolitan Cattle Market by Prince Albert in 1855, it once occupied thirty acres, but by the twenties its use had already diversified to focus on the second-hand and antiquarian stalls that drew crowds twice a week (it was actually held on Tuesdays and Fridays, but it falls on a Saturday in this book – I hope you can forgive that terrible inaccuracy).

In every newspaper article I read about it, a few key things were described. First came the characters who ran the stalls, shouting out for passing trade, then was the noise and bustle of the place, and last the number of toffs strolling about looking for a bargain with their antiques experts at their sides. Oh, and eels. I saw a couple of journalists refer to "the cult of the eel" and there are cartoonish drawings of people queueing ten deep to get a plate of jellied eels. There were also aerial photos in *The Graphic* in 1927 which show hundreds if not thousands of people filling the aisles of the open-air market stalls. It sounds like it was an interesting place, and I really enjoyed writing the scene with Bella and Marius exploring it.

The cast-iron central market hall looks in old drawings like a train station or a minor palace. All around it were pens for the animals and abattoirs on the outskirts – though more importantly, the land there was framed by five pubs. The market itself closed in the 1960s, but at least the ground was given over to making a park for the local community.

This is my... urmmm, give me a second... seventh Christmas book (including novellas and the first in this series which was actually set on New Year's Eve), and I still keep turning up interesting traditions, facts and anecdotes about the season. This time around, I tried to focus on what London would have been like in the 1920s. There are some incredible photo galleries online from the time. I particularly liked seeing pictures of what charitable foundations did to help the poor, sick and elderly celebrate, and Marius's depiction of the run-up to Christmas is all inspired by real information I found.

There really was a Christmas tree in front of St Paul's Cathedral which would be lit each day for spectators to enjoy. I didn't realise at the time that I wrote the scene, but you could definitely buy Christmas trees at Caledonian Market, too. There is a beautiful photograph from 1929 of a little girl looking at the camera as she carries a tree bigger than she is, while her foppish father and concerned grandparents look on.

For the most part, it doesn't seem that London went quite so crazy for decorations back then as we all do these days, but there were some exceptions. There are stunning images of Electric Avenue in Brixton decorated with about fifty Christmas trees and countless long natural garlands running up and down the street from one side to the other. This market street got its name as it was the first in England to have electric lighting. From what I've read in the past, electric Christmas lighting didn't become the standard until about the 1930s, but if you look at images of the street going right back to the 1890s the trees were already strung with fairy lights.

In terms of shop window decorations, Selfridges claims to have been the first to have themed displays back in 1935, though looking at photos from the decades before, decorations in windows were already common. Incidentally, my brother's ex worked for Burberry and one year it was his job to travel all over Europe organising the sponsored Christmas windows in places like Harrods and Galeries Lafayette. We saw the ones in Paris, and they were impressively complex, complete with moving figures and flying umbrellas.

The trend presumably came over from the States (along with Mr Selfridge himself) as, already in the 1920s, Macy's in New York had elaborate displays, with a huge sleigh dominating a run of windows. And if they weren't quite as we imagine them today, shops definitely covered their façades with advertisements for their sensational Christmas offers. There was one shop in particular that was well known for its seasonal offerings.

Gamages department store kept popping up in my research. Though it closed down in the 1970s, it served Londoners for nearly a hundred years and was particularly well known for its toy department and, as I saw in many photographs, its huge Christmas bazaar. Families would flock there to see an immense train set that was installed each year and had day and night modes. The shop was based in Holborn, just around the corner from Marius's publisher's office where this series of books began. While Gamages' flagship store was incredibly successful, whenever the owners tried to expand to a new location, spending a small fortune in the process, the venture would flop. They raised half a million pounds through the sale of shares to the public in 1928 to open a massive shop on Oxford Street, but it closed down just eight months later. I suppose its customers preferred the status quo.

I found two pictures online of the Children's Aid and Adoption Society at Leytonstone. The first is taken in 1931 and the second in 1938, and both show a Father Christmas dishing out presents to a group of orphans. The kids change – in the latter picture they're all wearing matching woollen hats so that they look like pixies – but the framing of the shot through a window and the man giving out presents remain the same, which I thought a nice metaphor for our attitude towards Christmas. I try every year to recreate the Christmases of my childhood, and yet every one is just about different enough to be unique.

There were lots of charitable Christmas traditions in London in the twenties and thirties. One thing I kept coming across was something called a "share-out". There are British Pathé videos and plenty of photos of the grandees of the Hammersmith Broadway Congregational Society standing with sacks of money and stacks of notes along with a police escort. From what I can tell, local people would invest in the scheme and, before Christmas each year, they would go to the local church hall to receive their dividends. It looks fun and community-spirited. I like the idea that a rising tide lifts all boats, and that seems to be that belief put into action.

I also came across another interesting charity from the time. The Hoxton Mission gets a mention in this book, and if you look for information online about it, you'll find lots of people still alive today whose then impoverished families benefited from the help it offered. It was set up in the 1880s as a soup kitchen and refuge by the Burtt brothers, two men who had themselves been born into poverty and were helped by local charities in that part of London. The mission was well known for its Christmas parties, with children queuing for a meal and presents and, of course, a Father Christmas there to lead the entertainment.

The concept of charity at the time could be quite different from today, and there was still an attitude embedded in society that the poor had brought their condition upon themselves. It's nice to read the comments from people whose parents or grandparents had fond memories of the mission from the twenties and thirties, as it speaks to the genuine kindness of the people who worked and volunteered there. I also discovered that one of the people who had used the mission as a boy went on to be one of the richest men in Britain today. So that's not bad going.

To finish off this chapter, and my Christmas considerations this time around, I'll leave you with a nostalgic article from the *Illustrated Sporting and Dramatic News* from 27th November 1926. What I like about it is that it is already nostalgic for a forgotten past, as it talks of the Romance of Christmas and says...

*We have travelled far from the Dickensian Christmas with the Yule-log mummers and the stage-coach and the accompanying stage-setting of snow and ice... However, there is one thing certain, and that is that Christmas will never depart, neither will the giving and receiving of gifts, for it is in this that the romance of Christmas lies.*

That's right, people, way back ninety-nine years ago,

Christmas was already fully commercialised! The article goes on to push silver cigarette boxes (hence Bella's purchase) and, in a nice coincidence, reversible Burberry coats. As Tiny Tim said, "God bless us, every one... Though what I'd really like for Christmas is a Hornby wind-up train for the bargain price of four and six at Gamages!"

# RESEARCH

Where to start? Where to start? Well, I turned up any number of interesting facts on a vast array of topics and I really can't promise there'll be much connection between any of them.

Let's begin with perfection. For the passing reference to a mother of pearl shell in Adele Leach's drawing room, I found myself reading about the chambered nautilus. A nautilus, as well as being the name of Captain Nemo's submarine in the Jules Verne novels, is a cephalopod with a large shell which, when cut open or X-rayed, can be seen as a near-perfect logarithmic spiral, an almost magical form that is greatly admired by mathematicians. There are fossils dating back 500 million years, and it is shaded in different ways on the top and bottom, so that it blends in with the light above to any predator below and the seafloor beneath for anything watching from above.

It is fitting that Verne chose the name he did, as the nautilus moves through the water much like a submarine, by pumping liquid between the various chambers within its shell to change its buoyancy. It also builds new chambers and seals off old ones as it grows so that its internal structure is like a personal history of its existence. They live at a depth of around 1,000 feet and their eggs have never been seen by humans in the wild. They also have the most beautiful nacreous coating inside their shells. Isn't nature wonderful?

Sticking with wildlife, green parakeets! I think I might have mentioned in these pages before, that in my garden in London, we have a colony of rose-ringed parakeets that are native to India and Africa. For years people have discussed the origins of these birds and there were rumours that Jimi Hendrix had released them in the sixties or that they had escaped from the set of *The African Queen* in 1951.

However, scientists have created a heat map of sightings over the last century to see when and where the most reports occurred. It seems that there were two key moments in the twentieth century when the birds started popping up. The first was in 1929–31 (the idea in this book being that the Baroness was responsible for their release a few months earlier). The scientists have applied a technique more commonly used by criminologists to identify repeat offenders and have worked out that the two periods coincided with a media panic over 'parrot fever'. It seems that pet owners became worried that they would catch a disease and so they left their poor parakeets to fend for themselves. The birds clearly adapted well, as recent estimates put the population at over 30,000 in Britain. Chirp away, little buddies!

From colourful birds to colourful jumpers... As I have written so many Christmas books, it is becoming more difficult to include traditions that I haven't already mentioned. One thing that was not particularly common in Marius's day was Christmas jumpers. However, they did exist in some form. Wintery jumpers seem to have originated in nineteenth-century Scandinavia, where people would wear thick, colourful sweaters in the run-up to winter. One pattern, known as *selburose*, features an eight-petalled, star-like rose repeated over and over and is commonly seen on mittens and jumpers. By the 1930s, these items were being produced by the hundreds of thousands, and the central Norwegian region where they're from now has the design on its flag.

The Christmas jumper benefited from the post-war interest in skiing, which spread winter fashions around Europe and, in the twenties and onwards, became increasingly brighter and more adventurous in design. By the fifties, the figurative patterns with snowmen, robins and Father Christmas that we still buy today were coming into existence. So, would Marius have ended up with a Christmas jumper from his previously unmentioned Aunt Clara? Well, it's more or less possible as she knitted it herself, so there's nothing truly anachronistic in it, but she would have been ahead of her time. Either way, I had to put it in. It wouldn't be a Benedict Brown Christmas book without at least one reference to *A Christmas Story*.

So much of the imagery in this book was inspired by old photographs I found. I have an amazing three-volume series called *Wonderful London: Illustrated* which was published in the twenties and contains thousands of photos of the capital. There are so many characters contained within it who simply don't exist anymore. People like dog meat boys and organ grinders, street hawkers and the toy man selling his wind-up soldiers have all disappeared from London streets. My mother remembers Breton onion sellers in the south of Wales when she was a child, and it's mind-blowing to think that people could make enough money from selling veg that it was worth the trip over from the continent. Even when I was a kid you could buy flipping toy dogs from men with blankets on Oxford Street – who would presumably pull up their wares if the police arrived. Obviously, some of this is a sign of improving living standards, and the image of the man who pushed the gramophone around for coins made me want to reflect on the mix of lavish living and poverty that was common in the 1920s (and much of history).

Speaking of forgotten members of society, I wasn't really sure what resources there were for veteran soldiers ten years after the Great War had concluded. I want these books to be about Marius's maturation as a person, and some readers found him selfish and immature in the first book – to the extent that they probably gave up on the series right then. But I couldn't start the story with a fully formed character or I'd have had nothing to write about. One way that he has changed is in his interaction with others. In this book, we find out that he goes to a veterans' charity to talk to the wounded soldiers there.

I came across the "Not Forgotten Association", which was founded in 1920 by Marta Cunningham, an American opera singer who lived in London, after she realised just how many men were still in hospital. In the early days of this organisation, she used her high-society contacts to throw parties and organise excursions for wounded servicemen. Looking in the newspapers in the twenties, I find lots of references to garden parties at Buckingham Palace, and there's even a photograph of Miss Cunningham decorating a Christmas tree there with her aristocratic friends.

I'm not going to lie, that tree is not up to my standards, but the association did a lot of good work for veterans and is thought to have helped 10,000 men in its first year. It continues to exist and has often had royal patronage as it seeks to address not just physical problems, but issues of loneliness, illness and isolation in former and serving soldiers. The Buckingham Palace parties are also still going strong – I can only hope that the decorations have improved.

From wounds and isolation to broken hearts. Could someone die of the kind of shock that Adele is subjected to? Well, yes, actually, they could. The American Heart Association explains that, while you're unlikely to keel over when someone comes knocking on your door on Halloween, pre-existing conditions and the sudden rush of adrenaline that an unwelcome surprise offers can combine to do a person in.

Not only can shock be a factor in sudden heart attacks, people die from far less. There is something called Broken Heart Syndrome, or more technically Takotsubo cardiomyopathy, which causes a weakening of the heart muscles that can lead to death. What's amazing about it is that it can be brought on not just by physical factors but emotional ones, too. Anything from the death of a loved one and the loss of a job or relationship can be enough to spark the condition, and even happy events like weddings or birthdays can be a trigger. It wasn't known about until the late 1960s when scientists noticed that the death of a loved one increases the risk of death. I know that my great-aunt Gwyneth died a year to the day after her husband Frank, and I've heard of other couples dying within an even shorter time. Fittingly for the events within this book, the condition is slightly more common in the cold of winter.

It occurred to me halfway through this book that I'd never taken much notice of my characters' blood alcohol levels when they are driving, so I decided to check on the laws from the 1920s. I don't think I've had anyone driving about half-cut, but I was interested to discover that the law only changed to outlaw drink driving in 1925. The maximum punishment at the time was fifty pounds or four months' imprisonment. That sounds pretty lenient, but I imagine general dangerous driving laws would have been stricter. I read a sad story about an ex-soldier who had just got engaged when he ploughed into and killed a police officer with his motorbike. The interesting part of the story was that the motorcyclist was obviously wealthy, as he donated £2,000 to the man's family, but the judge insisted that he should not get away with his crime just because he had the money to compensate for it. He was sentenced to eight months in prison. I wonder whether his fiancée waited for him...

Sticking with cars, I had no idea that the word chauffeur is the French word for *stoker*, as early cars were steam-powered and needed their drivers to stoke the engine. That's the only interesting thing that I found out about them, aside from the fact that, when cars were first produced, only the very richest in society had them, which is why it was briefly common to employ someone to drive for you.

When writing my London-set books, I spend half of my time checking the geographical history of the city to find out what was where and when. There's no question that the capital was changed immeasurably by the Blitz, but even before that, there was an incredibly high turnover of development. As Marius says, Highgate was originally entirely separate from London, but the city had been expanding outwards for decades and, looking at maps from the time, it had already been subsumed by the 1920s. In fact, you could drive your car from Highgate in the far north, to Wallington where I'm from sixteen miles south, without seeing much but shops, houses and the odd park in between.

One institution in particular that has come and gone in areas across London is the humble British police station. I was planning to set the main urban scene in this book in Highgate itself, but the closest nick to Holly Village at the time was at Archway Road. You can find detailed histories for the buildings of each part of London, and Highgate police station itself was hit by a V1 bomb in 1944. However, what I found most astonishing was the number of stations that have closed this century. From 160 police stations in London fifteen years ago, the number has plummeted to 36 now. That's kind of crazy, as there is no way that in-person crime has declined at a similar rate.

Another big change in London is the price of houses. It is estimated that the average property in the city has gone up by 3,000 per cent in a century, but in many cases it is far higher. Interestingly, we're able to make such calculations in part because Lloyd George, who went on to be prime minister, commissioned a survey of house prices back in 1910. Apparently, you could buy a house on Chancery Lane for £11,000, and a quick search on listing sites suggests you would pay around two million pounds for a flat there these days. That's an 18,100 per cent increase, and I know that my parents' house has gone up by around 2,000 per cent since they bought it in the eighties. It's really no wonder that one of my brothers still lives at home and the other rents (though they are both in their forties). London is insane!

Moving on to interesting people I encountered, let's go back to Catherine Dickens. I should point out that, unlike Chrissy in my Lord Edgington books, I'm honestly not obsessed with Dickens. I do really like his style and, if I weren't constantly writing mystery novels, I'd probably make more effort to read his novels that I don't know, but the only reason I mention him so often – beyond the indelible mark he left on Christmas – is because he pops up all over the place in my research.

His wife is a more discreet presence, but she had a fascinating life, nonetheless. She was a published writer in her own right as, under the pseudonym Lady Maria Clutterbuck, Catherine released a cookery book called *What Shall We Have for Dinner?* Similar in vein to *Mrs Beeton's Book of Household Management*, it offers a model for how middle-class women could live their lives and maintain a household. Catherine herself had ten children with Charles and was presumably pretty busy raising them when an eighteen-year-old actress caught his eye and he left his wife of twenty-two years.

There is some debate about why he left her – the couple had lost a baby girl seven years earlier, which had a major impact on Catherine's mental health – and even whether Dickens's relationship with the actress Nelly Ternan was anything more than platonic. What can't be denied is that, after their separation in 1858, Dickens went out of his way to cast his wife in a bad light. He accused her of being a bad mother, blamed her for their having so many children and sought to have her sectioned.

While Mr Dickens shaped the narrative of their relationship through press releases and his contact with relevant public figures, Mrs Dickens never spoke about what happened and was admired for her restraint. Even some of Dickens's closest friends turned against him. Elizabeth Barrett Browning was highly critical of his behaviour and, as we found out in the previous chapter, Angela Burdett-Coutts cut ties with him because of it. There were rumours that Dickens was having an affair with Catherine's sister – their housekeeper – and that Ternan was actually his illegitimate daughter. Catherine didn't seem interested in any of the chatter, and though her estranged husband did everything he could to keep their children away from her and treated her cruelly, on her deathbed, she still wanted to promote the idea that, for most of their married life at least, they had been happy together.

From authors to archaeologists. I wanted to check how realistic it would be for Adele Leach to have accompanied her husband on digs abroad in the late Victorian era, and I came across two really good examples. Hilda Petrie was married to "the father of Egyptian archaeology" Flinders Petrie. Hilda was at first employed as an artist and, within a year, married her illustrious husband. She would collaborate on digs with him in Egypt and Palestine and went on to give talks and publish on their subject. When he died in Jerusalem, his head was pledged to the Royal College of Surgeons, and there was a rumour that Hilda took it back to Britain in a hat box – though that doesn't seem to be true. On the darker side of things, Mr Petrie was a bit of a eugenicist and his racist views influenced his academic work.

Mortimer Wheeler was another complicated character, and another brilliant archaeologist who furthered the discipline in the twentieth century. Sir Max Mallowan (I need to have at least one Agatha Christie reference in these books!) described him as both delightful company and "a dangerous opponent if threatened with frustration".

He was something of an authoritarian, a real cad with the ladies, but he did form an important partnership with his first wife Tessa Wheeler, who worked with him on digs in the British Isles. She died young but pioneered some important excavation techniques, and it sounds as though she did a lot of the actual work while it was her husband's job to analyse results and publish papers on their findings. The things she achieved and the positions she held in her lifetime – all the while working in the shadow of her more famous husband – are truly impressive, and she clearly helped pave the way for other female archaeologists who would become famous in their own right.

After Tessa died, Wheeler married another intriguing character, though Mavis Wright was interesting in very different ways. She was born into a slightly mysterious working-class family and, having hitchhiked to London, took a job as a governess and became one of the Bright Young Things. She had an affair with the Welsh painter Augustus John before marrying the Irish hoaxer (and brother-in-law of Neville Chamberlain) Horace de Vere Cole. De Vere Cole was well known for his pranks and once, along with Virginia Woolf's brother, dressed up as a member of the royal family of Zanzibar in order to obtain a tour of the HMS *Dreadnought*. He also liked to embarrass well-known public figures, once held a party in which all the guests had the word bottom in their surnames and ended up getting himself and a politician friend arrested when he made it seem as if said friend were robbing him.

After he died, Mavis Wright married Mortimer Wheeler, but their tempestuous relationship included a proposed dual, domestic violence and divorce three years later. Yet, it was Mavis Wright's third husband who contributed what might be the most curious anecdote from her life. She married the impresario Baron Vivian in 1939 and, one night when he forgot his key to their house, she shot him as he climbed through the window. He was not fatally injured, but his wife was sentenced to six months in prison for intentionally wounding him. He was waiting for her when she got out, and the two lived (presumably) happily together for the remainder of her life.

Frederic Leighton is an artist who has popped up in my books before. He was hugely popular during his lifetime, which more or less spanned Queen Victoria's reign. However, shortly after his death, his classical and biblical paintings and sculptures swiftly decreased in value. He illustrated George Eliot's book *Romola*, was a keen volunteer soldier in the regiment known as the 'Artists' Rifles' which was set up to attract artistic types to be reserves in the army, and his paintings are very beautiful if you like rich, romantic Pre-Raphaelite art. He was made a baron the day before he died and, as he had no issue, the peerage is the shortest in history and immediately fell into abeyance.

Now, on to another once-beloved creative who has largely been forgotten. Walter de la Mare was a writer known particularly for his children's and supernatural fiction. I found him because I was looking for a Christmassy poem with a creepy slant and "Mistletoe", the one that John Presler reads, is just perfect. De la Mare also wrote a once-hailed novel called *Memoirs of a Midget*, which sounds like a Thumbelina tale for adults, and he had some interesting theories about the way our imaginations develop. He believed that most people let theirs fall to the wayside as we age, whereas we fancy-shmancy creative types hone ours into adulthood.

I do have a very active imagination, and I spend most of my time between writing and family duties daydreaming about future novels, so I found this very interesting. Sometimes my wife will talk to me after I finish a work shift (i.e. I've been making up silly stories on the computer for several hours) and it will take me some time to tune in to the real world again, much to Marion's annoyance. I must thank Walter de la Mare's estate and the always helpful Society of Authors for giving me permission to use the poem as, until the end of 2026, which will mark the seventieth anniversary of his passing, "Mistletoe" is still under copyright.

From authors to entertainers – are they the same thing? The life-size stone lion in Highgate Cemetery is a reference to a real grave which belongs to George Wombwell, the owner of Wombwell's Travelling Menagerie. He was a shoemaker who bought exotic animals from ships that docked in London and amassed a large collection which he took around the country. He became a real animal expert and was the first person to breed a lion in captivity in Britain. He was such a well-known entertainer in his day that he is even mentioned in a Sherlock Holmes story.

One last random interesting person, coming up! American Wilson Bentley was fascinated by snowflakes from a young age and set out, knowingly or otherwise, to become the first person to photograph them. He'd go on to record over 5,000 images after his first in 1885. He greatly influenced our understanding of their structure, and the book he published, *Snow Crystals*, is still in print today. Though he only had fairly rudimentary technology, the techniques he used are largely the same now, and it is said that no one tried to copy him for a century because the work he produced was so good. I only came across him because I wanted to check whether each snowflake really is unique or not. It is an idea that he popularised, and it seems that while it cannot be categorically proven that no two are the same, the chances of finding a pair is almost infinitesimal. However, they said the same thing about fingerprints and, I can't remember if I've mentioned this here before, but there's no definitive evidence that they are unique either.

Preliminary studies using AI have raised the possibility that fingerprints are not the infallible system for identification that scientists a hundred and fifty years ago decided that they were. But even before this new technology got involved, criminologists had moved towards DNA as the real determiner. While fingerprints are, of course, still used, partial or unclear prints are nowhere near as reliable as DNA evidence for determining a person's presence at the scene of a crime – and even then, DNA can be transferred or contaminated. There's an interesting article on the always excellent *Smithsonian Magazine* website which explains just how common DNA testing has become in policing and the impact of genetic databases on identifying criminals. So perhaps fingerprints aren't quite as distinctive as snowflakes, but – at an atomic level at least – each individual human is... (until our clones arrive). Aahhhhh!

I was going to talk about the long-gone tram system in London, how the royal wave developed to avoid wrist strain, how the Paris Bourse crash of 1882 led to Paul Gauguin leaving banking to pursue his art career, and Greyfriars Bobby, but it's gone ten at night, my kids are already asleep, and I want to watch something on telly before I follow them to the land of nod. And so I will finish with a couple of songs and bid you adieu.

"The Boar's Head Carol" is a truly odd Christmas song. It comes from at least the fifteenth century and describes a tradition that might actually date back to Anglo-Saxon times. Written in English, with the final line of each verse in Latin (as you do), it tells of the presentation of a boar's head for dinner, which was common during the Yuletide celebrations. In fact, the tradition is upheld in

Queen's College, Oxford. Former alumni are welcomed back, and a boar is roasted for the "Boar's Head Gaudy" celebration just before Christmas. I found pictures of a similar party in the Savoy Hotel in the twenties. Unappealingly, in 1921 their chef, François Latry, prepared a young *bear* for dinner. That's *bear* as in Paddington, not *boar* as in Asterix. The caption to the photo proudly states that the meal hadn't been served in Britain since the time of Henry VIII, which makes you think, *Hmmm... who thought it would be a good idea to bring it back?*

The tune of "Ding Dong Merrily on High" is almost as old as the previous song, but the words are comparatively modern for a Christmas carol. They only date to 1924 and were written by the Anglican priest George Ratcliffe Woodward. He compiled, edited and also composed carols and his song "Past Three O'Clock" featured in another of my books.

And lastly, "Deck the Halls" was originally a Welsh melody dating back to the sixteenth century (again). Both the original Welsh lyrics and the nineteenth-century English ones extol the virtue of sharing a drink at Christmas. It was well known enough as a Welsh New Year's song that Haydn created an arrangement of it way back in 1803 under the name "Nos Galan". Children would sing the song whilst carrying a decorated apple on New Year's Day and be given treats in exchange. Gift-giving in Wales at that time of year goes back centuries, though apparently nowadays people more commonly give bread and cheese. As I am a very ignorant (half) Welshman, I did not know this. The fact I've only spent two New Year's Eves in Wales in my life might have something to do with it.

These chapters added up to a mere 7,000 words this time. My audiobook narrator will be happy! I hope you have a very Merry Christmas and that this book has put you in the festive spirit. I'm sure I'll write another before very long.

## WORDS AND REFERENCES

Gadzookers – for mild surprise, like gosh. The first part of the word is the same euphemism that appears in Ye Gads! Now used humorously.

Sopwith Dolphin – the less famous sibling of the Sopwith Camel. A common fighter biplane from the First World War.

Lay some valuable item up in lavender – it can mean to put something carefully into storage, but also meant to pawn something. To tell the truth, it's probably too archaic for this book, but it's such a pretty phrase I used it anyway.

Axminster – a maker of fine English rugs founded in 1755 and still going, with a brief pause of 101 years before it was relaunched in 1929.

Do I know my grandmother? – this basically means, *Duh!* Used to point out that the person is stating the obvious.

Ivy had fallen head over heels with Bella – not a point of vocabulary. I'd just like to say that this was inspired by my wife, who everyone instantly falls in love with even though she's half as sociable as I am and generally prefers to hide from people. Our closest friends regularly confess how much they adore her, normally with a brief aside of, *Sorry, Ben!*

This sceptred isle – a famous expression from *Richard II*. Out of context it's probably a bit confusing, but it means a land invested with regal authority.

Blue-devilage – glumness.

Inherited the title from her father by writ – to inherit something by writ (written command) meant that it bypassed usual inheritance law and passed to the nominated person. It was not common but could be used to leave property/title, etc. to a chosen heir and in some cases female heirs.

Fumsup – a good luck charm in the shape of a baby that was often given to soldiers who were heading to war, or to children as a toy. Its name comes from a mangling of "thumbs up", another symbol of luck.

By Jove – another way of saying gosh, Jove is another name for the Roman god Jupiter. I came across the meaning in the Italian Edgington book as the local grape to Tuscany is called *sangiovese*, or blood of Jupiter.

Plus fours – a type of baggy golfing trousers that finish four inches below the knee – plus twos also exist. Tights or long socks are/were normally worn underneath.

Megrims – it can mean a number of things related to health, from headaches to depression, but in this case it refers to a non-specific illness.

Gun cotton – I came across this by chance somewhere quite unconnected to my books and thought it was interesting. Soldiers in the First World War would experiment making their own bombs when there weren't enough supplies. The cotton itself was soaked in nitrocellulose and put in a tin can with a fuse. Boom!

Lanchester armoured car – one of the most common British armoured vehicles, it was a converted Lanchester tourer with guns and armour added. They would often venture ahead of the main body of the army to scout and raid the enemy's defences.

Pedlars' market/rag fair – two terms for a flea market.

Bonzo – a common name for a dog, I didn't realise it came from a 1920s comic strip by George E. Studdy in *The Sketch*. It was a big hit and Bonzo went on to be one of the first animated cartoon characters.

Chisel – another word for cheat or defraud.

Revelation suitcase – a make of suitcase at the time which had an innovative design that could expand and (apparently) fit twice as much inside.

Bow Bells – (for those not from Britain) a true Cockney is said to be someone born within hearing distance of the bells of the church of St Mary-le-Bow in East London.

Isle of Dogs – a part of East London with an interesting history that I forgot to include in the research section.

Swizzle – slang for an alcoholic drink.

Troul – to pass something around (as in the bowl of drink) but also to sing in the round, which is presumably the case in the song.

Fluster – to move agitatedly or swagger about.

Great Scott of the Antarctic – not a common expression, but I thought it fitted well together.

We had biscuits and jam, a little cheese and mustard – I looked up the real rations of a First World War soldier and they were particularly poor at first but improved as supply lines opened and the war wore on.

Wellington chest – a tall, thin chest of drawers.

Hackdom – not a word. I made it up! Hopefully understandable in context to mean the realm of poor writers.

Crabstick – a crabby person.

National Gallery of British Art – the contemporary name for what is now Tate Britain on Millbank near Pimlico.

Flighty – it can mean "given to flights of the imagination" which I thought was a pretty definition.

Parlour-jumper – someone who robbed opportunistically by climbing or leaning in through a window.

Factory and Workshop Act – this was the act that forbade Sunday trading. Funnily enough, when I looked for an example of its being mentioned in the papers in the twenties, the first that came up was about a florist who made his staff work illegally.

Caen Wood Towers – a handily located manor house that belonged to the managing director of Shell in the twenties. It is now known as Athlone House and belongs to a Russian oligarch who, to give him his dues, saved the house from ruin.

Lickspittling – to flatter, suck up to someone.

Homburg – a felt hat with a dent down the middle that was popularized by Edward VII when he was Prince of Wales. Churchill often wore one too.

I don't give a fig's end – I don't care.

Renter/petticoat pensioner/gigolo – slightly different but linked terms. Renter suggests that jumpers were definitely removed and services rendered. The other two are more innocent and just implied a male companion or toyboy.

Footsicles – not a word. I think I might have used it before though, either in my books or just when talking to my children.

Glaikit ouf – I asked my Scottish uncle for an appropriate insult, and this is what he gave me. It basically means "silly oaf" in Scots.

George Eliot and Mary Ann Cross – some readers didn't understand this reference. George Eliot was the author of *Middlemarch* and *Silas Marner*, among other great books. She was born Mary Ann Evans and her husband's name was Cross, so she has both her married name and the pen name she used to make people think she was a man on her tombstone.

Gino Severini – an Italian futurist painter who painted the Hall of Masks in Montegufoni Castle which features in my Lord Edgington book "Murder in an Italian Castle". That story didn't mention Severini, so I thought I'd drop a reference to him here. He didn't really paint a picture of a fictional British baroness and half her husband, but he had already exhibited his work by 1928 and was developing a new style away from futurism.

# CHARACTER LIST

Old Favourites

**Marius Quin** – he's there on the cover! You must know him by now!

**Lady Bella Montague** – Marius's former girlfriend, sleuthing partner and close friend.

**Inspector Valentine Lovebrook** – a happy-go-lucky officer who befriended Marius & Co. in the first book of the series.

**Bertrand Price-Lewis** – Marius's larger than life editor.

**Marius's mum** – Marius's mum, Mary.

**Uncle Stan and Auntie Elle** – Marius's dad's brother and his wife. They run a bakery in Hurtwood Village.

New Favourites

**Adele Leach** – a treasured family friend of Bella's.

**Maggie** – her maid.

**Ivy Frazel** – frazzled and peculiar neighbour to Adele. She lives at number 1 Holly Village.

**The Baroness** – a rather magisterial old lady who lives at number 2 with her husband.

**Herbert Wandle** – her husband, an antiquarian and carpenter. He was also a childhood confidante of Bella's.

**Sergeant Bulmer** – the unhelpful local policeman.

**Constable Pike** – his unhelpful constable.

**Ruth Haskell** – a bit of a busybody who has charged herself with being the social secretary of the village. She lives at number 6a.

**Caretaker – Hamish Dumfries** – a tetchy Scot who looks after the village and runs errands if you're willing to pay him enough.

**John Presler** – a somewhat mysterious figure who lives at number 3. He is a more recent arrival in Holly Village.

**Silva Presler** – his wife who comes from a working class though wealthy background.

**Freddy Pointing** – a particularly cantankerous resident who lives at number 7b.

**Other neighbours** – Clive Whitworth (number 6b), Betty (4), Carrie (7a).